"Don't you know the more you fight a man, the more determined he'll be to conquer you?"

Murdock arrogantly raked his eyes over her. "And, Cat, honey, you have a knack for verbal sparring that can really turn a man on."

That was it! Catherine had had it with this big, smart-mouthed wise guy! With her hands balled into tight fists, she took that one step that separated them, then lifted her gaze to make direct eye-to-eye contact. That's when she realized she'd made a mistake. A huge mistake. Murdock was looking at her as if she were the last drop of water in a sweltering, dry desert.

"What the hell," he said as he reached out and jerked her into his arms. "We might as well get this over with."

Dear Reader,

Happy New Year! Silhouette Intimate Moments is starting the year off with a bang—not to mention six great books. Why not begin with the latest of THE PROTECTORS, Beverly Barton's miniseries about men no woman can resist? In *Murdock's Last Stand,* a well-muscled mercenary meets his match in a woman who suddenly has him thinking of forever.

Alicia Scott returns with *Marrying Mike... Again,* an intense reunion story featuring a couple who are both police officers with old hurts to heal before their happy ending. Try Terese Ramin's *A Drive-By Wedding* when you're in the mood for suspense, an undercover agent hero, an irresistible child and a carjacked heroine who ends up glad to go along for the ride. Already known for her compelling storytelling abilities, Eileen Wilks lives up to her reputation with *Midnight Promises,* a marriage-of-convenience story unlike any other you've ever read. Virginia Kantra brings you the next of the irresistible MacNeills in *The Comeback of Con MacNeill,* and Kate Stevenson returns after a long time away, with *Witness... and Wife?*

All six books live up to Intimate Moments' reputation for excitement and passion mixed together in just the right proportions, so I hope you enjoy them all.

Yours,

Leslie J. Wainger
Executive Senior Editor

Please address questions and book requests to:
Silhouette Reader Service
U.S.: 3010 Walden Ave., P.O. Box 1325, Buffalo, NY 14269
Canadian: P.O. Box 609, Fort Erie, Ont. L2A 5X3

$\mathcal{B}$EVERLY BARTON
MURDOCK'S LAST STAND

Published by Silhouette Books
America's Publisher of Contemporary Romance

To Connie,
whose mind is filled with fanciful,
magical and intriguing ideas.
This "protector" is for you.

 SILHOUETTE BOOKS

ISBN 0-373-07979-6

MURDOCK'S LAST STAND

Copyright © 2000 by Beverly Beaver

This edition published by arrangement with Harlequin Books S.A.

Visit us at www.romance.net

Printed in U.S.A.

BEVERLY BARTON

has been in love with romance since her grandfather gave her an illustrated book of *Beauty and the Beast*. An avid reader since childhood, she began writing at the age of nine and wrote short stories, poetry, plays and novels throughout high school and college. After marriage to her own "hero" and the births of her daughter and son, she chose to be a full-time homemaker, aka wife, mother, friend and volunteer.

When she returned to writing, she joined Romance Writers of America and helped found the Heart of Dixie chapter in Alabama. Since the release of her first Silhouette book in 1990, she has won the GRW Maggie Award and the National Readers' Choice Award and has been a RITA Award finalist. Beverly considers writing romance books a real labor of love. Her stories come straight from the heart, and she hopes that all the strong and varied emotions she invests in her books will be felt by everyone who reads them.

IT'S OUR 20th ANNIVERSARY!
We'll be celebrating all year,
starting with these fabulous titles,
on sale in January 2000.

Special Edition

#1297 Matt Caldwell: Texas Tycoon
Diana Palmer

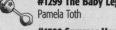
#1298 Their Little Princess
Susan Mallery

#1299 The Baby Legacy
Pamela Toth

#1300 Summer Hawk
Peggy Webb

#1301 Daddy by Surprise
Pat Warren

#1302 Lonesome No More
Jean Brashear

Intimate Moments

#979 Murdock's Last Stand
Beverly Barton

#980 Marrying Mike... Again
Alicia Scott

#981 A Drive-By Wedding
Terese Ramin

#982 Midnight Promises
Eileen Wilks

#983 The Comeback of Con MacNeill
Virginia Kantra

#984 Witness... and Wife?
Kate Stevenson

Romance

 #1420 The Baby Bequest
Susan Meier

#1421 With a Little T.L.C.
Teresa Southwick

#1422 The Sheik's Solution
Barbara McMahon

#1423 Annie and the Prince
Elizabeth Harbison

#1424 A Babe in the Woods
Cara Colter

#1425 Prim, Proper... Pregnant
Alice Sharpe

Desire

#1267 Her Forever Man
Leanne Banks

#1268 The Pregnant Princess
Anne Marie Winston

#1269 Dr. Mommy
Elizabeth Bevarly

#1270 Hard Lovin' Man
Peggy Moreland

#1271 The Cowboy Takes a Bride
Cathleen Galitz

#1272 Skyler Hawk: Lone Brave
Sheri WhiteFeather

Prologue

Sweat dripped off his forehead and down into his eyes, blurring his vision. Using the back of his hand, he swiped away the moisture. The oppressive heat coated his body, filled his lungs and dulled his senses. He had been in some bad situations before, endured sweltering temperatures just as deadly and lived to tell the tale. But his gut instincts warned him that this time was different. From the minute he and Lanny arrived in Zaraza, he'd had an uneasy feeling that their luck had finally run out. He'd known that sooner or later fate would catch up with them and they'd wind up paying with their lives. He just hadn't thought it would be this soon. Hell, he was only twenty-six. He was too young to die. Besides, wasn't there an old adage that said only the good die young? If that were true, he'd live to be a hundred.

"No way we're both going to get out of this alive, Bubba," Lanny said.

Murdock lifted his gaze from the tip of his M-16 to

*his old buddy's dirt-streaked face. Lanny McCroskey
was a good ol' boy from Tennessee, who had lost his
soul back in Nam and had been searching for it ever
since.*

"We've been outnumbered before. We'll figure a way
to get out of this one." *Even as the denial came from
his mouth, Murdock knew Lanny was right. They were
trapped! And even for a couple of highly trained mercenaries like them, it would take a miracle for both of
them and Sabino's troops to all escape.*

"The information has to get back to Burdett." *Lanny
opened his canteen, then lifted it to his lips. After taking
a hefty swig, he recapped the canteen.* "One of us has
to hightail it out of here, while Juan and his boys keep
Ramos's men occupied."

"Whoever stays is a dead man," *Murdock said.*

"You go. I'll stay." *Lanny chuckled.* "We both know
that I've been living on borrowed time ever since Nam.
You're different. You're a young man. You've still got a
chance to have a normal life, if you get out of our line
of work."

*Before Murdock could reply, before he could protest
leaving his former army sergeant behind, a barrage of
enemy gunfire exploded around them. As the ragtag
band of rebel soldiers retaliated against the Zarazaian
troops, Juan Sabino crawled through the thicket and
eased up beside Lanny.*

"We can hold them off for a while longer," *Juan said
in his native Spanish.* "One of you must go now, if there
is any hope of getting that information to Burdett."

"Murdock's going," *Lanny said.*

"Sí. He is younger and stronger than you and has the
best chance of getting through." *Juan's large, dark eyes*

gazed directly at Murdock, the look a mixture of fear and hope and pleading. "Vaya con Dios, amigo."

Murdock opened his mouth to protest, but stopped short of uttering a word. He knew that Lanny and Juan were right. And he didn't have time for long farewells. No time to tell Lanny what the man already knew—that he cared for him like a son cared for his father.

While Juan's battered and bruised teenage soldiers held the mighty Zarazaian army at bay, Murdock slipped into the thicket of vines and gnarled trees that led into the jungle. He didn't think, didn't feel and didn't look back. On his belly, he made his way over the rough forest floor until he knew he was out of sight and out of range. Just as he rose into a crouching position, a thunderous explosion rocked the earth beneath his feet. He froze to the spot. His heartbeat drummed in his ears. His blood ran cold.

Murdock retraced his path, racing toward the men he'd just left. Pausing briefly as he neared the site, he breathed deeply and pleaded with God. But it was a prayer he already knew wouldn't be answered. Finding shelter and a modicum of safety behind a stand of massive carnauba palms, Murdock forced himself to face the truth. Billows of black smoke rose into the sky where the explosion had hit. Pieces of trees mingled with body parts. There was nothing he could do to help Lanny and Juan or the boy soldiers.

Lanny! Murdock cried silently. *Lanny was dead!*

Murdock's eyelids flew open. He shot straight up. Moisture coated his body as if he'd just returned from the Zarazaian jungle a few minutes ago instead of twenty years ago. Kicking the wrinkled, tangled covers off his feet, he slid out of bed. He padded on bare feet across the wooden floor as he made his way out of the bedroom,

*down the hall and into the living room. What he needed
was a shot of whiskey.*

*He retrieved a bottle of Jack Daniel's from the make-
shift bar on the sofa table by the windows that overlooked Locklin Street. After pouring himself a liberal
amount of the liquor, he flopped down in his favorite
chair, a brown overstuffed leather seat. As he lifted the
glass to his lips, he stretched out his long legs and rested
his feet on the huge leather ottoman.*

*Why the hell had he dreamed about Lanny? About
Juan and his soldiers? After twenty years, why couldn't
he forget the past?*

*Liking the taste of the whiskey, he savored it in his
mouth a few seconds before swallowing. The liquid
burned a trail down his throat and hit his stomach like
a ball of fire, warming his insides.*

*For the first five or six years after his escape from
Zaraza, he'd had the dream on a regular basis, but as
time went by, the dream had become less frequent. This
particular nightmare hadn't awakened him once during
the past ten years. So why tonight?*

*An uneasy feeling gnawed away at him. Something
was wrong. But what? He was a man who had survived
by taking heed when his gut instincts warned him. When
he'd been a green kid of eighteen, he had come through
the final days of the fighting in Nam without a scratch.
He had survived over twenty-five years as a mercenary
and a freelance CIA operative by a combination of good
instincts and being a damn lucky son of a bitch.*

*There had to be a reason why he'd dreamed about the
last day he had seen Lanny McCroskey alive.*

*Murdock's hand accidentally brushed the television
remote control. His nerves zinged. That was it! On the
world news he'd watched right before going to bed last*

night, there had been a report about the twenty-year war in Zaraza and how the rebel army had grown in size and strength over the years. The journalist had said that the old regime, controlled by General Ramos, was in a panic. For the first time since the beginning of the civil war, the rebels had a real chance to take over the government.

Murdock downed the last drops of whiskey, set the glass aside and closed his eyes. Lanny, Juan and a bunch of teenagers masquerading as guerrilla soldiers had sacrificed their lives that day—for the cause. And by dying, they had saved Murdock. Saved him to deliver a message to their CIA contact, Rick Burdett.

In the dark, lonely moments when a man questioned what his life had been worth, Murdock asked himself why he'd been the one spared. What made him so all-fired special that God had let him live when better men had died? But he'd never found the answer.

Chapter 1

Catherine Price rose from her chair, smoothed the wrinkles from her blue linen skirt and squared her shoulders. The moment the door to her office opened, she took a calming breath and prepared herself to meet the government official who had telephoned her that morning. Rickman Burdett had identified himself as a CIA Deputy Director.

"I have information about your father," the man had told her. "This is something I prefer to discuss with you in person."

Jane Farr, Catherine's secretary, ushered the gentleman into her office. Mr. Burdett was a tall, slender gentleman with a mane of white hair and a set of piercing brown eyes. Except for those cold, calculating eyes, he looked like any ordinary, grandfatherly businessman.

As Catherine rounded her desk, she extended her hand in greeting. "Mr. Burdett."

Burdett clasped her hand in his. His cool, slender fingers gripped loosely, his handshake reserved. "I appreciate your seeing me, Ms. Price. I realize that I probably made this matter sound mysterious when I phoned you and for that I do apologize. However, the news I have for you is the kind that should be delivered in person."

Catherine had no idea what this man would tell her about her father. After all these years, she didn't really care. Lanny McCroskey had been dead since she was sixteen and hadn't really been a part of her life even before his death. His military career had sent him to Vietnam when she was a mere child and when he had returned, he'd been a stranger to her and to her mother. Her parents had divorced five years before her father's mysterious death in Zaraza and during those five years, she hadn't seen her father once.

"Won't you sit down." Catherine waved her hand in a well-mannered invitation.

"Thanks."

Burdett waited for her to return to her tufted-leather chair behind her antique oak desk before he sat.

"Now, what is this information you have about my father that prompted you to fly to Tennessee to tell me in person."

"Have you been watching the televised reports on the war in Zaraza lately?"

"Not really. I don't watch much television. I prefer to spend my leisure hours reading."

"Then let me bring you up to date on what's going on there."

"Is that really necessary?" Catherine glanced at her diamond-studded gold watch. Whatever this man had to tell her, she hoped he'd make it quick. She had a busy day ahead of her and she hated the thought of wasting time listening to some old war story about her father.

"Ms. Price, what if I told you that your father didn't die in Zaraza twenty years ago?"

"What?" A nervous unease fluttered in her stomach.

"We have reason to believe that Lanny McCroskey was taken alive by the Zarazaian government and has spent the past twenty years in prison there."

Catherine laid her tightly balled fists on top of her desk. She had understood Mr. Burdett's words, but her mind refused to accept their meaning. "What makes you think that my father is a prisoner in Zaraza?"

"We received a letter—" Burdett reached into the inside pocket of his coat and pulled out a tattered envelope "—from General Ramos, the Zarazaian dictator." Burdett held out the missive toward Catherine.

She stared at the envelope. She didn't want to touch it. Didn't want to become involved in whatever game this man was playing. Her father had died twenty years ago. The U.S. government had officially informed her mother of that fact.

"I don't believe my father is alive and I have no intention of sitting here listening to any wild stories you've fabricated about—"

"Lanny McCroskey is alive!" Burdett lifted a photograph from the envelope. "He's twenty years older and looks like hell, but I recognize the man in this picture. It's your father, Ms. Price." He laid the six-by-four-inch color snapshot on her desk.

Catherine fought the urge to swipe the picture off into the trash. But despite her doubts that it was possible for her father to still be alive, she couldn't seem to stop herself from leaning forward slightly and glancing quickly at the photograph. Her heart caught in her throat as she looked at the vaguely familiar face. Without hesitation, she snatched the snapshot from her desk and lifted it for closer inspection.

The man's hair was gray, as was his beard and mustache. He was thin, haggard, weary. Slumped shoulders. Hollow eyes. An aura of defeat surrounded him. This was an old man. A pathetic old man. This wasn't the Lanny McCroskey she remembered. Big, robust, intimidating. Gone was the tanned skin and black hair. Gone was the virile, almost swaggering persona that had been a part of her army sergeant father. But the eyes were the same. A pure sky blue. Despite the misery she saw in his expression, she couldn't mistake the resemblance between her own eyes and those that stared back at her from the photograph she held in her trembling hand.

"My God!" She clutched the picture with both hands, then brought it upward to cover her mouth with it as she closed her eyes. Tears lodged in her throat.

Burdett stood abruptly. "General Ramos is asking $100,000 in exchange for Lanny's release."

Catherine's eyelids flew open. "What—what did you say?"

"It seems General Ramos is well aware that his dictatorship is nearing its end, so he's selling his foreign prisoners back to their families for as much cash as possible. The asking price for Lanny's freedom is $100,000 in U.S. currency." Burdett offered Catherine the letter once again.

"Officially, we—the U.S. government—can't become involved. But unofficially, I want to help you and am willing to put up part of the money, if—"

"I have the money," Catherine said, her voice a mere whisper. "I can give you a check today."

"I'm afraid it's not quite that simple." Burdett frowned, wrinkling his brow and deepening the lines around his mouth. "If you'll read the letter, you'll see that, in Lanny's case, General Ramos is demanding that you deliver the money in person to the capital city of San Carlos. This holds true for all the political prisoners the governor is selling. By extorting money from individuals and not governments, he stands a better chance of finding a government that will give him asylum when he flees Zaraza."

Catherine grabbed the letter from Burdett, unfolded the wrinkled page and scanned the message hurriedly. The conditions of the exchange were spelled out quite succinctly. No room for doubt. One hundred thousand dollars, U.S. currency, hand delivered by Lanny's daughter, Catherine McCroskey Price, directly into General Ramos's hands.

"I'll provide the money, Mr. Burdett, but I will not take the money to Zaraza." Lanny McCroskey *was* her father, she reminded herself, and she'd never miss the hundred thousand, which was only a pittance in comparison to the ten million Rodney had left her. But she didn't really owe her father anything. And she certainly wasn't ready to risk her life entering a South American country embroiled in a twenty-year civil war. "Surely you can send a female agent into Zaraza. Someone who can pose as Lanny's daughter."

"Ms. Price, if General Ramos knows you exist, knows your name, then our guess is he has a way to identify you. Perhaps recent pictures of you."

Catherine shuddered. The thought that some stranger working for the Zarazaian government might have snapped her picture without her being aware of it both frightened and outraged her.

"Are you saying that the only way I can save my father is by actually going to Zaraza?"

"Yes, I'm afraid that's exactly what I'm saying," Burdett told her. "Of course, it's your call, Ms. Price. We can't force you to rescue your father. However, if you decide to go, I can guarantee you a professional bodyguard to accompany you on the trip."

"A professional. Do you mean a government agent?"

"No. As I told you, the government can't become involved in this." Burdett cleared his throat. "The man I have in mind has worked for Dundee Private Security and Investigation for over a year now, but before that he was one of the best mercenaries around. If anyone can get you in and out of Zaraza safe and sound, it's Murdock."

"Murdock? Aloysius Murdock?" Catherine asked.

A hint of a smile curved Burdett's lips. "No one calls him Aloysius and lives."

"This Murdock was in Vietnam with my father, wasn't he? And he was in Zaraza with him twenty years ago, too! I vaguely remember my mother mentioning once that Mr. Murdock paid her a visit after my father was killed."

"Will you go to San Carlos and deliver the money to General Ramos?" Burdett asked. "Remember, you'll have Murdock at your side the whole time."

"If Mr. Murdock is a contemporary of my father, then he must be at least in his early sixties. Do you honestly think he's physically capable of—"

"Murdock's forty-six. He was just a green kid in Nam, not a career soldier like your dad. And believe me, I doubt any man half his age is in as good a shape as Murdock. Take my word for it, he's a man of steel."

The last thing on earth Catherine wanted to do was travel to a third world, war-torn country to rescue the father who had deserted her and her mother long before he'd been reported killed. Why should she risk her life for a man who'd walked out on her without a backward glance? Christmas and birthday presents didn't really count as far as she was concerned. The fact that he'd sent gifts up until he'd supposedly died in Zaraza hardly made up for his absence.

"I can withdraw the money from my bank this afternoon," Catherine heard herself saying, despite her uncertainty. "When can you arrange for me to meet Mr. Murdock?"

Dinner had been on the Dundee Agency tonight. Once a year, Sam Dundee dragged himself away from Le Bijou Bleu, his island retreat in the Gulf Coast, to come to Atlanta and inspect the troops. Or, at least, that was the way Murdock thought of the big boss's visit. The rest of the time, Ellen Denby, Dundee's CEO, was in charge. Ellen had been the one who had hired Murdock, as well as most of the other current employees, and she was the one who made the decisions. But Sam still owned the agency, despite his retirement several years ago.

A private room at Peaches, a local downtown Atlanta bar and grill, had hosted the crème de la crème of private security agents. Murdock glanced around the table as Sam handed his credit card to the waitress. Over a year ago, after deciding he was getting too old for a life of constant danger, Murdock had retired from his career as a soldier of fortune and come to work for Dundee. The men congregated here tonight were cut from the same cloth as he. Former mercenaries, special forces members, lawmen and government agents. And not a guy under thirty-five in the bunch.

One man—Egan Cassidy—was Murdock's age and a

former Nam vet. Their paths had crossed more than once in the years they'd both been mercenaries. The youngest of the bunch was Joe Ornelas, a former Navajo policeman who had just turned thirty-five.

Murdock had a passing acquaintance with all the Dundee employees, but Cassidy, Ornelas and four others were men whose expertise Murdock knew firsthand and for whom he had the greatest respect. Matt O'Brien, a pretty boy with a mind like a computer. Hunter Whitelaw, the silent, deadly type. Jack Parker, a deceptive charmer. And David Wolfe, a mystery man, who'd been hired personally by Sam Dundee.

And of course, there was Ellen, who was an enigma. Ultra feminine. Beautiful face. Built like a brick outhouse. Yet tough, shrewd and a match for any man.

When Jack proposed a final toast, this one to the lovely Ellen, Murdock lifted his beer mug and joined in the good-natured fun. Despite her knockout good looks, Ellen fit in with the crowd of macho men as if she were one of them. She could outdrink, outcuss and outsmart every last one of them and they all knew it.

Murdock had learned about Dundee's from an old buddy, Gabriel Hawk, who had once been a freelance CIA operative and with whom Murdock had occasionally worked on assignments, especially in the Caribbean and Central and South America. He and Hawk spoke Spanish like natives.

Hawk had left the agency after marrying his last assignment, a former missionary who had tamed one of the baddest of the bad boys when she landed Hawk. Murdock never thought he'd live to see the day a woman would be able to wrap Hawk around her little finger. He'd been wrong.

Murdock had been kicked more than once where it

hurt, the first time as a teenager, the last time as a grown man who should have known better. After Barbara, a society beauty who'd used him for "a walk on the wild side", he'd sworn off relationships.

With the check paid and the last round of beers drunk, the agents began milling around the room, shaking hands and saying their good-nights. Murdock enjoyed a social occasion from time to time, but usually he preferred the solitude of his loft apartment in an old renovated building. Sometimes Cassidy would drop by for a game of pool or several of the guys would come over for poker, but the rest of his free nights, Murdock spent alone. He liked to read, a passion of his since childhood. And sometimes, when he had the urge, he'd find himself a willing woman. One who didn't mind that he'd leave afterward, long before daylight, and probably wouldn't call her for a second date.

As they headed out the door, Murdock laid his hand on Cassidy's back. "I hear you got stuck with teaching the ropes to the new Dundee recruits."

"Yeah, I drew the short straw."

Cassidy grinned, something Murdock had seldom seen the man do in all the years he'd known him. Cassidy was a somber man, with some sort of demon chasing him.

"You on for pool tonight?" Murdock asked.

"Not tonight," Cassidy replied, the smile still in place. "I have all-night plans with a lady."

"A lady, huh? Well, be careful, Bubba. Ladies are the most dangerous kind of female known to man."

"Speaking from experience?"

"A gentleman never gets kicked where it hurts and tells." Murdock slapped Cassidy on the back as the two men chuckled.

The cool autumn air hit Murdock the minute he stepped out onto the Atlanta street. He threw up his hand to wave goodbye to Cassidy and the others, then headed for his Camaro.

The drive home to Locklin Street took less than fifteen minutes. He parked the Z28 in the tenants' garage that took up the entire ground level of the old building. Besides his loft apartment, there were four other apartments below him, two each on the second and third floors. Using the service elevator, which none of the other residents used, Murdock headed upward. The moment he emerged from the elevator, a sense of unease hit him square in the gut. He lifted his jacket back over the hip holster and unbuckled the flap. He hadn't lived forty-six years, most of it in life-threatening situations, without acquiring a keen instinct for danger.

"No need to draw your weapon," the familiar voice said.

Recognizing the voice, Murdock released a tightly indrawn breath and turned to face his former CIA contact. "What the hell are you doing here, Burdett?"

After glancing around at the darkened corridor, Burdett nodded toward the door of Murdock's apartment. "I just drove over from Huntington, Tennessee, and I've been waiting for you here nearly an hour. Before we talk, I need to see a man about a dog and then I wouldn't object to a drink or two."

Murdock chuckled as he unlocked the door and ushered Burdett inside the open expanse of his private domain. After flipping a light switch that controlled the recessed wall fixtures and illuminating the huge living room, he locked the door behind them.

"Bathroom's through those double louvered doors."

Murdock used his thumb to point the direction. "Jack Daniel's is all I'm drinking these days."

"Fine with me. Make mine neat."

While he prepared the drinks and waited for Burdett to emerge from the john, Murdock wondered why a CIA Deputy Director was paying him a nighttime visit. He hadn't seen or heard from Rick Burdett in nearly two years.

When Burdett came out of the bathroom, he glanced around the apartment, his gaze taking leisurely note of everything from floor to ceiling. "Don't tell me you decorated this place yourself."

"All right, I won't tell you." Murdock handed Burdett his whiskey. "So, are you going to tell me what you're doing here or are we going to play nice-nice all night?"

Burdett took a sip of the liquor, then without invitation, sat on the tan leather sofa that rested on the wooden floor, squarely in the middle of the large room.

"Lanny McCroskey is alive."

"What?" Murdock felt as if he'd been hit on the head with a sledgehammer.

"Lanny didn't die twenty years ago the way we thought he did, the way you said he did." Burdett took another sip of whiskey. "We figure he was wounded. Hurt pretty bad. But he lived, God bless his damned soul. He's spent the past twenty years in a Zarazaian prison."

"How do you know? Hell, don't answer that! Just tell me if you're sure. One hundred percent sure."

Rick Burdett pulled a photograph from his coat pocket and handed it to Murdock. "This was taken less than a week ago."

Murdock studied the snapshot of a skinny, old, gray-haired man. If not for the eyes, he wouldn't have recognized his former sergeant. "God! He'd have been better off if he'd died."

"Have you been keeping up with the latest news on the Zarazaian civil war?"

"Yeah. I know Juan Sabino's kid has taken over where his old man left off and he's whipping Ramos's ass."

"Ramos is preparing for the worst and he wants to make sure that if he has to abdicate his position, he can take as much money with him as possible. He's asking $100,000 in exchange for Lanny."

"Jeez!" A hundred thousand was a lot, but by cashing in some bonds, emptying his savings and, if necessary, selling his new Camaro, he could scrape up the cash. "I can get my hands on that much, but it could take me several days."

"Lanny's daughter has the cash and she's willing to pay for his release."

"Lanny's daughter?" Murdock frowned, remembering. "Oh, yeah. He talked about her all the time. Her and her mother. He really cared about his ex-wife and about his kid, too. So, the girl's all right, huh, if she's willing to help—"

"Catherine Price is no girl," Burdett said. "She's thirty-six, a widow and was reluctant at first to even talk to me about her father."

"Thirty-six. Damn. Guess I still thought of her as a young girl."

"Here's the deal," Burdett said, as if he didn't want to waste any more time. "Ramos is demanding the money in cash."

Murdock let out a long, low whistle. "That's a lot of

money for one of your men to carry around in a briefcase all the way to Zaraza.''

''There's a bigger problem. One of my men won't be taking the money. Catherine Price will be.''

''Why the blue blazes would you—''

''Ramos's stipulation. He's demanded Lanny's daughter bring it herself. For each prisoner, Ramos has asked that a specific family member bring the ransom money. He's a wily old fox trying to cover his ass by not getting any governments directly involved in the exchange.'' Burdett paused momentarily, but when Murdock didn't respond, he continued. ''I told Ms. Price that you would accompany her to San Carlos for the exchange. She'll arrive tomorrow evening, escorted by one of our agents, who will turn her and the hundred thousand over to you.''

''I don't like it. Taking Lanny's daughter into that cesspool. The last thing he'd want would be for that girl of his to put her life in danger to save him.''

''She's going to Zaraza to get her father out of prison. She's the type of woman who's doing this because it's the honorable thing to do, not because she loves Lanny. But regardless of her motivation, she needs a bodyguard. I was sure you'd want to be her protector.''

''What time does her flight arrive?''

''Five-thirty.'' After finishing off his whiskey, Burdett set the glass on a brown marble coaster that rested on the big, square, oak coffee table. ''You two will fly straight to Peru day after tomorrow. Arrangements have been made to then take you and Ms. Price, by private plane, directly into San Carlos. One of our contacts will meet you at the airport down there.''

''And I suppose since she'll have cash on her, Ms. Price will be under my protection from the moment she arrives tomorrow. Which means Lanny's daughter will be staying here with me until our flight for Peru.''

"Yeah. And you better roll out the red carpet while she's here. Catherine Price is the type of woman who expects first-class treatment. She's a thoroughbred. A Southern lady, through and through.''

"Just like her mother.'' Murdock remembered how Lanny had gone on and on about his Mae Beth. *She's too good for me,* he'd said. *Don't know what a lady like her ever saw in an ole Tennessee hillbilly like me. But damn if she didn't love me as much as I loved her.*

"You knew Lanny's ex-wife?'' Burdett asked.

"I met her once. After I came back from Zaraza. I went to see her, to tell her about Lanny's last day. And about how much he still cared about her and their child. She didn't shed a tear, but I could tell she was hurting bad. My guess is that she still cared about him, too. Maybe when Lanny comes back, the two of them can—''

"Mrs. McCroskey died nine years ago.''

"Then Catherine is all Lanny has left.'' Murdock sighed. With a look of resolve he said, "You can be damned sure I'll take good care of her.''

Catherine scanned the airport crowd, searching for Murdock. Although she knew the agent who'd accompanied her would know Murdock on sight, she wondered if she could pick him out from all the other men. A former mercenary. A man like her father, to whom killing was second nature. Surely, that kind of life would show on his face.

Placing his hand under her elbow, the young agent urged her forward. "There he is,'' Agent Hendricks said.

"Where?'' Catherine asked.

"Straight ahead, on the left."

A dozen men waited for disembarking passengers. After surveying several, her gaze halted on one man. She instinctively recognized Aloysius Murdock. A knot of apprehension formed in the pit of her stomach. And a purely feminine unease settled deep within her. He was everything she had expected. And everything she had feared. Big. Burly. Indeed, a mountain of a man, with enormous shoulders and huge arms. He stood at least six foot six, towering over the others. And there was a world-weary look in his hazel brown eyes as their gazes locked. A shudder rippled through her at his intense scrutiny. And she realized in that one instant that the man who was going to be her bodyguard on a trip into hell had recognized her just as she had him—instinctively.

Chapter 2

He would have known her anywhere. Could have picked her from a lineup of a hundred women. She had class written all over her. Catherine Price might as well have had twenty-two Karat Gold stamped on her forehead. She was the genuine article. He had known enough women in his time to recognize a real lady when he saw one. He remembered Lanny saying his little girl was beautiful, just like her mama, but he hadn't paid much attention to a father's praise of his only child. Murdock had no idea what she'd looked like as a kid, but Lanny's little girl had grown up to be one fine-looking woman.

Her gaze met his and locked instantly. An odd sensation hit Murdock in the gut, as if a hard fist had knocked the air out of him. Her blue eyes, so much like her father's, held him spellbound for a split second. She tilted her head, and he noted an air of snobbery in her expression, as if she'd just encountered something unpleasant and couldn't quite figure out the mannerly way to react. With mixed emotions bombarding him, he shook off the crazy feelings swirling around inside him and marched forward to meet Lanny's daughter.

Agent Hendricks, carrying a briefcase manacled to his wrist, followed Catherine's quick steps as she headed straight toward Murdock. He realized that, without introductions, she knew exactly who he was. She'd recognized him instantly, as he had her.

When she drew nearer, he noticed how tall she was, a good six feet in her sensible two-inch navy heels. And although she was trim in her simple navy suit, her hips and breasts were rounded nicely, accentuating her tiny waist. Her shiny brown hair was secured in a large, neat bun at the base of her neck. A pair of large gold hoops shimmered in her earlobes and a heavy gold bracelet dangled on her left wrist.

"Mr. Murdock?" she inquired as she paused directly in front of him.

"Just Murdock, Ms. Price."

Agent Hendricks stepped in front of Catherine and extended his hand. "Brian Hendricks," he introduced himself. "As soon as I see your ID, I can hand Ms. Price and her briefcase—" he lifted his wrist to display the brown leather satchel "—over to you. Just standard procedure."

Murdock whipped out his Dundee's identification badge. Hendricks inspected the ID quickly.

"You have the key, don't you, sir?" Hendricks asked.

Swallowing hard as she broke eye contact with Murdock, Catherine watched his huge hand as it delved into his pocket and produced the handcuff key. Then hurriedly, she rummaged in her purse for the key to the briefcase, wanting to make sure it was safe.

"Is that the key to the briefcase?" Murdock asked.

"What?" Momentarily flustered, Catherine hesitated before she replied. "Yes. Why?"

Without asking permission or making any comment, Murdock took the key from her. His big, callused fingertips brushed over the soft, smooth flesh of her palm. She sucked in a deep breath at the contact.

"Better let me keep that." He realized that she'd felt it, too. That electrical current snapping between them at a mere touch. Damn! He didn't like this. The last thing he had expected was to be attracted to Lanny's daughter.

Catherine glowered at him, but didn't respond.

Hendricks cleared his throat. Murdock hurriedly uncuffed the man and took possession of the briefcase containing a hundred thousand dollars in U.S. bills.

"Good luck, Ms. Price," Hendricks said.

"Thank you." Catherine extended her hand to the agent.

The minute Hendricks took her hand in his, the urge to grab her away from the drooling boy made Murdock act hastily. Without so much as a goodbye, he slid his arm around Catherine's waist and drew her to his side. She tensed immediately and released Hendricks's hand. Before she could voice a protest, Murdock maneuvered her around swiftly and headed her toward the baggage claims area.

"I don't think it's necessary for you to manhandle me, Mr. Murdock!" Catherine pulled away from him and stopped dead still.

Oh, but that was where she was wrong, he thought. You started out with a woman the way you intended to go. Catherine needed to realize that, from here on out, he was running the show.

"I didn't realize I was manhandling you. I saw no reason to prolong your goodbyes to Agent Hendricks."

Murdock took a couple of steps forward, then paused when he noticed Catherine hadn't moved. "The sooner we get you and this briefcase out of the airport, the better."

She moved then, quickly and straight to his side. "You don't honestly think I'm in any danger here in the Atlanta airport, do you?"

Murdock placed his arm around her again. This time she didn't protest and fell into step beside him.

"You're safe, as long as you're with me."

"Confident, aren't you, Mr. Murdock?"

"Just Murdock, Catherine."

He grinned when he felt her flinch at his use of her given name. Surely she didn't expect him to call her Ms. Price. He wasn't one of her students and he sure as hell wasn't one of the refined Southern gentleman she dated.

He liked the fact that she was tall. Most women barely came to his shoulder, even in heels. But standing only six inches shorter than he, Catherine could look him square in the eye. Close enough to spit, he thought. And something told him that during this trip together, the time might come when she'd do just that—spit in his eye! Catherine might have been raised to be a lady by her Southern belle mother, but there had to be something of Lanny in her. Some streak of wildness. He'd bet his last dollar that a hot-blooded woman was hidden beneath that cool, controlled facade.

At the baggage claim, she pointed out her black suitcase and Murdock lifted it quickly, then hurried her out of the airport and to his car.

On the drive to Murdock's apartment, their conversation consisted of such mundane matters as the details of their 8:00 am flight to Peru and the weather. When the silence between them reached the awkward stage,

Murdock turned on the radio, setting the dial to a jazz and blues station. A mournful voice sang about love, loss and heartbreak.

Occasionally Catherine stole quick glances at Murdock's chiseled profile. Hard chin and jaw. Clean shaven, with only a hint of a light aftershave. Short, neat, dark-brown hair. Confined alone with him in the small quarters of the car's interior, she felt overwhelmed by his massive size. Aloysius Murdock was huge. And every ounce was pure muscle.

He was a much larger man than her father, who, although tall, had been lanky. But the aura of danger and power that surrounded Murdock reminded her of Lanny McCroskey. She had adored her big, macho father, even though she'd seen little of him during her young life. He had called her his kitten and even after the divorce, he had remembered her with expensive birthday presents, Christmas gifts and occasional phone calls. She had tried to hate him, had pretended that she never wanted to see him again, but when the news came that he'd been killed in Zaraza, she had mourned his death. Even now, after twenty years, she had conflicting feelings about the man who had fathered her. She both hated and loved him. But despite everything, she was willing to pay a hundred thousand dollars and perhaps risk her life to save him.

Something told her that men like her father—and men like Murdock—inspired those mixed feelings in their women. Their wives, daughters, sisters, lovers and perhaps even their mothers. Most women were drawn to big, bold, dangerous men and yet their common sense warned them to flee from the bad boys of this world. Her mother had learned, the hard way, that loving such a man caused immeasurable heartache.

Catherine had avoided men who even vaguely reminded her of Lanny, choosing instead to date the academic types. Rodney Price had been Lanny's exact opposite. A quiet, gentle, soft-spoken gentleman who had enjoyed a night at the ballet as much if not more than an afternoon at a football stadium. She and Rodney had been a perfect match and she had been happy during the four years of their marriage. Her one regret, after Rodney's death, was that he hadn't left her with a child.

"We're here," Murdock said, his voice a baritone roar.

Catherine jumped at the sound. Jerked abruptly from her thoughts, she glanced through the windshield just in time to catch a glimpse of the renovated brick building. Murdock wheeled the Camaro into the ground-level garage and whipped it into a parking slot.

After lifting the briefcase from the floorboard, he rounded the hood and opened the door for Catherine. She mouthed a thank you, but refused his offered hand. He dropped his big paw, grinned and left her standing by the open car door. She slammed the door shut when he walked toward the trunk, then waited at his side until he'd retrieved her suitcase.

"I've got the loft apartment," he said. "So, I use the old service elevator. Just follow me."

"Have you lived here long?" Making conversation was something Catherine excelled at as a normal rule. Years as a teacher at Huntington Academy before she'd become headmistress of the school had taught her the art of speaking. She had charmed many a student and many a parent.

"I moved to Atlanta about eighteen months ago and found this place about a year ago." He didn't tell her that he'd bought the old building as an investment. "I completely renovated the loft." He opened the iron-bar door of the service elevator and stood back, waiting for her to enter. When she eyed the contraption and hesitated, he chuckled. "I promise it's safe."

Reluctantly, she entered the elevator, then plastered a phony smile on her face, as if to say, *See, I'm not afraid.* But she suspected that he knew she was leery—of the elevator and of him.

The smooth ride up to the loft surprised her, but not as much as the spacious, tastefully decorated apartment that spread out before them when Murdock unlocked and swung open the double entry doors. The living room, kitchen and dining room were one huge area of painted white walls on the interior and old brick on the exterior side. Gleaming hardwood covered the floor and big wooden beams ran the expanse of the ceiling. An overstuffed leather sofa and twin chairs created a cozy, yet masculine living area in front of the floor-to-ceiling windows. Pleated shades allowed for privacy or sunlight. On the opposite side of the room an oil painting of a clipper ship tossing about in a storm hung on the wall behind the black lacquer table which was surrounded by six brass-and-steel chairs that mimicked Victorian bentwood chairs.

"Your apartment is…well, it's wonderful." Catherine wished she had been able to keep the surprised tone out of her voice. "You didn't do this yourself. I mean, surely you hired someone to—"

Murdock slammed the door. Catherine jumped. Dammit, why was she so nervous? she wondered. Every unexpected sound made her overreact.

"Why do you assume I hired a decorator? Don't you think a guy like me could put together something like this?"

"I'm sorry. I didn't mean to imply that you—"

"Sure you did." Murdock walked past her. "No need to be on your best behavior around me or try to be mannerly. We don't know each other, but you've drawn some conclusions about me, just as I have about you. You figured a former mercenary who's now a professional bodyguard has more brawn than brains and would probably live in a cluttered dump, with hot-and-cold running bimbos."

"I didn't say one word about bimbos!"

Murdock laughed, the sound like rumbling thunder. "Sit down and make yourself at home. I'll put your suitcase in the bedroom." He caught the startled look on her face and before she could protest, he said, "There are two bedrooms, so don't be concerned that you'll have to share a bed with me. Besides, why would I need you when I keep a bimbo on call twenty-four hours a day."

Catherine's eyes rounded into wide, startled, blue saucers. As Murdock disappeared behind a glass-block partition, she gritted her teeth. Only her strong willpower prevented her from stomping her foot. Damn the man! He enjoyed teasing her—another typical male trait she remembered Lanny McCroskey had possessed. She recalled when her mother had complained about his constant teasing, he'd said a man only teased a woman he liked. Then he'd kissed her mother and said *or a woman he loves*.

Did that mean that Murdock liked her? *What did it matter?* her inner voice questioned. *He doesn't have to like you to accompany you to Zaraza and act as your bodyguard. And you don't have to like him. As a matter of fact, you'd be better off not liking him.*

Just as she sat in one of the leather chairs, Murdock returned, minus his jacket. He had rolled up the sleeves of his white shirt to his elbows, revealing large, hairy forearms. A bevy of tiny nerves sent off shock waves inside her stomach. The man was so big, so overwhelmingly masculine that he took her breath away. Dear God, he intimidated the hell out of her.

"Want something to drink?" he asked. "Coffee? Tea? Cola? Whiskey?"

"Tea would be nice."

"Hot or cold?"

"Uh-huh." As if entranced in a hypnotic spell, she couldn't take her eyes off him.

"Which?"

Warmth crept up her neck and into her face. Stop this right now! she warned herself. You're acting like an idiot. So he intimidates you. Big deal! There is absolutely no reason to be afraid of him. Remember, he is supposed to be your protector.

"Hot tea, if it's not too much trouble." She deliberately avoided direct eye contact.

"Earl Grey?"

"Yes, that would be lovely." Once again Murdock surprised her. She'd never have thought he would have Earl Grey tea in his cupboard. "By the way, did you put the briefcase in the bedroom, too?"

"I put the hundred thousand in the wall safe in my bedroom."

"Oh."

"You can trust me with the money, Catherine. There's no one who wants to get Lanny out of that Zarazaian prison more than I do."

"I wasn't implying that you'd—"

"Sure you were, but don't let it bother you. Despite the fact that Lanny is your father and was once my best friend doesn't mean you and I have to be friends. Actually, to accomplish this mission, we don't even have to like each other. All that's necessary is for you to co-operate with me and follow my orders.''

"I'm well aware of the fact that you're a professional, with years of experience in matters like this." Catherine's right hand fluttered nervously at her neck as her fingers toyed with the collar on her white silk blouse. "I have no intention of giving you any trouble, Mr. Murdock. I'm perfectly willing to accept your leadership in this matter.''

"Well, that takes a load off my mind, Catherine." He emphasized the use of her given name and took great delight in the displeased look she gave him. But instincts warned him that her giving lip service to his leadership and actually following his orders were two different things entirely.

Murdock filled a kettle with tap water, then placed it on the stove eye to heat. Taking two black mugs and a small box from an upper cabinet, he set them on the counter and then removed a couple of tea bags and placed them in the oversize cups.

"I'd like to freshen up," Catherine said.

"Bathroom is to your right, between the two bed-rooms. Can't miss it.''

"Thank you."

She found the bathroom and hurried inside, then closed the door behind her. She slumped against the wall, letting her head rest on the cool glass-block surface that enclosed the small room. What was she doing here, in this man's apartment, making preparations to fly away with him on a dangerous trip into foreign country? She didn't have an adventurous bone in her body. All her life, she had taken the safe path, avoiding all unneces-sary risks. And here she was, putting her life in this stranger's hands, gambling her very existence on his ability to keep her safe. Had she completely lost her mind?

If you don't go to Zaraza, your father will die in prison, her conscience taunted her. *You have no choice, but to do the right thing.* Somehow she knew that if her mother were alive, her mother would risk anything to save the man she had cut out of her life ages ago— A man whose name Mae Beth McCroskey had whispered with her last breath. If her mother had loved her father that much, then Lanny had to be worth saving.

Catherine wet a washcloth and patted the cool dampness over her face as she gazed into the mirror. She hadn't slept well last night and it showed in the faint darkness under her eyes. After washing her hands, she left the sanctuary of the bathroom and returned to the kitchen area of Murdock's apartment.

As she approached him, she said, "You knew my father very well, didn't you?"

"He was my sergeant in Vietnam," Murdock said. "That's where we met. And then later, we worked together."

"As mercenaries?" Catherine pulled out one of the round-back metal stools that lined the wide bar which separated the kitchen from the rest of the open space.

Murdock didn't answer her immediately. Instead, he rummaged around in the refrigerator. When he turned to face her, he held a plate of sliced ham, a head of lettuce and a ripe red tomato. "Want a sandwich? It's nearly dinnertime."

Murdock placed the dish on the counter, puzzling over her sudden curiosity. Just what did Catherine want to know about her father? he wondered. How much did he dare tell her about Lanny's life? About the assignments they had shared, the risks they'd taken, the bloodbaths they had been a part of more than once. He didn't think Lanny would want his little girl to know the details of his soldier-of-fortune life.

"I know that after my father returned from Vietnam, he resigned from the army and became a mercenary," she continued. "His job choice was one of the reasons he and my mother eventually divorced."

"Then why ask me, if you already know?"

"Because I never *really* knew Lanny McCroskey." Catherine eased down on one of the stools and hooked her feet beneath the circular rounds on the bottom. "I was barely eight years old when he came home from Vietnam and in those eight years, he'd been away from us more than he'd been with us. Then three years later, he and my mother divorced. I never saw him again." She paused, waiting for Murdock to comment. He didn't. Instead he laid plates on the counter and opened a loaf of bread.

"Ham sandwiches okay with you?"

"Why don't you want to talk to me about my father?"

"Mustard? Mayonnaise? Both?"

"Are you deliberately trying to irritate me?"

"All I'm trying to do is fix you some tea and a sandwich."

Catherine stared at the big man. The expression on his face one of total calm, Murdock met her gaze head-on and didn't so much as flinch. What was it that he was determined not to tell her? Why was he being so evasive?

"I'll take both mayo and mustard," she replied. "But please, let me help." She knew there was nothing she could do to persuade this man to talk to her, to tell her about her father. All she could do was cooperate. After all, whether she liked it or not, she needed Murdock to go with her into Zaraza and bring her father back alive. He could well be her father's only hope for survival—and her only hope, too.

"Sit tight," he told her. "I can throw a couple of sandwiches together."

She nodded her agreement. They exchanged brief, hesitant looks. But she understood the significance of his quick yet penetrating stare. And she suspected that he knew exactly what she was thinking. They were strangers, two people joined in a common cause—saving Lanny McCroskey's life. After all, her father was their only bond, the only reason they'd met. Neither wanted or needed to become better acquainted. Each feared the other, on a purely primitive level. And despite their shared interest in Lanny's welfare, they didn't quite trust each other.

Silence separated them as surely as if it were a tangible wall. Murdock prepared the sandwiches and tea, then placed a plate and mug in front of Catherine. He eased his large frame down beside her on one of the stools, then lifted the thick sandwich to his mouth. She sipped the tea and eyed the man-size sandwich he'd made for her.

"The war messed your father up pretty badly." Murdock laid down the sandwich and lifted the mug in both hands, gripping it firmly. "You know. Mentally and emotionally. It wasn't that he didn't want to be the man he'd been before...he just couldn't be."

"Why didn't he get help? A psychiatrist could have—"

"All the doctors in the world couldn't have put Lanny McCroskey back together. Believe me, Catherine, he wanted to be a good husband and father. And he did try.

For a couple of years. But once he realized he was hurting your mother…and you…by being in your lives, he split.''

"And became a mercenary?" Catherine nervously circled the rim of her mug with the tip of her index finger.

"He was a trained soldier. It was the only life he knew. And…" Should he tell her? Murdock wondered. It wasn't as if she were still a kid who needed protection from the truth. She was a grown woman. "I think your old man had a death wish."

Her full, pink lips formed an oblong oval as she gasped softly. "A death wish?"

"I was with him the day he…well, the day I thought he died. One of the last things he said to me was that he'd been living on borrowed time ever since Nam."

"You were with him when—"

"We were on an assignment in Zaraza. We were trying to get through enemy lines in order to get a vital message to a contact." He couldn't tell her details of the mission or explain that the U.S. government had been playing a part in the ongoing revolution for the past twenty years. "Your father sent me with the message, knowing that by staying behind, he was saving my life and sacrificing his. So you see, if he's still alive and there's some way I can get him out of Zaraza, then I'm going to."

"Because you owe him your life?"

"Yeah. Because I owe him my life."

Catherine lifted the mug to her lips and sipped the tea. She preferred it with neither cream, sugar nor lemon and apparently Murdock liked his the same way. They ate and drank in silence, each avoiding any eye contact. After Catherine ate half her sandwich and drank all her tea, she slipped off the stool and, with her back to Murdock, made her way across the room.

She paused momentarily and asked, "Which bedroom should I use?"

"The one on the left of the bathroom," he told her.

"Then if you'll excuse me, I'd like to be alone for a while."

He watched her disappear into the small guest bedroom that he used mostly as a study. Perhaps he should have given her his room, which was larger and less cramped. But the bed in the extra room was an old double bed, which meant his feet would hang over the footboard. One of the drawbacks of being six foot six.

Busying himself cleaning up the kitchen, Murdock started trying to figure out just how to handle Catherine Price. A man would have to be dead not to notice how attractive she was. But a smart man would keep his distance from a lady who so obviously considered him as nothing more than a necessary means to an end. No doubt, she wouldn't give him the time of day, if she didn't need him to get her and her hundred thousand into Zaraza and secure her and Lanny's safety.

He had known her type back in Mississippi, where he'd done yard work for rich families when he'd been a teenager. Sweet little innocent Southern belles liked to flirt and give poor boys ideas. And Barbara had been the society type, too. Rich and pampered. She'd led him on, making him believe she loved him, when all along she'd had no intention of making a commitment to him. That had been years ago, but he'd learned his lesson well. Barbara had been an excellent teacher.

He knew Catherine wasn't Barbara. Physically they didn't resemble each other at all. But her superior attitude, her air of snobbery, the slightly condescending way in which she looked at him reminded him of a woman he thought he'd long since not only cut out of his heart, but exorcised from his soul. *Like the demon she had been.*

If he didn't owe Lanny McCroskey his life, no amount of money could induce him to spend the next few days with Catherine. She was the kind of woman he avoided, at all costs. The moment he'd seen her, he'd known they would mix like oil and water. He might not be the smartest guy on earth, but he had sense enough to know that dealing with Lanny's daughter was going to be one big headache.

Even though she'd promised to take orders, something told him that if she ever disagreed with his commands, she'd buck him. Before they left for Peru, he had to make certain she truly realized the dangers that confronted them and that one wrong move could cost both of them their lives.

With loud, marching steps, Murdock stormed across the room and into the square hallway that separated the two bedrooms. The guest room door stood open just enough to give him a glimpse of Catherine lying across the bed, the red spread in place beneath her. He paused, his hand hovering in midair. Maybe she was asleep, he thought.

Their talk could wait, couldn't it? She'd be in a better mood once she'd rested, perhaps more willing to truly accept his leadership in their joint venture. If she were a sensible woman, she'd realize that following his instructions could easily mean the difference between success and failure, between life and death—for her and her father.

The moment Murdock walked away from the bedroom door, Catherine opened her eyes. She had sensed his presence and feigned sleep. She couldn't deal with Murdock. Not now. Later perhaps. She knew it was only a matter of time before they would have to discuss their trip to Zaraza. She suspected she would have no choice but to accept Murdock's being in command. She dreaded the thought of letting him boss her around. She'd been an independent woman all her life. Even as a teenager, she'd made her own decisions and taken care of herself. Her mother had been dear and sweet and kind. But Mae Beth McCroskey had been a weak woman whose life had crumbled into loneliness and misery once she lost her husband. But Catherine was made of stronger stuff. She had sworn no man would ever have that much power over her—enough power to break her heart and destroy her life.

She had never needed anyone. Not even Rodney. Her husband had understood and accepted her need to control every aspect of her own life and he had never asked for more than she'd been willing to give.

Catherine sat up and scooted to the edge of the bed, then let her bare feet touch the polished hardwood floor. Rising from the bed, she stretched, then lifted her suitcase and set it on the arms of the wooden rocker in the corner. The best way to avoid Murdock tonight was to take a bath and go to bed. Tomorrow morning would be soon enough to deal with the big man again.

She removed her toiletries case and set it on the small, cluttered desk to her right, then lifted her pajamas, robe and slippers from the suitcase. As she reached down for the vinyl case, her hand accidentally knocked a manila folder off the desk and onto the floor. With her clothing draped over her arm and her slippers secured in one hand, she reached down and picked up the folder, intending to return it to the desk. But just as she lifted it, she noticed her name scrawled across the top in a large, bold handwriting that she felt certain belonged to Murdock. Tossing her clothing and slippers on the bed, she flipped open the folder. As she scanned the thick report, her hands tightened around the folder, crushing the edges of the papers she held.

Damn him! How dare he! What gave him the right?

In her bare feet, Catherine stormed out of the guest room and ran into the living room. Murdock sat in one of the big leather chairs, his feet resting on the matching ottoman, a book in one hand. He glanced up at her, his gaze casual.

"I thought you were sleeping," he said.

Catherine held up the crumpled file folder as if she were confronting him with a murder weapon in a trial. Her gaze narrowed angrily on his expressionless face.

"Is something wrong?" He slid his feet off the ottoman and onto the floor, then laid his book on the arm of the chair and stood to face her.

"This is a report on me," Catherine told him, her voice trembling with rage. "You know every detail of my life from birth to the present. You have a copy of my birth certificate, my marriage license, even my dental records. How dare you invade my privacy this way?" She rushed toward him, flung the file folder in his face and screamed, "You had no right to do this!"

"You're getting yourself all worked up over nothing."

She hated the calmness in his voice, hated the rational, emotionless way he was acting. "How would you like it if I'd had an extensive report compiled on you? Would you like for me to know everything there is to know about you?"

Murdock moved forward, bringing his body within inches of her. When he looked down at her, she noticed gold specks in his hazel-brown eyes. She stepped backward. He lowered his head a fraction, then reached out and grasped her shoulders.

"All that's in the report on you are facts and figures." He glanced meaningfully at the scattered papers lying on the floor. "Those don't tell me everything there is to know about you. Only you can do that."

Garnering all her willpower, she forced herself not to tremble at his touch, not to allow his massive size and imposing self-assurance to intimidate her. "Why did you have the report compiled?"

"I'm going to be responsible for you, for keeping you safe, from now until we bring Lanny back to the United States. When I take an assignment, I always do my homework. When I become someone's bodyguard, it's my standard procedure to find out as much as possible about them."

Titling her chin, she glared into his eyes, seeking and finding the truth of his statement. She believed him, and yet she couldn't let go of her anger. If it was Murdock's standard procedure to have a report compiled on all of his clients, then why did she still feel as if his knowing the details of her life was tantamount to his having stripped her naked?

He made no move to release his hold on her. His big, callused hands clutched her shoulders with gentle strength.

Feeling as if they were in a contest of wills, she refused to be the first to break eye contact. "Somehow it doesn't seem quite fair that you know so much about me and I know so little about you."

Easing one hand down and around her waist, while

the other wound around the back of her neck, Murdock lowered his head farther, until his mouth was a hairbreadth away from hers. "Just what do you want to know about me?"

Chapter 3

The flight from Atlanta to Peru had taken off precisely at eight. Catherine hadn't known that they would be flying on the Dundee private jet—just one of many things Murdock hadn't bothered explaining. Their confrontation last night had ended in a stalemate. He hadn't won the battle. And she hadn't actually lost it. In retrospect she could admit to herself that she'd never been as frightened or as excited by a man as she'd been when Murdock had almost kissed her. If she hadn't withdrawn, hadn't pulled back, hadn't broken eye contact, she wasn't sure what might have happened.

The logical part of her personality felt a great sense of relief that she'd had the good sense not to allow her emotions free rein. But the purely female aspects of her mind and body couldn't forget the way she'd felt and longed to feel again.

"How about some breakfast?" Murdock unhooked his seat belt, then rose and headed toward the galley.

"There's coffee and sweet rolls and muffins. What'll you have?"

Catherine released the catch of her seat belt, stood and stretched. She had chosen brown pants and a tan jacket of a nonwrinkle material for the long trip, planning to use the outfit more than once. She had packed light. After all, this was supposed to be a quick trip in and out of Zaraza. All they had to do was pay the ransom money for her father and then bring him out of the country as fast as possible.

Without replying to Murdock, she made her way to the galley and poured her own coffee, picked up a paper napkin and then chose a sweet roll from the assortment. She didn't bother even looking at her bodyguard. To be honest, she was having a difficult time facing him this morning, after the way she'd run from him last evening. He had to be aware of the way he'd affected her—of the reason she'd run from him.

"Giving me the silent treatment today?" Murdock filled his cup, grabbed two rolls and watched Catherine as she sat and crossed her ankles in a demure, ladylike fashion.

Was she upset with him? he wondered. Still angry that he'd compiled an extensive report on her? Or was her attitude the result of something a little more basic? She had run from him last night, as if he'd been a monster ready to devour her.

"I'm more than willing to talk to you." She tilted her nose just enough to imply superiority. "As a matter of fact, I have dozens of questions and I'd very much like some answers."

Murdock sat beside her, then lifted his coffee mug in a salute. "Fire away. What do you want to know?"

Eyeing him suspiciously, she picked up the roll from

the napkin on her knee, brought it to her mouth and took a bite. After laying the roll back on the napkin, she took a sip of coffee. "Since we're using the Dundee jet, why aren't we flying directly into Zaraza today?"

"Because only Zarazaian planes are allowed in and out of the country right now. Even the commercial flights have been canceled temporarily."

"Then how are we going to fly into—"

"Arrangements are being made for us to take a Zarazaian plane. Hopefully, by tomorrow morning, we'll be in San Carlos."

"Hopefully? Do you mean there's a chance we—"

"My contact in Lima should be able to arrange the flight," Murdock told her.

Catherine glowered at Murdock. "Would you mind allowing me to finish one sentence without interrupting? Don't you have any manners at all?"

Murdock chuckled. Manners? Had she actually said *manners?* "Sorry, ma'am. I'm afraid not spending much time around ladies, I have forgotten my manners."

"I don't appreciate your sarcasm, either!"

"You don't appreciate much of anything about me, do you, Cat?"

"Cat!"

"Yeah, honey, that's what you remind me of—a spitting, hissing she-cat, who has her claws drawn and is ready to fight, even with very little provocation."

"My name isn't Cait or Cathy and it most definitely isn't Cat. It's Catherine. Do I make myself clear... Aloysius?" Her lips curved in a self-satisfied smile. She could tell from the sudden tension in his jaws and the narrowing of his eyes that her use of his given name had accomplished the desired effect.

"Nobody calls me Aloysius." His voice roared, deep, throaty and harsh.

"Then we have a deal—you don't call me Cat and I won't call you Aloysius."

"So, the lady knows how to fight dirty." Setting his mug and roll on the tray in front of him, he turned to her. She visibly cringed when he settled his gaze directly on her face. "In case you didn't know it, that was a compliment...Catherine."

"Thank you." She wished he'd stop inspecting her so thoroughly.

His big hand came toward her so quickly that she had no time to withdraw before he wiped the corner of her mouth with the tip of his index finger. She sucked in her breath and held it until her lungs ached for release.

Her startled eyes expressed what she felt. Murdock realized touching her had been a mistake. One he shouldn't make again. He sensed a hunger in Catherine that could be dangerous for both of them. "You had sugar from the sweet roll on—"

She released her breath and glowered at him. "Next time, just tell me. I'm perfectly capable of wiping my own mouth."

He stood abruptly. With his back to her, he said, "You're perfectly capable of doing a great deal, I'm sure."

Why was she allowing this man to have such a negative effect on her? she wondered. Just because she found herself attracted to him, on some purely primitive, animalistic level, didn't mean she would ever act on those unwanted feelings. And there was no excuse for her taking out her frustration and anger with her father on Murdock, no matter how alike the two men were. This man meant nothing to her and never would.

"Murdock?"

His big shoulders tensed, but he didn't turn around. "Yeah?"

"Let's call a truce," she said. "I admit that I've been deliberately difficult, but so have you. Can't we be more pleasant to each other and agree to disagree on certain issues? After all, we have to put up with each other for only a few days. Just long enough to rescue my father."

Hell! She's right, he thought. Just because she pushed all his buttons didn't mean he had to react like an idiot when she irritated him. So what if her superior, lady-of-the-manor persona reminded him of Barbara the Beast. So what if she'd made it abundantly clear that she didn't like him. So what if she was a good-looking woman and when they came into physical contact with each other, sparks flew.

He turned slowly and by the time he faced her, he had a forced smile in place. "No more squabbles. We have a mission to accomplish together, whether we like it or not."

"Do you think we'll run into any major problems once we arrive in San Carlos?" she asked, wanting to focus on their joint venture and not on the man himself.

"Anything can happen once we cross the border over into Zaraza. That's why it's imperative that you don't question any command I issue. If I tell you to jump off a bridge, then by God, you jump off that bridge without hesitation. Do you understand?"

Every muscle in Catherine's body stiffened. She despised the thought of mindlessly following anyone's lead. But her common sense told her that in this case she needed to make an exception. "I understand."

He eyed her skeptically.

"Really. I do understand. I won't like it," she admitted. "But I will do whatever you tell me to do."

"Without asking me a bunch of dumb fool questions?"

"Yes."

"Then there's a good chance that you and Lanny and I will be on a plane out of Zaraza by day after tomorrow."

The six-and-half-hour flight to Peru seemed much longer. She and Murdock had talked very little, each aware that by not conversing, they were less likely to argue and break their new pledge of cooperation and cordiality. She'd tried to read the paperback novel she'd hidden away in her purse, but had been unable to concentrate. However, Murdock hadn't seemed to have any trouble concentrating on the two action-adventure movies he'd watched to pass away the time.

When the pilot announced their imminent arrival at the Jorge Chavez International Airport, Murdock reached over and secured Catherine's seat belt. Words of chastisement had been on the tip of her tongue. Instead, she forced a smile. After all, he was just doing his job, wasn't he? Just taking care of Lanny's daughter.

"Look out the window," he said.

"Why?"

When he lifted his eyebrows, she clenched her jaw. Damn the man!

"Excuse me. Was that an order?"

"Just a suggestion," he replied.

One glance out the window and she realized why Murdock had *suggested* taking a look at the city. A soft, hazy mist blanketed the entire area with a dreamlike atmosphere.

"What is it?" she asked. "Some sort of fog?"

"It's the *garúa*," he said. "A fine mist that settles over the city from May to October. The residents don't seem to mind at all."

"You've been here before then?"

"Yeah, I've been here before."

"With my father?"

"Yeah, twenty years ago. And a couple of times since."

"On mercenary assignments?"

"Catherine, stop asking me about my life as a mercenary. Believe me, you really don't want to hear any details and if you keep asking, eventually you might irritate me enough that I'll tell you."

"Is our truce over already?"

"No."

"I won't ask about your past again."

"Good."

Although a line of taxis waited in front of the airport terminal, Murdock steered her toward a waiting rental car. The way he casually carried the briefcase filled with $100,000 surprised her. He acted as if the satchel contained nothing more than easily replaced business documents. He popped the trunk, dumped her suitcase and his vinyl bag inside, then opened the door for her. There was something unnerving and yet reassuring about the way he placed his hand on the small of her back. She glanced over her shoulder at him, but could detect not the least bit of emotion on his face.

Once inside the vehicle, he laid the briefcase between them, then reached across her and opened the glove compartment. She gasped when she saw the gun. He took the weapon into his hand, then lifted his jacket and placed it inside a hip holster.

"How did that gun—" She bit down on her bottom lip. "I know. I know. Don't ask."

"You're learning."

"When do you meet your contact? Or is that top secret information, too?"

"Tonight, at the restaurant," he said. "You'll like Jose. All the ladies do."

"You mean I'm actually going be allowed to hear what the man has to say? Gee whiz, I'm honored."

"Hmph!" Murdock kept his gaze on the road.

"I don't understand why all this cloak-and-dagger stuff is necessary." When he didn't respond, she continued. "I mean it seems fairly cut-and-dried to me. General Ramos wants the money. We want Lanny. A simple exchange. Right?"

"When it comes to Zaraza, General Ramos and the rebel army, nothing is simple."

"Meaning?"

"Meaning this is a game I've played before. I know the rules. You don't. Why do you think Rick Burdett included me in this little scenario?"

Catherine huffed loudly. "I'm not a complete idiot! I do understand that we're going into a country that's still involved in a twenty-year civil war and I realize how dangerous it could be for me. What I'm asking is why we seem to be taking the long way around. And why are you being so secretive with me? I'm not the enemy."

Gripping the steering wheel with white-knuckled fierceness, Murdock gritted his teeth. "I'm not used to having to explain my actions, but here goes. I suppose by not enlightening you on every little detail, in not exposing you to all the so-called secrets, I feel as if I'm protecting you.''

"Protecting me from what?''

"From the rotten, stinking, ugly side of life. The life I've lived for the past twenty-odd years…the life your father once lived. I just figured Lanny would rather his little girl not know everything about the way he made his living.''

Strangely enough, Catherine felt duly chastised. She actually believed Murdock meant what he'd just said. Perhaps he was right. Perhaps it was better if she never knew everything there was to know about the world of the mercenary soldier. After all, why not simply accept Murdock at face value—a professional bodyguard, with an unsavory past. A civilized man. Although not quite a gentleman, not a ruffian either. A man who lived in a tastefully decorated apartment, drove a new sports car and dressed well. There was absolutely no reason why she should ever know anything more about him.

On the drive to Miraflores, the central cultural district, they passed *penas*—bars—open marketplaces and numerous restaurants. Despite its ancient past, Lima was a metropolitan area, similar to most large cities throughout the world. But uniquely, Lima pulsed with a slower, calmer rhythm created by the more traditional aura of its warm and friendly citizenry.

The Pacifico Hotel was on the corner of de Julio Avenue and had a wonderful view of the ocean.

Catherine soon learned that everything had been arranged per Murdock's instructions and that the assistant manager, Hugo Mendoza, and her bodyguard were old acquaintances. Although her knowledge of Spanish was minimal, she discovered that Murdock spoke the language fluently. She couldn't help wondering just how many hidden talents this mystery man possessed.

The briefcase containing the ransom money went into the hotel safe before Hugo escorted them to the elevators. Catherine listened intently while the two men conversed. She could make out a few words, but derived as much from their body language and facial expressions as from what they said. She clearly heard Murdock refer to her as *mi mujer,* which she was sure meant *my woman.*

Hugo grinned broadly and slapped Murdock on the back. *"Ella es muy hermosa y muy alta."* He whispered something to Murdock that she couldn't hear and the two men laughed. Then Hugo snapped his fingers for the bellboy, who appeared to be no older than eighteen.

Okay, *muy hermosa* meant what? she contemplated. *Very beautiful?* How nice. What a lovely compliment. But what did *alta* mean? Think, Catherine, think!

Hugo reached out, took Catherine's hand and brought it to his lips. "I hope your stay at our hotel will be a pleasant one, *señora.*" His English was on the same level as her Spanish, so she assumed the wishes were a statement he had memorized and recited to all the female guests.

She only nodded and smiled, as her mind continued puzzling over the word *alta* and also tried to figure out why Murdock had referred to her as his woman and why the two men had exchanged such boisterous laughter. Some macho thing, she supposed. Had Murdock been simply trying to impress another man or had he been placing boundaries around her? She had every intention of asking him, as soon as they were alone.

When they arrived at their suite, Murdock instructed the bellboy in his native language, apparently telling him which bag went to which bedroom. After the young man opened the doors onto the terrace overlooking the ocean, Murdock tipped him and from the wide grin on his face, she assumed the tip had been a generous one.

"You've got time for a bath and nap before dinner," Murdock told her. "We're meeting Jose upstairs in the Roof Garden at eight."

"What does the word *alta* mean?" she asked.

"Tall."

"Oh."

The corners of Murdock's mouth quivered, but he didn't smile. "Hugo said that you were very beautiful and very tall."

"What else did he say that you both thought so funny? And why did you refer to me as your woman?" Catherine stuck out her chin and squared her shoulders.

Murdock wondered if she knew how much a defiant woman tempted a man to try to control her. Probably not.

"Dammit, you can ask more unnecessary questions that any woman I've ever known!"

"And you're the most secretive man I've ever had the misfortune of meeting!"

Murdock removed his sport coat and tossed it on the sofa. "Get used to my referring to you as *mi mujer,* because for the duration of this mission, that's what you'll be—my woman!"

"Now, wait just one minute. If you think—"

"I think, but you don't. You jump to conclusions."

Steam rose inside her, fueled by pure anger. She was doing it again—allowing Murdock to enrage her and make her feel foolish. "Excuse me. Why don't you explain the situation, *if* I've jumped to the wrong conclusion."

"Despite how very beautiful and desirable you are, the only brand I'm putting on you is a verbal brand. Jose and a few people in Zaraza know what our real mission is, know why we're here in Lima and why we're going to Zaraza. The simplest way to explain our being together and also to announce that you're under my protection is for me to say you're my woman. Understand?"

"I think so." Okay, so once again she'd been wrong in assuming Murdock was just being an arrogant jackass.

"If that's settled, then why don't you—"

"What were you and Hugo laughing about?"

"Good God, woman! Do you have to know everything?"

"Humor me."

Murdock raked his cupped hand across the faint stubble on his lower jaw. "Hugo made a comment about your long legs wrapping around me when I screwed you."

Catherine gasped loudly.

"You asked. So I told you. Don't go getting outraged and giving me hell for telling you what you demanded to know."

"Are all your friends that crude?"

"Men are that crude, honey."

"All men aren't."

"Oh, just men like me and my friends and your father, huh?"

"My husband would never have made an inappropriate remark about a woman, especially not in her presence."

"Well, bully for your husband," Murdock said. "But in Hugo's defense, he didn't realize you knew any Spanish. And he assumed you and I were lovers."

"Which we are not!"

"Which we most definitely are not!"

They stood there face-to-face, staring each other down, like two Old West gunfighters preparing for a high-noon showdown. Catherine's chest rose and fell dramatically with each labored breath she took. Everyone who knew her, knew Catherine had a temper. But as a general rule it took a great deal of aggravation to rile her. She had learned over the years to control all her emotions, and seldom allowed anyone or anything to irritate her to the extent Murdock did.

The pulse in Murdock's neck swelled and throbbed. She could tell that he was as upset as she and trying just as hard not to explode. Usually, she was the person others feared, the one in charge, the one who had the power to make underlings shake in their boots. She certainly wasn't accustomed to having some big, overbearing man running roughshod over her and making all the decisions.

"You bring out the very worst in me," she told him. "And I don't like it. However, there's not much I can do about it, but endure your presence until we have my father safely out of Zaraza. Then I hope I never see you again as long as I live."

"Believe me, nothing would suit me better. Your attitude isn't conducive to winning friends and influencing people. And there's no place in my world for uptight, snobby, prudish women who are out to emasculate every man they meet."

"*Conducive.* My, my. What a big word for such a small mind." Catherine flashed her adversary a wide, eat-dirt-and-die smile. "And if my aim was to emasculate men in general, I wouldn't waste my time on you. But, I must admit, the thought of dropping a stick of

dynamite into your pants and blowing your...your mas-
culinity to smithereens, gives me immense pleasure.''

"Ouch, Cat, your claws are not only showing again,
they're scratching me.'' His smile matched hers in sheer
brilliance and outmatched hers in pure devilry. "And if
you want to drop something into my pants, I have a
much better idea.''

Gritting her teeth and huffing, Catherine closed her
eyes to shut out the blazing red glare that blinded her.
The man was insufferable! Was her father really anything like Murdock? If so, how could her sweet, genteel
mother have endured being married to the oaf?

"In your dreams,'' she said, under her breath, then
opened her eyes and gasped when she realized that he
had silently crossed the room and stood within an arm's
length of her.

"Don't you know that the more you fight a man, the
more determined he'll be to conquer you? And, Cat,
honey, you have a knack for verbal sparring that can
really turn a man on.''

That was it! She'd had it with this big, smart-mouthed
wise guy! With her hands balled into tight fists, she took
that one step that separated them, then lifted her gaze to
make direct eye-to-eye contact. That's when she realized
she'd made a mistake. A huge mistake. Murdock was
looking at her as if she were the last drop of water in a
sweltering, dry desert.

"What the hell,'' he said as he reached out and jerked
her into his arms. "We might as well get this over
with.''

Chapter 4

Catherine didn't know what hit her! Murdock's big arms tightened around her in an embrace that made escape impossible. In that one instant before his mouth closed over hers, a dozen different elements swept through her consciousness. The sexual glint in Murdock's hazel eyes. The faint scar on his left cheek. The musky scent of his masculine body. The sound of his accelerated breathing. And the width of his massive shoulders.

With her mind overloaded by exciting, threatening sensations and her body betraying her by pressing against Murdock's rock-hard frame, Catherine opened her mouth to object. But before she could utter a word, he speared his fingers into her hair and gripped the back of her head solidly in one huge hand. Immobilized by shock and a primitive awareness, she could do nothing more than whimper when he took her mouth in a overpowering kiss. The ravaging attack possessed a tantaliz-

ing tenderness that she hadn't expected. And that hint of
gentleness was her undoing. All thoughts of protest vanished as she eagerly responded with a fierceness that
equaled his. Lost to rational thought, removed from logical action by the all too human instincts controlling her,
Catherine reached up and clasped Murdock's shoulders,
clinging to him as he deepened the kiss.

He walked her backward, up against the wall, and all
the while devoured her mouth greedily. She trembled
with expectation when she felt the thick, swollen hard-
ness of his sex pulsing against her belly. Her short, round
nails bit into the cloth of his shirt, trying to draw him
closer.

Their tongues plunged, swiped and sampled, partici-
pating in a prelude to actual mating. When he buried his
face against her neck, his lips searing her flesh, his teeth
nipping, she drew in a deep, shuddering breath. Shivers
of desire rippled along her nerve endings when his hand
covered one breast and kneaded softly.

He thrust himself hard against her mound. Shock
waves of fear and longing flooded through her. She
gasped audibly, but made no move to stop him.

"Do you want to take this farther?" Murdock asked,
his voice ragged with arousal. "If we don't stop now,
I'm going to have you right here, up against the wall. Is
that what you want?"

Yes. Sweet mercy, yes! That's exactly what she
wanted. She wanted him inside her. Pounding. Throb-
bing. Filling her completely. Loving her as she'd never
been loved.

"This is insane!" She loosened her tight grip on his
shoulders. "How—how could I have let this happen?"
She had been on the verge of having sex with Mur-

dock—a man she neither liked nor respected. Had she lost her mind?

"You didn't *let* it happen, honey." Murdock eased his body away from hers and took a step back, allowing her breathing room. "I could see this coming a mile off. It's been there, between us, ever since we recognized each other at the airport in Atlanta yesterday."

Catherine shook her head as if to dislodge irrational thoughts and better comprehend what he'd just said. "I don't know what you're talking about."

Running his hand across the back of his neck, Murdock snorted. "I'm talking about this sexual thing between us. And don't even try to deny it."

She glared at him, but didn't contradict him. "I want you to know that I don't usually…that I never act this way. You took me by surprise and didn't give me time to think. I'm not accustomed to being treated like a…a…"

"Like a woman?" Smirking, he narrowed his gaze as he scanned her body from hips to breasts to face.

"Like a tramp!" she corrected.

"I've never treated any woman like a tramp, even if she was one. What we just shared was mild compared to heavy-duty loving. Something you have obviously never experienced."

Squaring her shoulders, Catherine forced herself to move away from the support of the wall. "My sexual experience is none of your business and I have no intention of discussing it with you."

"Fine by me. No need to bore me, is there?"

He grinned at her then, and she wanted nothing more than to pick up the nearest deadly object and toss it at his head. The man was insufferable! And so damn sure of himself!

"You've proved your point," she told him. "For some unfathomable reason, there's this raw, primitive attraction between us. But I hate it. Do you hear me, Murdock? I hate that feeling!"

"Yeah, something like that can be a damned nuisance, can't it? Especially if the other person isn't your type."

"Then we understand each other perfectly, don't we?"

Apparently feeling more confident and in control by the minute, Catherine dared to walk right up to him and stick her snooty little nose in the air. He grinned broadly, amused by her foolish assumption that stating the truth now made her immune to him.

"This will not happen again," she informed him.

Unable to resist proving a point, Murdock skimmed her cheek with the back of his hand. She sucked in a harsh breath. Her eyes widened, as if she'd been greatly surprised that a mere touch could ignite such powerful feelings inside her. He knew exactly how she felt because he felt it, too. Every time he got near her.

"Powerful stuff, sexual attraction." His throaty, gravelly voice added a highly sensual tone to his words.

"Don't ever touch me again." She hated the way her voice quavered when she issued the order.

When he laughed, she sensed he was laughing at her, right in her face. How could she possibly be attracted to such a man? He was everything she disliked. Aloysius Murdock was the same type of human being Lanny McCroskey had been. A person capable of deserting a wife and child. A soldier to whom killing was second nature. A brutal, insensitive, uncaring bastard!

And a lover capable of breaking a woman's heart and yet at the same time securing that woman's love until the day she died.

"You're safe from me, Cat, as long as you don't throw yourself at me," he said. "But if you ask for it, you just might get it. So be careful about sending out those sexual signals."

"I didn't send out any sexual signals…Aloysius!"

"You did, just then," he told her. "You like to provoke me. To see just how far you can push me."

"This conversation is over! I'm going to my room until it's time to meet your Mr. Jose."

She snapped around and marched into the bedroom where the bellboy had taken her suitcase. When she slammed the door, Murdock shook his head. Catherine Price was a time bomb, waiting to explode. They'd both be better off if they just went ahead and *did* the nasty and diffused the tension between them. But he suspected that Ms. Uptight wasn't into casual sex. Too bad.

The Roof Garden on the twelfth floor overlooked a breathtaking view of the bay and offered a sophisticated national and international menu. Catherine felt slightly underdressed, but her casual attire matched Murdock's. And Jose Alverez's black suit, gray shirt and burgundy silk tie complimented his date's slinky black dress, which left absolutely nothing to the imagination. Charo, a bosomy brunette with huge cow eyes, didn't speak a word of English, but she managed to convey her interest in Murdock by body language alone.

"It bothers, you, *señora,* that my little Charo is so taken with Murdock?" Jose reached across the table and lifted Catherine's hand in his, as they watched the other couple on the dance floor. "Believe me, it is harmless. A mild flirtation. After all, why would Murdock want any other woman when he has you?"

Catherine forced a smile. She wanted to scream, *But*

he doesn't have me! "I could care less what Murdock does or doesn't do with your little Charo, but I'm tired of wasting time. I thought we were having dinner with you to discuss our trip into Zaraza. Instead we've eaten a huge meal, drank expensive wine and now we...*he* is dancing the night away."

Jose exposed a sparkling set of perfect teeth when he smiled. He brought Catherine's hand to his lips. "A little pleasure mixed with business. It is the way I prefer doing things. Makes life so much more pleasant."

Just as she was about to demand information about their flight into Zaraza, Murdock brought Charo back to the table. She all but had herself draped around him. A vulgar, disgusting display, Catherine thought.

"Your Catherine is much distressed," Jose said. "I fear she is not a party girl."

"Been giving you a hard time, has she?" Murdock cast her a teasing glance.

"She wishes to discuss business," Jose said.

"I simply want to know what arrangements have been made to fly us into Zaraza." Catherine tapped her fingertips on the table, the sound muffled by the crisp, white linen tablecloth.

"Ease her mind, *amigo,*" Murdock said. "Tell her what the plans are."

"I have arranged for two seats aboard a seven o'clock flight in the morning," Jose said. "You will reach San Carlos in a little over an hour and the American ambassador will meet you at the airport. He will have a car and driver waiting for you to take you to General Ramos's home. A perfectly natural way to handle things, do you not think so, since you and Murdock are American citizens and so is Mr. McCroskey?"

"Thanks." Murdock smiled at Jose. "And who's my contact to get us a flight out of the country?"

"The proprietor of *Hotel Dulce de Rosa* will provide you with whatever assistance you need. If not personally, then through friends." Jose glanced around the room, checking to see if anyone seemed interested in their conversation. "You must get in and out of Zaraza quickly. Within a week, two at the most, the war will explode again."

"So, now is the calm before the storm," Murdock said.

"Sí, la calma antes de la tormenta."

"Do you have any word on Lanny's condition?" Murdock lowered his voice to a deep whisper.

Apparently feeling neglected while the others conversed in a language she didn't understand, Charo scooted her chair closer to Jose and murmured something in his ear. Jose slipped his arm around the woman's bare shoulders and said something to her that obviously pleased her, because she giggled and tap danced her fingers up his arm and neck and into his hair.

Jose glanced at Catherine, his black eyes filled with hesitation. "He is alive, but not well."

Catherine suspected that he knew more, but chose not to burden her with the complete truth. Another macho man *protecting* the weak woman!

Jose turned to Murdock. *"El puede morir."*

Murdock's facial muscles tensed.

"What are y'all not telling me?" Catherine asked.

Jose looked to Murdock for permission to speak. Murdock nodded.

"El puede morir. He could be dying," Jose translated. "Your father is very sick, very weak. Malnourished and...and suffering from tuberculosis."

"Oh."

"Once we get him back home, we'll get him the best medical treatment possible," Murdock assured her. "Don't worry about anything now, except getting him out of Zaraza."

"You're right," she agreed. "One problem at a time."

The flight to San Carlos had been uneventful, except for the rocking of the small plane from air turbulence. Murdock had cautioned her before takeoff to let him handle everything, since he knew the language and she didn't. However, she suspected that even if she'd been fluent in Spanish, he would have insisted on her keeping quiet. Under normal circumstances, she wouldn't have allowed him—or anyone—to control her actions. But nothing was normal about this trip or her part in it. She was out of her league and she knew it.

The two-engine plane landed at the small airport just outside the capital city. She held her breath when an inspector eyed the leather briefcase containing the ransom money. But he passed it along without opening it and they were whisked through customs without a moment's delay.

Murdock placed his hand in the small of her back and pressed gently. She understood that he was silently praising her for keeping her composure. At that moment, she was thankful for Murdock's presence. Despite her nervousness, she felt reassured by his cool, calm demeanor. He's done this before, she reminded herself. This type of danger is nothing new to him.

When a rotund, bald, red-faced man introduced himself as Ambassador Hadley, Catherine breathed a sigh of relief. Everything seemed to be running smoothly, going according to schedule.

Terrence Hadley exchanged a handshake with Murdock, then turned to Catherine. "I have a car waiting to take you directly to General Ramos. He has been notified of your arrival."

"Have they brought my father here to San Carlos?" she asked.

Hadley shook his head. "No, I'm afraid Mr. McCroskey is still in *Prision de las Puertas al Infierno.* There will be no exchange until General Ramos has the money."

Hadley ushered them through the airport and out into the warm, tropical air. A native in his late forties waited beside an older model black sedan. When he saw them approaching, he rushed forward and took the bags from Murdock, then placed them in the trunk.

"Manuel will take you to the general's home." Hadley smiled nervously. "It's been arranged for him to be your driver while you're in Zaraza." Then just as Manuel opened the door for her, almost as an afterthought, Hadley said, "He works for the owner of the *Hotel Dulce de Rosa.*"

At the mention of the hotel, Catherine's eyes widened as she snapped her head around and she and Murdock exchanged a meaningful glance. She understood that Manuel was no ordinary driver, but a member of whatever group worked within the capital city with and for the rebel army, and that the Hotel Dulce de Rosa was a safe haven for rebel sympathizers.

Once enclosed within the car, Murdock laid the briefcase across his knees. Catherine glanced down at the ransom, then quickly looked away when Manuel slid behind the wheel and started the engine. Before he pulled out into the traffic, Manuel lifted a box off the front seat and handed it to Murdock. Without saying a word, Murdock accepted the box, then laid it in the floorboard. Catherine watched while he removed the lid and retrieved the handgun inside. She bit down on her bottom lip. Another weapon!

"I thought you already had one," she whispered.

"That one was for while we were in Lima," he told her. "Couldn't take it aboard the plane this morning."

"Are you never without a weapon?"

"Only when I'm buck naked. And then I usually have one close by." He slipped the handgun into his hip holster.

Catherine wished she hadn't asked, especially when she heard the gruff chuckles coming from Manuel. Damn! The man understood English.

As they drove along the main thoroughfare of San Carlos, Manuel—in heavily accented English—noted points of interest, as if he were a tour guide and not some sort of undercover agent. When they crossed a Spanish colonial bridge, spanning one of the smaller tributaries of the mighty Amazon, Catherine felt as if she'd stepped back in time. Dwellings spread out over the nearby hillsides and sheep grazed in verdant pastures.

Within minutes they left the tranquillity of the outer valley and entered the municipality, which reminded Catherine of a small, pre-World War II city, dotted with remnants of a wealthy past. From gemlike churches to foliated Baroque portals, San Carlos hinted of a time when she had been a city of good breeding and great style. Although no ravages of war showed on her face, the capital of Zaraza was a beauty well past her prime.

"Less than thirty miles outside San Carlos there is a jungle," Manuel said. "Remember, *señor,* that the Rio

Negro can lead you deep into the rain forest. Taking a boat downriver is a good way to travel.''

''That's something I'll keep in mind,'' Murdock said.

Catherine grabbed the sleeve of his jacket. ''Why did he remind you about alternate modes of travel? Is there any reason why we won't be able to fly out of here?''

''No reason I know of,'' Murdock told her. ''But I can't be sure of anything, until we're safely across the border.''

Within five minutes they arrived at General Ramos's home, a three-story structure situated on the main street in the old part of San Carlos. Catherine sucked in her breath as she studied the magnificent building, a true masterpiece of late colonial Baroque. Huge, ornately carved wooden doors were crowned by equally intricate patterns that spiraled and curved with elaborate design. Rows of *miradores*, designed to overlook the town square, hovered above the first-floor windows.

The moment Manuel stopped the car at the front entrance gates, a uniformed solider stepped forward to inspect the vehicle's occupants. He spoke rapidly in Spanish, directing his inquiries to Murdock, who responded in a distinctive, authoritarian voice. With a wave of his hand, the solider motioned for the gates to be opened. Catherine wanted to ask all sorts of questions, but opted to keep quiet and, per Murdock's instruction, let him do all the talking. Once through the closely guarded entrance, Manuel pulled the old sedan up to the front door. Murdock got out, then assisted Catherine.

''I will wait there.'' Manuel nodded toward a row of empty parking places to the left of the home.

With the briefcase in one hand and the other resting against the small of Catherine's back, Murdock guided her up the steps. Before they reached the top, the double doors creaked open and another uniformed soldier met them.

Again Catherine remained quiet, listening while Murdock told their names, which she easily understood, but the rest of his conversation was entirely in Spanish, so she assumed that he was informing the soldier that General Ramos was expecting them.

Once allowed into the house, they were led through the rotunda area and down a long hallway. Catherine hastily absorbed the inner decor and assessed it as being opulent, the furnishings and artwork worth a small fortune. With all this wealth, why did the general need more money? Perhaps because he wouldn't be able to transport the contents of his mansion, if he had to escape the country quickly.

The soldier knocked before entering, then when a verbal response came from inside, he opened the door for Murdock and Catherine to enter. She heard the heavy *rat-a-tat-tat* of her own heartbeat and willed herself to be brave. The man she was about to meet held her father's life in his hands.

Two armed guards flanked the Zarazaian dictator, their rifles ready to defend him at a moment's notice. She wasn't sure what she'd been expecting, but the tall, elegant man standing behind the massive mahogany desk looked more like an aging Latin movie star than a dictator. His white hair swept away from his face in thick waves. A neatly trimmed gray mustache arched over full, smiling lips. And a pair of large, luminous, brown eyes glistened with vibrance.

"Please, Señora Price, come in. You are most welcome." His command of English was excellent, flawed by only the slightest accent.

Catherine cleared her throat, but before she could utter

one syllable, Murdock stepped between her and the general.

"Ms. Price has brought the money you requested for Mr. McCroskey's release. Let's dispense with any courtesies, General, and make the exchange."

"*¡Ustedes los norteamericanos!*" General Ramos sighed dramatically. "Always in such a hurry." He flashed Catherine a brilliant show of pearly white teeth. "But of course, Señora Price is anxious to see her father again, after so many years."

Murdock slapped the briefcase down on the desk, removed the key from his pocket, then unlocked and unsnapped the closures. "One hundred thousand in U.S. currency, just as you requested."

Catherine's mouth rounded in a silent gasp. *Why are you giving him the money now?* she wanted to scream. *Wait! Wait until we know my father is safe.* But she remained quiet.

The general reached out and ran his long, ring-adorned fingers over the neatly stacked bills. After picking up one bound bundle, he flipped the edges.

"Feel free to count it," Murdock said. "But I'm sure you know we wouldn't try to cheat you. Ms. Price has no hidden agenda. All she wants is to take her father home with her."

"Yes, of course." Ramos's smiled turned sinister as his heavy-lidded eyes narrowed. "But what about you, Señor Murdock? I know who and what you are. Why should I trust you?"

"I'm just one man, General. What could I possibly do?"

Ramos's smile lightened. "You are right. You could do nothing without forfeiting your own life." He called out loudly in Spanish and a small, bespectacled man came running into the room. The general motioned to the briefcase. The little man hurriedly removed the cash, laid it out on the desk and began counting.

Murdock glanced at Catherine, giving her a warning look. *Stay calm. Keep quiet.* Moments ticked by, seeming more like hours, while they waited for the general's accountant to finish his job. Without a word, the little man returned the money to the briefcase and nodded to the general.

"Your father is in *Puertas al Infierno,* a facility just outside the city. You can be there in fifteen minutes."

The general opened a desk drawer, removed an official-looking document, then swept an ink pen up into his hand and placed his signature at the bottom of the page. He brought the papers with him as he rounded the side of his desk. Catherine stepped forward, but once again Murdock blocked her path.

"You wish me to give this to Señor Murdock?" the general asked. "This document is your father's official pardon. Show this to Colonel Salvatore and he will release your father immediately."

Catherine nodded agreement. "Yes, please give the document to Mr. Murdock."

The moment the pardon was in Murdock's hand, Catherine sensed the room beginning to spin around and around. I will not faint. I will not faint. She repeated to herself, as if somehow the litany would protect her.

"Gracias." Murdock eased his arm around Catherine, giving her trembling body the support he knew she needed.

Murdock realized she was close to fainting—pretty damn close, if the paleness of her face was any indication. Without any farewells to the general and his private guard, Murdock guided Catherine slowly from the room and out of the grand mansion.

Manuel whipped the sedan up to the front of the house. Murdock jerked open the back door and shoved Catherine inside, following her immediately.

"Take us to *Puertas al Infierno*," Murdock said.

"*Sí, señor.*"

Manuel motioned for the guard to open the gate, which he did. The car flew through the entrance and out onto the street.

Murdock turned to Catherine. "Are you all right?"

"I will be, as soon as I see my father and we get him out of this godawful country."

"You did good in there, honey. You kept your mouth shut and let me handle everything. And I know how hard that must have been for you."

"Why did you just give him the money? How could you be sure he'd sign the pardon and free my father?"

"I couldn't be sure. But once we entered San Carlos that hundred thousand was already the general's property." Murdock grasped her chin between his thumb and forefinger. She stared at him with wide, misty blue eyes. Her father's eyes, Murdock thought. "I admit it was a gamble just coming to Zaraza, but the odds were in our favor. By releasing your father, Ramos thinks he's buying himself a little goodwill with the U.S. After all, he's going to need somewhere to go when this war finally ends. Believe me, he won't stick around for the final showdown." He released his hold on her chin, but let the back of his hand skim the length of her smooth neck.

She swallowed hard, then asked, "You don't honestly think our government will give that man sanctuary, do you?"

"It's possible."

Turning from Murdock, Catherine leaned her head back against the seat and looked out the window. Already they were zipping down a back street, heading out of town. In a few minutes she would see her father again. After twenty-five years!

Murdock demanded that she stay in the car and wait. She started to protest, but one good look at the gray walls of *Prision de las Puertas al Infierno,* which Murdock had told her meant Hell's Gate Prison, and she acquiesced willingly. Just the name of the prison conjured up horrific images. The thought of what her father might have experienced during his twenty years of imprisonment behind those high walls nauseated her.

Before he left her, Murdock gave Manuel instructions in Spanish. By translating the few words she knew, she suspected he had told Manuel that if he didn't return, to get Señora Price to safety as quickly as possible. Murdock leaned into the back seat, clasped the back of her neck in his big hand and drew her to him.

"It's been real interesting getting to know you, Cat."

The kiss was fast, hard and breath-robbing. Before she could pull herself together for a response, he shut the door and walked away.

She rolled down the window and called out to him. "Aloysius!"

He glanced back over his shoulder.

"I'll be waiting for you…and my father."

Chapter 5

Catherine checked her watch for what seemed like the hundredth time. The minutes passed slowly, every second a nerve-racking eternity. Murdock had been inside the prison for nearly an hour. Dear God, what if something had gone wrong? What if her father was dead? What if they had detained Murdock with the intention of keeping him? No matter what happened, she couldn't just leave them here. If something had gone wrong and Murdock didn't show up soon, she'd ask Manuel to drive her back to San Carlos to the American Embassy. She would demand help from Terrence Hadley.

"*Señora,* you wish music?" Manuel looked at her with concern and compassion.

"Music?"

"*Sí,* the radio." His brown fingers twisted the dial of the car's radio. "Good music."

"Oh. No. *Gracias.*" She realized that the man was trying, by whatever means necessary, to take her mind off their long wait. "Manuel, do you suppose something's gone wrong?"

He shook his head. "No. Nothing is wrong. Señor Murdock, he be back soon."

She forced a weak smile to her lips. Did Manuel believe what he'd said or was he simply trying to convince her?

"How—how long did Mr. Murdock tell you to wait, before…before…"

"Do not worry. I will take you to *Hotel Dulce de Rosa* to keep you safe. In two hours." Manuel tapped the face of his wristwatch. "One hour more."

Even with all the windows rolled down, heat inside the car became stifling. Sweat coated her skin. Beads of perspiration speckled her forehead and collected beneath and between her breasts. She removed a tissue from her purse and wiped her face.

With each anxious heartbeat, the blood rushing through her veins sang loudly in her ears. She could also hear Manuel's breathing, as if the stillness surrounding them somehow intensified the sound. Somewhere in the distance a clap of thunder echoed. And nearer, the call of an unknown bird carried shrilly on the warm, humid wind.

She opened the door, to let in more air. Manuel stirred, but didn't speak when he saw that she remained in the back seat. Glancing outside on the ground, she noticed a small, black insect crawling over the gravel. The bug was helpless against animals and humans alike, all capable of ending its life with one stomp of a large foot. She sympathized with the tiny creature, for at that very moment she felt entirely helpless, completely at the mercy of others.

Suddenly the gates through which Murdock had been

admitted over an hour earlier opened to reveal three prison guards. When Catherine thrust her legs out of the car, Manuel reached across the seat and grabbed her arm. When she glanced back at him, he shook his head.

"Wait, *señora*."

She waited. The guards separated. Two flanked the open gateway, their rifles held across their chests, while the third marched toward the sedan. Catherine held her breath. What was happening? she wondered.

And then she saw Murdock emerge from behind the prison walls. Her heart leaped into her throat and stopped beating for one infinite second. Time stood still. Murdock carried something in his arms. Merciful God, he was carrying a man. A scrawny, gray-haired man dressed in rags.

Her father!

Catherine jumped out of the car and rushed toward Murdock. The third guard stepped out of her way, allowing her to run past him. She stumbled once, her footsteps hindered by the rough gravel road. When she neared Murdock, she slowed her pace. Their gazes met and locked. A sadness almost beyond enduring passed between them.

"Get back in the car," he told her. "In the front seat with Manuel."

She hesitated, wanting to see her father, wanting to find out if he was dead or alive and if she could do anything to help. *Not now. Later!* an inner voice cautioned her. *Follow Murdock's instructions. Don't question his authority.*

Catherine scurried quickly back to the car. She slid into the front seat and watched, while Murdock eased her father's frail body into the back seat and then climbed in beside him. Murdock handled her father gently, as if he were a small child. The tender compassion with which this big, robust man cared for his friend revealed an unexpected side of Murdock's personality that touched her heart.

"Go. Now!" Murdock ordered.

As Manuel backed up and headed the car away from *Prision de las Puertas al Infierno,* Catherine turned around in her seat and took a good, hard look at Lanny McCroskey. Or what remained of the man she remembered as Lanny McCroskey. A horrible stench filled the interior of the vehicle. A combination of sweat, soured food, human waste, and dried blood clung to her father's clothes and body. Catherine covered her nose and mouth with her hand. Nausea rose in her throat.

Her father's head lay in Murdock's lap. Lanny's hair had grayed and thinned and hung in long, matted strands over his shoulders. Deep crevices lined his once handsome face. Skin that years ago had been tanned and healthy was now parchment thin and sallow. His filthy shirt and pants, constructed of some coarse, tan cotton fabric, contained numerous rips and tears.

Once again, Catherine's gaze locked with Murdock's. He noticed the tears in her eyes and wanted to tell her to go ahead and cry. Cry her heart out. And while she was at it, cry for him, too. Seeing his old friend's pathetic condition ripped him apart inside. If he'd been the one who had stayed with Juan Sabino and his young soldiers twenty years ago, then this would have been his fate. He and not Lanny would be the battered shell of a once strong warrior.

"Is—is he alive?" Catherine asked.

"Barely," Murdock said. "As soon as we get to the hotel, I'll arrange for a doctor. Lanny's been severely beaten recently. Last night. Maybe earlier today. My guess is he's been unconscious for hours. Maybe longer.''

"Is there anything I can do...now?" Tears trickled down her cheeks.

"You can pray, if you think praying will help."

The *Hotel Dulce de Rosa,* a two-story structure of cream stucco, slightly grayed by time and weather, sat on the corner of a back street in San Carlos. Tattered, white shuttered doors closed off rooms from the wrought-iron balconies and protected the interior from the sweltering sun. Manuel circled the block, then drove the car into a back alley. After parking the car behind the hotel, he jumped out and came around to open the door for Murdock, who issued an order in Spanish. Manuel quickly disappeared through a back entrance to the hotel.

With her legs feeling as if they were weighted with lead, Catherine emerged from the vehicle just as Murdock reached back inside the vehicle and pulled out a lifeless Lanny. Hoisting the body of skin and bones up into his arms, Murdock turned his head and took a deep breath, seeking a breath of fresh air.

"Get the door for me," he told her.

She ran to do as he had requested, but just as she touched the handle, the door swung open. A short, stocky man wearing a wrinkled white suit dashed outside to greet them.

"I am Andres. The proprietor of *Hotel Dulce de Rosa.* Rooms are being prepared. Come this way."

He led them inside, through the kitchen and up the rickety back stairs. The large, second-story room, containing two full beds, faced the alley. The curtains were drawn and the shuttered doors to the balcony were closed. A young girl turned down the bedcovers, picked up her broom from the corner and slipped quietly from the room.

With Lanny still in his arms, Murdock turned to Andres and said in Spanish, "We need a doctor."

"*Sí, señor*. Manuel has gone to bring Dr. Constantino."

While Murdock lowered Lanny to the bed, the young girl reappeared, a bucket of water in one hand and a stack of towels, washcloths and two bars of soap in the other.

Catherine stood by, her hands at her sides, her nails biting into her palms, while Murdock stripped Lanny's filthy clothes from his emaciated body. Cringing, she cried out when she saw the multitude of bruises, in varying shades from black to pale purple, marring his skin. The young girl set the bucket on the floor beside the bed, then turned and handed the other items to Catherine, before she rushed away again.

"Give me a hand," Murdock said. "Let's get him cleaned up a little before the doctor gets here."

"I will find something for him to wear," Andres said.

Murdock tossed Lanny's ragged garments to Andres. "Burn these."

"*Sí, señor.*" Andres grabbed the nasty clothing, then excused himself with a low bow, followed by a swift exit.

Together Catherine and Murdock washed the pale, wrinkled flesh clinging to Lanny's bones. She could hardly believe this pathetic creature was her father. Her memories of him were a child's idolization of her big, handsome father, who had tickled her chin, kissed her cheeks and called her his precious little kitten.

"You may not remember that your father was once a

damn good-looking man.'' Murdock removed a pocket knife from his pants, opened the blade and lifted the long, dirty strings of Lanny's hair. "It makes me sick to see him like this!'' God only knew what the man had lived through these past twenty years! The very thought of the indignities Lanny must have suffered made Murdock want to rip off heads and gun down armies.

As soon as Murdock cut off the matted locks of Lanny's hair, Catherine took a soapy wash cloth and lathered her father's head. While washing his hair, her gaze lingered on his haggard face, his sunken cheeks and closed eyelids. She couldn't hate this man, this pitiful wretch, no matter what he had done in the past. At this precise moment, she neither hated him nor loved him. The only emotion that surfaced and took hold inside her was simple compassion.

By the time Andres returned with a pair of soft, white cotton pants and matching shirt, Murdock and Catherine had completed their chore. While Andres removed the murky wash water and soiled towels, Murdock put the clean pants on Lanny and Catherine eased him into the billowy shirt and buttoned only the bottom three buttons.

Twenty minutes later, the doctor arrived. Elderly, with wisps of thin white hair sticking out from his short ponytail, Dr. Constantino entered the room with the grace and flare of a bullfighter entering the ring. He shook hands with Murdock, bowed to Catherine and proceeded with the examination of his patient.

Murdock wrapped his arm around Catherine's shoulder and led her across the room toward the balcony. After opening the shuttered doors, he drew her outside with him. The stifling air hit them full force. Murdock urged her to sit down on the old wicker settee, then leaned his hip against the iron railing encircling the balcony and faced her.

"You realize we probably can't leave San Carlos today or even tomorrow." Murdock crossed his arms over his wide chest. "I doubt Lanny would survive the plane ride to Lima."

"Then we'll stay until he's able to travel."

"I can stay." He paused momentarily, then said, "I want you to leave. This afternoon, if Andres can arrange it."

"No. No! I'm not leaving my father here in Zaraza. I'm staying until I can take him home."

"It isn't safe for you here. The longer we stay, the more likely we are to get caught in the middle of things when Vincente Sabino leads his rebel forces against the capital city."

"I understood the risks when I agreed to come." But had she? Catherine asked herself. Had she truly understood the horrors of war? Seeing what being a prisoner of war had done to her father made her realize that she had understood nothing about the true dangers that faced them.

"If anything happened to you, Lanny would never forgive me," Murdock told her. *And I'd never forgive myself,* an inner voice warned.

"I want to be here when my father regains consciousness. I want him to know that I didn't desert him." She reached out and placed her hand over Murdock's. "I know you can make me leave, but please, don't. Let me stay."

He glanced down at her hand. Soft, white and delicate. Long, slender fingers. Neatly manicured nails. No rings. He flipped her hand over, then ran his index finger over her palm. She shuddered.

"You can stay. At least until tomorrow. Then, we'll see."

"Thank you."

He released her hand and stood abruptly, then turned his back to her and gazed out over the alley. Catherine rose to her feet and just as she reached out to lay her hand on Murdock's broad back, Dr. Constantino joined them on the small balcony.

"Señor McCroskey needs rest and nourishment. He is half-starved and has several broken ribs." When Catherine bit down on her bottom lip in an effort not to cry, the doctor shook his head sympathetically. "I have no way of knowing, without X rays, but I believe his tuberculosis is quite advanced. Even with proper care and medicine…" He allowed his sentence to trail off into silence.

"We had planned to fly to Lima as soon as possible," Murdock explained.

"You can't move your friend," the doctor said. "To do so now might kill him. It's possible that in a few days, I can arrange something. I'm afraid I have limited medical supplies, due to the war, but I was able to…cr…confiscate one bag of glucose solution. After it is used up, try to get some broth down him as often as possible. I'm afraid I won't be able to bring any more glucose. More would be missed and its absence questioned." He held up a bottle of small white pills, then handed them to Catherine. "These may help ease your father's pain a little. I'm afraid that is all I can do. We don't dare take him to the hospital."

Catherine grasped his hands in hers. "Thank you. We'll take good care of him. And if you can help us get him out of San Carlos, I'll be eternally grateful."

Dr. Constantino squeezed Catherine's hands. "I

cannot come back again. But as soon as I have made the arrangements, I will send word by Manuel.''

In the late afternoon, Murdock persuaded Catherine to eat some of the food that Andres had brought up on a tray. She agreed to eat, only if he joined her. They sat across from each other on the bed, the tray between them, and dined on fresh fruit, thick slices of crusty bread and cheap domestic wine.

''I wish there was something more we could do for him.'' Catherine's gaze lingered on the still-unconscious man lying in the other bed. ''If only we could take him to a hospital. Maybe…''

''The glucose should help,'' Murdock said. ''And we'll make sure to keep him as comfortable as possible, continue with the pain medication and hope he comes to, soon. Getting some food into him will help him regain his strength.''

''Would you have recognized him, if you hadn't known this man was Lanny McCroskey?'' She lifted the glass of wine to her lips. She hated the taste, but it was wet to the mouth and soothing to the stomach.

''Not with his eyes closed. But if I could see his eyes, I'd know him anywhere.'' Murdock looked at her and smiled. ''You've got his eyes. The same blue, blue color. Even the same expression.''

''You really care about him, don't you?'' She pressed the wineglass against her cheek and studied him. Murdock nodded, clamping his lips together. Then seeing her eyelids flutter as she yawned, he said, ''Why don't you take a nap? I'll be right here, if Lanny needs something.''

''You'd do anything for him, wouldn't you?'' She set the glass on the tray, kicked off her shoes and curled her legs up under her, as she dug out a nest for herself near the head of the bed.

Murdock pulled down the spread, jerked up a pillow and slid it between her back and the headboard. "I owe your father my life. So, yeah, I'd do *anything* for him."

Catherine reclined against the pillow, letting her head fall back against the headboard. "Tell me about him. About the Lanny McCroskey you knew."

Murdock lifted the tray off the bed and placed it on the floor, then braced his back on the headboard. He reached down and picked up his wineglass from the tray. "I didn't know Lanny before Nam. But I realize the war did something awful to him. Changed him from the man he'd once been. It messed him up—" Murdock tapped his head "—like it did so many other soldiers. I came in at the tail end of that war and got off damn lucky. But guys like your dad saw the worst of it. Friends blown to pieces right in front of their eyes. Women and children shot down because they were being used by the enemy."

"I remember when Daddy first came home." Catherine closed her eyes as memories flooded her mind. The good memories came first. Her mother's tears of joy. The way her father had clasped them tightly in his arms and told them how much he loved them. But the bad memories quickly overshadowed the good ones. Her father's manic temper tantrums. Her mother's pleas and quiet weeping. Slamming doors. Long silences. The dead look in Lanny's eyes when he withdrew into himself and became a stranger to his wife and child.

"No matter what he did or didn't do, Lanny was a good man. Inside. Where it counts." Murdock laid his tightly drawn fist over his heart. "He did what he thought was best for you and your mother. He left before he... Well, he knew you'd both be better off with him out of your lives.''

"He left before he did what?" After opening her eyes, she directed her gaze on Murdock's face.

He took a deep breath. "Before he physically hurt your mother or you."

"He struck my mother once." Catherine had tried so hard to erase that memory from her mind. "She didn't know that I saw it happen. I...I pretended that I hadn't."

"He told me." Murdock looked away from her, not wanting to see the pain in her eyes. "One time when he was talking about your mother." Murdock lifted the glass to his lips and finished off the wine. "He said he'd rather have cut off his right arm than to have struck her. He didn't realize what he'd done until she screamed. He left the next day."

"And he never came back. Not even once. You know, he didn't say goodbye to me. No explanation. No, 'I'm sorry.' One day he was there and the next he was gone."

"The Lanny McCroskey I knew was kind, good-hearted, loyal to his friends." Murdock lifted the wine bottle from the tray and refilled his glass. "Want some more?"

"I don't think—"

He handed her his full glass. "Drink it. It'll help you sleep. You rest now. I'll rest later. We'll take shifts with Lanny, if necessary."

She accepted the wine. When their hands touched briefly, they avoided direct eye contact, but the electrical sensation was there between them all the same.

"My mother divorced him but she never remarried. And...when she was dying, she called for him. I think she never stopped loving him." Catherine brought the glass to her lips and tasted not only the wine, but Murdock.

"My bet is that Lanny still loves your mother. He left her because he loved her. Because he didn't want to put her through the mental and emotional hell he was living in. He wanted to protect his wife and child."

"He's my father—" she glanced over at the silent, unmoving figure on the other bed, the skeleton connected to an intravenous tube "—and I don't know anything about him. My mother couldn't talk about him without crying, so we didn't discuss him."

"Lanny liked beer better than wine or whiskey. He sang off-key. His favorite food was fried chicken. He snored like a freight train. And he had a weakness for blondes." Murdock shook his head. "Your mother was blond, wasn't she?"

"Yes." Tears lodged in Catherine's throat. She bit down on her bottom lip in an effort not to cry.

He ran his hand up and down her arm, from shoulder to elbow and then back up again. "Get some rest."

When he eased up and off the bed, Catherine slid down enough so that her head rested on the pillow. She closed her eyes. A short nap would do her a world of good, she thought.

She awoke with a start, shooting up in bed and looking around in a panic. Murdock realized Catherine was slightly disoriented. He hadn't turned on a light after sunset, so the darkness probably surprised her. After she'd fallen asleep, he'd pulled a couple of chairs up by Lanny's bed, sat in one and propped his feet on the other. He had finished off the bottle of wine, napped on and off, waking once when Lanny had moaned and his breathing had become erratic.

Right now, moonlight flooded the room, shining through the open balcony doors and spreading across the floor like shimmery golden water. A soft breeze cooled the air as a languid hush settled over the back streets of San Carlos.

Murdock's neck ached and his legs were stiff. He was too damn big to try to sleep in a chair. He had no idea what time it was. Nearly nine o'clock would be his guess. He checked his watch. The illuminated numbers told him it was 8:20. He glanced at Lanny and noted that the glucose nourishing his old friend was almost gone. He'd have to remove the needle from Lanny's arm soon and dispose of it, along with the tube and the empty bag.

When he shoved the chair back, it scraped along the wooden floor. Murdock cursed under his breath. He stood and stretched, then rounded the end of Lanny's bed and went to Catherine.

''Are you okay?'' He hovered over her, his gaze seeking hers in the semidarkness.

She nodded her head, then ran her hands over her face. ''How long have I been asleep?''

''About three hours. Feel better?''

''I'm not sure. Why didn't you wake me to take a turn keeping an eye on my father?''

''No need. He hasn't come to. He got restless once and he was breathing rough, but I figured he was hurting. I crushed up one of those pain pills and put it in his mouth.''

Catherine scooted to the edge of the bed, flung her legs off the side and looked up at Murdock. ''I don't suppose there's any chance I could get a bath?''

''I don't see why not.''

''But there's no bathtub or shower in the bathroom.''

She inclined her head toward the tiny, connecting half bath.

"Yeah, but there's a bathroom down the hall with a big old claw-foot tub in it."

"How do you know?"

"I asked Andres when he came back for the tray. He says there's a lock on the door. But you probably won't need it. There are no other people on this floor."

Murdock grabbed her around the waist and brought her to her feet, sensing she was still unsteady with exhaustion. He held her for a split second, his gaze boring into her with heated intensity. She started to shove him away, but he released her before she touched his chest. Moving around him, she headed toward her suitcase resting on the floor across the room. She undid the case, pulled out clean underwear and a white slip, then rummaged through the other garments until she found a lightweight cotton robe. Hurriedly, she gathered up a towel, a washcloth and the unopened bar of soap.

"I won't be long," she said.

"Take your time."

Thirty minutes later, she returned to the room to find one small lamp on the dresser burning and Murdock stretched out in the bed, his shirt off and his gun lying on top of the spread near his right hand. Why did he have the gun so close? Was he expecting trouble?

"I can stay with my father now, if you'd like to take a bath," she said.

"I'll wait. Manuel will be back early in the morning. I'll bathe then. I hope you don't mind sleeping beside a sweaty man."

"What do you mean, sleeping beside? Are we sharing

the bed? I thought one of us was going to stay awake and—''

''I've removed the intravenous tube,'' Murdock said. ''Your father is still unconscious. If you want to sit up with him for a while, fine. But we'll both be better prepared for tomorrow, if we get as much rest as possible.''

''Do you intend to sleep with that gun?''

''Yes.''

''The gun bothers me more than your being sweaty.'' *And your naked chest bothers me more than the gun!* she thought, but would never have said so. ''Can't you just lock the door?''

''I'll lock the door, but the gun stays under my pillow.''

''Fine.'' Catherine laid her dirty clothes in a neat bundle alongside her suitcase.

''Hang the towel and washcloth on the balcony,'' he told her. ''They'll be dry in a couple of hours.''

''Good idea.''

She felt him watching her and somehow his close scrutiny made her feel naked. Foolish thought! She wore underwear, a slip and a thin robe. And still she was hot—heated by the tropical night and seared by Murdock's fiery gaze.

Once out on the balcony, she laid the towel and washcloth over the iron railing, then forked her fingers through her damp hair. The sweet breeze caressed her face and neck. She unbuttoned her robe and spread it apart, allowing the air to cool her.

Murdock's big hands came down on her shoulders. She tensed. He eased her robe from her shoulders and tossed it aside, onto the tattered wicker settee behind them. Every nerve in her body zinged. Her muscles froze.

"You'll be cooler without it."

He slid his hands down her arms, wrapping her in the vastness of his big body, cradling her in his protective embrace. She shivered.

The only thought in her mind at the moment was that she would like to stay this way forever. Held and comforted. Protected and cherished.

He pivoted her around, slowly, with the utmost tenderness, until they faced each other and her breasts pressed against his bare chest. In her peripheral vision she caught a glimpse of his gun, lying beside her robe on the settee.

He lifted her arms up and of their own accord, her fingers splayed out across his muscular chest. He glided his hands down over her back and across her hips to cup her buttocks and lift her into his arousal.

He was big and hard and hot. And she wanted him. Desperately.

Chapter 6

Damn, he wanted this woman! Wanted her naked and begging him to love her. Wanted her crying out his name when he pleasured her. He longed to bury himself deep inside her and make her his. Her fingers caressing his flesh, threading through his damp, chest hair aroused him painfully. He throbbed and pulsed with a powerful need.

He was used to getting what he wanted, especially when it came to women. But Catherine wasn't just any woman. Not the one-night-stand type. Not one of the good-time girls he preferred. She was the kind who would regret acting impulsively. The type who'd convince herself that if she gave herself to a man then she must love him.

But first and foremost, she was Lanny's daughter. The little *kitten* he'd heard all about whenever Lanny had been in a mellow, self-pitying mood. Usually when they'd been drinking heavily.

You didn't screw around with an old friend's daughter, especially not when you owed that friend your life.

He knew what he had to do. Now. Before this went any further and he lost control. He had nothing to offer Catherine, except sex. She deserved a better man. A man the exact opposite of him.

He sensed that she expected him to kiss her, and it took every ounce of his willpower not to give her what she wanted. But heaven help him, if he kissed her, he'd take her. And he couldn't let that happen.

Abruptly, while he could still manage rational thought, Murdock grabbed her shoulders and gently shoved her away. She gasped. Her eyes rounded in surprise. And her arms reached out for him.

"You don't belong here, honey." He eased back against the stucco wall. "Not in this godforsaken country. And not with me!"

Catherine felt as if he'd dashed a bucket of cold water on her. How could he do such a drastic about-face in what seemed to her like a split second? How could he just turn off his feelings and toss her aside? She ached with the kind of sexual need that wouldn't just vanish, the kind she couldn't simply will into oblivion.

She searched his face for an explanation, but saw only a deadly controlled withdrawal. "Is it because I'm Lanny's daughter?"

He looked away, his gaze traveling the length of the bougainvillea vine clinging to the balcony railing. What should he tell her? How did he explain? *Try telling her the truth,* his conscience suggested.

"Yeah, it's partly because you're Lanny's little girl," he admitted. "But...it's more than that."

She took a hesitant step toward him, uncertain why she didn't just thank her lucky stars that he had called a halt to the insanity. Why did she feel compelled to press him for an explanation of his rejection?

"The truth is that I'm not fit for any decent woman." Murdock's eyes narrowed to tight slits when he glared at her. "I'm exactly what you think I am, Catherine. A soldier, a killer and a heartless son of a bitch. Not to mention a womanizer. You don't want a man like me. You deserve better."

Crossing her arms over her waist, she clasped her elbows. Suddenly she felt chilly. Cold, in fact. "You're right." Her voice quavered ever so slightly. "I don't want a man like you. I never have."

He hated himself for wanting her and hated her for wanting him, despite what she'd just said. Her logical mind might not want him, but he knew that her body yearned for his as much as his body yearned for hers. Just tough it out, he told himself. Once this mission is over, you don't ever have to see Catherine again.

When he noticed her shiver, he picked up her robe from the settee and walked toward her. She backed away from him until her hips pressed into the balcony railing. Taking her hand, he drew her away from the railing, just far enough so he could wrap her robe around her shoulders. His hands lingered. She gazed at him, anger—and something more—in her eyes. The smoldering embers of passion still glimmered there.

He withdrew from her, retrieved his gun from the settee, then turned to go into their room. Halting in the doorway, not looking back, he said, "Don't stay out here too long."

She didn't reply. Instead she whirled around and grasped the railing, clutching it tenaciously. Anger and hurt swirled around inside her, combining with the aftershocks of a powerful sexual desire that wouldn't relinquish control over her body. Of all the men in the world, why did she feel this unrelenting sexual hunger for Aloysius Murdock? He was the last man on earth she would have chosen for herself. So why did she want him more than she'd ever wanted any man in her entire life?

Because you're an idiot! her inner self screamed. *You'd have to be an idiot to fall for a man who, by his own admission, is a womanizing, heartless son of a bitch who has spent his life as a mercenary! He's right—you deserve better! Be glad he stopped things before you had sex with him. Before you fell in love with a man like your father. A man incapable of making a lifetime commitment.*

Listen to yourself, Catherine Price! Do you hear what you're saying? Just because you want Murdock to make love to you doesn't mean you want anything else from him. You don't want to wind up like your mother—on your deathbed, crying for the man who deserted you.

"Catherine!" Murdock's strong, loud voice called out to her. "Catherine, get in here right now!"

Snapped from her thoughts by his harsh command reverberating inside her head, Catherine hesitated. She needed to do what he said, without question, she reminded herself. They were still in Zaraza and he's still the one in charge.

When she entered the room, she found Murdock sitting on the side of Lanny's bed, her father's hand in his. Her heartbeat accelerated. Her feet turned to stone, refusing to budge. Oh, dear God, had her father died? All the energy within her focused on one single prayer. *Please, don't let him be dead.*

"Is he—?"

"No," Murdock said. "He's conscious."

An incredible sense of relief swept over her as she released a long, grateful sigh. *Thank you, God.*

"Get over here," Murdock snapped at her.

Nodding in agreement, she tried to move, but couldn't. For the past twenty years she had believed that her father was dead. But he wasn't. He was alive. And she could see him, talk to him, be with him. All she had to do was walk the few feet that separated her from his bed.

"What's wrong with you?" Murdock glared at her, his eyes narrowing and his brow wrinkling.

"Nothing. I'm just a little nervous."

She forced herself to take that first step. And then another and another. Until she paused beside the bed. Murdock released Lanny's hand, stood and then grasped her shoulders, placing her in front of him. She looked down into a pair of blue eyes staring up at her. Eyes so like her own. But weakness and illness dulled the bright luster she remembered in her father's gaze.

She tried to speak, to say Lanny or Daddy or to tell him who she was. But her throat closed up with emotion, making speech impossible.

Those bloodshot blue eyes seemed unfocused as Lanny's gaze darted right and left, up and down and then finally settled once again on Catherine's face.

"Mae Beth." The barely audible voice spoke her mother's name.

"Oh, Daddy!" The heart-wrenching cry came from deep within her soul, from the little eight-year-old girl who had adored her father. Her heart wept for all that was lost. All that could never be retrieved. Mentally, she wrapped her arms around her father and held on tight. *Don't leave me. Please, don't ever leave me again,* the child inside her pleaded. Tears gathered in Catherine's eyes. She swiped them away with her fingertips.

"Mae Beth, is that you?" he asked, apparently deaf to Catherine's cry. His bony fingers twitched, as if he were trying to lift his hand.

Catherine leaned over, gently clasped his hand in hers and said, "Lanny, it's me. It's Catherine."

"Catherine?" He coughed. He wheezed. His rail-thin body shook.

"Yes. Catherine. Your daughter."

"Kitten?"

She sucked in a loud, weeping gasp. *No, please, don't call me kitten,* she wanted to scream. *Don't take me back there. Don't make me feel what I felt then. Don't make me love you. Please, Daddy. Please. I couldn't bear to love you again and then lose you a second time.*

Murdock draped his arm around her shoulder. "Hey, there, bubba. Remember me? Murdock."

"Murdock? Catherine?" A confused frown squinched his face.

"Yeah. Your daughter and I came to Zaraza to get you out of prison." Murdock felt the shudders racking Catherine's body. He tightened his hold around her shoulders. "You're free, Lanny. And we're taking you home. Back to the States."

"Where—" Cough. Wheeze. Cough. "Where are we?"

"We're in San Carlos, in a hotel," Catherine said.

"Go. Now." Lanny lifted his head a couple of inches off the pillow as he pressed his fingers into Catherine's hand, squeezing weakly. "Not safe. Get her out of here." Cough. Hack. Wheeze.

Murdock dropped his arm from Catherine's shoulders,

veered around her and placed his open palms on Lanny's heaving chest. "Take it easy, bubba. Take it easy."

"Not safe," Lanny whimpered like a frightened child. "No place for my kitten."

Murdock patted Lanny on both shoulders. "She's safe with me. I promise. You're too sick to travel yet, and your daughter wouldn't leave without you."

"She shouldn't be here," Lanny mumbled. "Never wanted her to know...to see me like this." With a surprising strength, Lanny lifted his bony arm enough to grab the front of Murdock's shirt. "Take care of her. Take care of my little girl!"

His fingers unwound and released Murdock's shirt. His arms drifted down to the bed, on either side of him. He heaved a loud, harsh sigh and fell backward, unconscious again.

"Lanny!" Murdock grabbed his wrist to check for a pulse.

"Is he—"

"No. He has a heartbeat." Murdock clenched his jaw, anger tightening his facial features. "Damn! There's no telling how many times he's been beaten into unconsciousness over the years. But this last time they nearly killed him."

"Do you think he'll—"

"He'll probably drift in and out of consciousness for a while."

"It's a good sign that he came to, even for just a few minutes."

"Yeah, it's a good sign."

"He knows who he is and who you are and...and he remembers me."

"He thought you were your mother at first." Murdock cupped and tilted her chin so that she faced him. "Except for your blue eyes and your size, you do look a lot like her. She was a beautiful lady.''

''Yes, she was very beautiful. Outside and inside,'' Catherine said. ''I have his eyes, his height and my hair's a little darker than hers, but I've been told that I have her facial features.''

''He's not going to want you to stay.'' Murdock skimmed his index finger over her cheek. ''When he comes to again, he'll tell me to get you out of Zaraza as soon as possible.''

''If he were your father, would you leave him?'' Catherine asked.

Murdock had no answer for her.

One night turned into two and two into three. Murdock knew letting Catherine stay was a huge mistake. Each morning she had pleaded to stay—just one more day. And each day, as Lanny drifted in and out of consciousness, he seemed to be regaining strength. Sometimes he knew where he was, knew who Murdock was and would ask half a dozen questions in rapid succession. At other times, his mind was back in Nam or back in *Prision de las Puertas al Infierno*. And once or twice he comprehended that Catherine was his little girl, all grown up now. But most of the time he called her Mae Beth and begged her not to leave him.

What puzzled Murdock most about Lanny's delusional ranting was when he kept talking about warning Vincente. Warn Vincente, the young rebel leader, about what? Murdock wondered. Maybe Lanny was getting Vincente and Vincente's father Juan Sabino all mixed up in his mind. After all, Lanny seemed confused about so many things.

Each night he and Catherine had shared a bed, lying

stiffly alongside each other. He hadn't dared touch her, hadn't dared give in to the desire that rode him hard. Sometimes, when she thought he wasn't looking, she'd steal a glance at him. That's when he'd all but unraveled, wanting to reach out for her. It didn't matter what she said, or how she avoided touching him, even in the most innocent way. She was still hungry for him. And he wanted her so bad it was killing him.

Standing in the doorway to the balcony, he watched her as she cleared away the soup bowl that had contained the broth she'd fed her father over two hours ago, before he'd drifted off to sleep. They'd learned to crumble the pain medication into the watery chicken broth Andres brought to the room at regular intervals. Every time Lanny was conscious, Catherine forced more broth down him. It was as if she thought she could force him to live, force him to get well, by lavishing attention on him.

If Mae Beth McCroskey had been anything like her daughter, it was no wonder Lanny had loved the woman so much. Only now did Murdock truly understand how difficult it must have been for Lanny to leave her. But he had loved her too much to stay. If he'd been smart, Lanny never would have gotten married in the first place. Murdock himself knew better than to saddle some good woman with a man who led a life such as he and Lanny did.

"He ate all the broth this time," Catherine said. "His appetite is getting better."

"Yeah, I think he's improving. His face has a little color in it now."

She gazed longingly at Murdock, a faint smile curving the corners of her mouth.

Dammit, woman, don't look at me like that, he wanted to shout. Don't you realize that what you're feeling shows plainly in your expression? A man can stand only so much before he breaks. Lying beside you at night without touching you is torture, but seeing the yearning in your eyes every time you look at me is almost more than I can take.

"I think I'll go sit out on the balcony for a while, now that it's almost dusk," she said.

Yeah, honey, get away from me, he thought. Go somewhere—anywhere I can't see you. "Go ahead. I'll kept an eye on Lanny."

"He'll probably sleep for hours."

Before Murdock could respond, a loud knock sounded at the door. His hand drifted to his hip holster.

"Señor Murdock," Manuel said through the closed door.

Murdock unlocked the door. "Yeah, come on in."

Manuel entered the room, then shut the door behind him. "I have word from Dr. Constantino."

"Has he made arrangements for us?" Catherine asked.

"*Sí, señora.*" Manuel turned to Murdock and speaking in Spanish, gave him the doctor's instructions.

Catherine hurried to Murdock's side. "What's he saying?"

He shushed her. She gritted her teeth and huffed. Manuel and Murdock continued their conversation.

"He said we have to bring Lanny to the hospital at dawn tomorrow," Murdock translated. "Dr. Constantino will place him with patients being flown to Lima for surgeries that can't be performed at the hospital here. Jose will meet the plane in Lima and stay with your father until we arrive."

"What do you mean 'until we arrive?' Aren't we going with him?"

"No. There's no way we can go with Lanny. Dr. Constantino is sending a dead man's papers along with Lanny to get him out of Zaraza on a medical flight. You and I will leave later tomorrow afternoon, on a regularly scheduled flight back to Lima."

"Why does my father need a dead man's papers to leave Zaraza?" Catherine asked.

Murdock frowned. "Seems General Ramos never intended for Lanny to leave the country alive. He personally ordered his last beating. He assumes Lanny will die."

"But why? I don't understand."

Murdock stiffened and she could tell by the look in his eyes he was uncomfortable discussing the subject.

"Let's just say that Ramos is a bastard and leave it at that."

She realized that it would be useless to probe for more information. Murdock would tell her only what he wanted her to know.

"I don't like the idea of our being separated from my father."

"If I had control over the situation, it wouldn't be my first choice either, but this is our only option."

"I understand. I just wish…" Catherine smiled at Manuel. "Thank you. *Gracias*. And please, thank Dr. Constantino. I'm grateful to both of you."

"*Sí, señora*. I will tell the doctor."

When Murdock followed Manuel out into the hall, Catherine knew something was wrong. There was bad news and neither man wanted her to know. Damn! She hated being kept in the dark this way, hated being *protected* from information, no matter how disturbing.

Lanny groaned. Catherine glanced at her father. His

eyelids fluttered and opened. He lifted his head, then bracing his hands on the bed, he tried to sit up.

"What are you doing?" She rushed to him, intending to force him gently back down onto the bed.

"Don't fuss so, kitten." He grabbed her forearms. "Help me sit. I need to talk to you and Murdock."

Her father was more lucid at that very moment than he'd been any other time since Murdock carried him out of the prison in his arms. His gaze seemed focused, not jerkily darting about the room. Without the least bit of slurring or vagueness, his words were clear and distinct. And physically, he was so much stronger.

She eased him into a sitting position and propped pillows behind his back. He grabbed her arm. Their gazes met and held. He tugged on her arm, urging her to sit beside him.

"We're leaving San Carlos tomorrow," she said. "Dr. Constantino has arranged for you to fly out to Lima with some hospital patients. Then Murdock and I will follow on a later flight."

"Who is Murdock talking to?" Lanny asked.

"Manuel. He's been a great deal of help to us."

"He's Murdock's contact?"

"I think Andres, the proprietor of this hotel, and Manuel are both involved with the rebels and—"

As Lanny squeezed her hand tightly, his body trembled and he coughed several times. "When this Manuel leaves, I have to talk to Murdock. Alone."

She eased her hand from his fierce grip. "What's wrong? Why are you so upset? Getting this agitated isn't good for you."

"I'll be all right. And it's not me I'm worried about. It's you."

"We're all going to be fine. I'll have you back home

in Tennessee soon and I'm going to get you all the medical help you need to fully recover.''

The minute Lanny saw Murdock close and lock the hotel room door, he held up his skinny arm and motioned to him. ''We need to talk, bubba. Just you and me.''

''Lanny?'' Murdock hadn't expected his old friend to be sitting up in bed and looking, surprisingly, so alert.

''Don't know what you two have been doing to me, but I'm beginning to feel human for the first time in I can't remember when.'' Lanny's smile deepened the heavy wrinkles in his face. ''I don't remember your getting me out of prison. How long have we been here, at the hotel?''

''This is the third day,'' Murdock said.

''You were terribly malnourished and very weak when Murdock carried you out of...'' Catherine patted her father's shaky hand. ''You're trembling again. Are you all right?''

''I wouldn't mind some more of that broth and some bread to go with it,'' Lanny said. ''Maybe you could get me some, while I talk to Murdock.''

''Andres will be bringing supper in a little while,'' Murdock said. ''I don't want Catherine going downstairs alone.''

''Things that bad, huh?'' Lanny's glance scanned the room. ''Kitten, how about you going outside on the balcony for a few minutes and give me a chance to—''

''You two are so much alike!'' Catherine jumped up. ''Protect the poor, helpless female from knowing too much about what a big, hairy, freaking mess we've landed right in the middle of. God forbid either of you be totally honest with me about anything!'' She whirled around and flew out of the room, then slammed the louvered balcony doors, placing a barrier between them.

"A big, hairy, freaking mess? That is what she said, isn't it?" Shaking his head, Murdock snorted. "You should have taught your daughter how to cuss."

"Girl's got my temper." Lanny chuckled, but the laughter cost him. He coughed and wheezed until his face turned red. "Damn TB!"

Murdock pulled up a chair by the bed, then crossed his right leg over his left, ankle to knee, and rested his hands on his thighs. "Need some water?"

"Nah, I'll be okay." Lanny nodded toward the balcony. "She's a beauty, isn't she?"

"Yeah."

"Why the hell did you let her come with you?" Lanny's expression sobered as his gaze pleaded for an explanation. "I knew you'd come, once Ramos started selling off prisoners, but why bring Catherine with you?"

"Ramos's stipulation. Ransom for every prisoner had to be paid personally by a family member," Murdock told him. "Catherine had to deliver the hundred thousand herself."

"Damn that sorry bastard!" Lanny's face contorted into a vicious frown. "Did you say a hundred thousand? What did you do, hock your soul to get your hands on that much cash?"

"It was Catherine's money. Seems her husband left her millions."

"Left her millions, huh?" Lanny asked. "Is my kitten a rich widow?"

"Yeah, she's worth about ten mil. And her husband died about four years ago. He was a straight-arrow guy. Good breeding. Fine old Tennessee family."

"That's the kind of man Mae Beth should have married. Not some ole dumb hillbilly boy like me."

"From what Rick Burdett told me, your daughter didn't hesitate about offering to pay the ransom money Ramos demanded."

"Damn Ramos! Bubba, saving me wasn't worth putting Catherine at risk. If anything happens to her—"

"I won't let anything happen to her. I promise."

"I'll hold you to that promise. Nothing is more important to me than my girl. If you think you owe me anything, then repay me by protecting Catherine."

"Is that what you wanted to talk to me about?" Murdock asked. "About keeping Catherine safe?"

"Swear to me that you'll get her back to the States safe and sound." Lanny sought Murdock's hand.

"I swear." Murdock clasped Lanny's hand in his and held it with the force of his vow.

"Good." Lanny heaved a sigh of relief. "Now, I need you to get a message to Vincente Sabino. Send it through Manuel or Andres or whoever the hell you know you can trust."

"What sort of message?"

"Recently in *Prision de las Puertas al Infierno,* I got hold of some interesting information." Lanny's gaze searched the room as if checking for hidden spies. "You know that Juan Sabino's brother Raul kept the rebel forces united after Juan's death."

Murdock nodded. "Yeah, and I know that Juan's son Vincente pulled the rebels together when he was just a kid and kept the fight going after his uncle Raul died."

"Without Vincente, the rebels would break up into factions and Ramos could regain control of the entire country. The people must have a Sabino to follow."

"Everyone knows that Juan's son is the glue that

holds all the rebel factions together,'' Murdock agreed. ''His taking over after Raul's death is what saved the independence movement in Zaraza.''

Lanny motioned for Murdock to come closer, so Murdock leaned over, in order to hear Lanny, who had begun to whisper.

''There's an assassination plot against Vincente.'' Lanny grabbed Murdock's shirtfront. ''If someone doesn't save that boy's life, then everything they've been fighting for these past twenty years will have been for nothing. Juan Sabino would have died for nothing! I would have spent twenty years in hell—for nothing!'' Another hacking fit overcame Lanny. His sunken cheeks swelled. His eyes watered. And his pale face flushed with color.

When the spell eased, Murdock poured Lanny a glass of water and held it to his mouth. ''How did you find out about the plot to assassinate Vincente?''

Lanny sighed as the aftereffects of his painful coughing subsided. ''In prison, you learn quickly who you can and cannot trust,'' he said. ''Your life depends on it. My friendship to old Juan Sabino is widely known. When it was learned that I might be released, this information was passed along to me by a recently imprisoned rebel. The man hoped that I might find a way to get word to Vincente.''

''Do you know the details about the assassination plot?''

Lanny sipped the water Murdock had offered, then shoved the glass away. ''One of Vincente's right-hand men is a traitor.'' Lanny lowered his voice to a barely audible whisper. ''Domingo Sanchez. Vincente's most trusted bodyguard.''

"Do you know when the attempt on Vincente's life is planned to take place?" Murdock asked.

"For the day he officially takes control of San Carlos." Lanny gripped Murdock's shoulder. "Find a way to save Juan's son."

"We can't trust this news to anyone," Murdock said. "How do we know that Manuel and Andres can be trusted one hundred per cent? They're rebel sympathizers, but are they loyal to Vincente or would they side with Sanchez? There's only one thing for me to do and that's go to Vincente myself and expose this Domingo Sanchez."

Lanny tightened his hold on Murdock's shoulder. "No! Don't go yourself. Don't get back in the middle of this war down here. You aren't a young buck anymore. If you're ever going to have a life, you ought to be finding yourself a good woman and settling down. Don't you think that if I thought I had a chance with Mae Beth, I'd crawl back to her on my hands and knees?"

"Lanny, about your ex-wife…"

"You don't have to tell me, bubba. I know she's dead. I've known it, in here—" he thumped his chest "—for a long, long time."

"Well, you've got a second chance with your daughter. She may huff and puff a lot, but she loves you. She's been taking care of you, day and night."

"You gotta trust somebody. Either Andres or Manuel. You've got to get word to Vicente, before it's too late." Lanny laid his hand over Murdock's cheek. "But don't you go hunting Juan's boy out there in his jungle stronghold. You get my Catherine out of this damn country. Nothing's more important than that. Do you hear me?"

"Yeah, Lanny, I hear you."

Murdock knew what he had to do. He owed Lanny his life. But he owed his life to Juan Sabino and the ragtag band of teenage soldiers he'd left behind that day twenty years ago. He couldn't trust Vincente's life to anyone other than himself. Despite what Lanny said, Murdock knew he had no way of knowing who he could trust. Any rebel sympathizer could as easily be a Domingo Sanchez backer as they could be completely loyal to Vincente.

Murdock had never forgiven himself for living when others had died—died to save his life so that he could get vital information through to the CIA. He owed something to those boys, to their cause, to the country they had lived and died for.

But there was no reason to worry Lanny, no reason to share his plans with his old comrade. No need for either Lanny or Catherine to know that Manuel had told him that the first advance of Vincente's troop were headed toward San Carlos at that very minute. And within the week, Vincente would follow, with the bulk of his rebel forces.

First thing in the morning, they would take Lanny to the hospital so that Dr. Constantino could slip him aboard the medical flight. Then he would personally put Catherine on the afternoon plane from San Carlos to Lima. Once he'd kept his promise to Lanny and made sure his little *kitten* was safely aboard that flight, he could finally even an old score and repay a twenty-year-old debt.

He would go up the Amazon and into the jungle to find Vincente Sabino.

Chapter 7

Catherine kissed her father's cheek, then released his hand and watched while Manuel wheeled him into the hospital's back entrance. She couldn't bear saying good-bye and leaving Lanny's care to someone else. But she had no choice. She couldn't go with him; she could only follow. She had spent a lifetime wishing things could have been different with her father and now they were being given a second chance. But only if they both got out of Zaraza alive.

Murdock gripped her shoulder. "We'd better go. And don't worry, you'll be with Lanny again tonight."

"I know. It's just so difficult to watch him leave without me."

Slipping his arm around Catherine's waist, Murdock led her away, back toward the old black sedan parked a block away in a dead-end alley. "Come on. Let's head back to the hotel. We can pack our bags and eat a bite of lunch before we go to the airport. We have about seven hours to kill before our flight takes off.''

Reluctantly, Catherine slid into the front seat of the car, but couldn't help glancing over her shoulder at the hospital. She cautioned herself not to waste time and energy on needless worry. There was nothing more she could do for her father until he was safely out of this horrible country. To her, Zaraza had always been just a tiny South American country, a dot on the map, the place where her father had died twenty years ago. But Zaraza was more than that to her now. Much more. This wasn't where her father had died; it was where he'd been held prisoner and subjected to inhumane conditions. Starved. Beaten. Tortured.

Her ambivalent feelings about Zaraza had changed dramatically. She was no longer uncertain. No longer ignorant of the truth. She had always doubted the horror stories reported on the news and had often wondered if her father had died fighting for an unjust cause. But now after seeing, firsthand, the results of General Ramos's brutality to his captives, her opinion had done a 180-degree turn.

Once Murdock started the car's engine, Catherine snapped out of her troubling thoughts. She glanced over at the big man beside her. Her father's old friend. Her highly trained bodyguard. Was there any hope for Murdock or was he lost forever to the harsh world of violence? She'd be a fool to take a chance on caring for a man so much like her father, a man who could probably never be satisfied with the safe, the sane, the ordinary.

''You're mighty quiet,'' Murdock said, but didn't take his gaze off the road ahead of them.

''Just thinking,'' she replied. ''By the way, what did Manuel tell you last night?''

Murdock shrugged, implying he didn't understand her question.

"Don't play dumb with me. I know something's wrong. Don't you think I have a right to know?"

"It isn't something that should affect you...affect us," he told her. "What's the point of my worrying you with it?"

"So there is something to worry about."

"Why can't you just leave it alone and stop asking questions? Lanny will be headed out of Zaraza within the hour and you'll...we will be joining him in Lima by late afternoon. So what happens here in San Carlos won't concern you."

Murdock kept to the back streets, knowing danger might meet them at any turn. There were no guarantees, no assurance of safety—not in San Carlos. Not anywhere in Zaraza. Once he put Catherine on the plane to Lima, he'd breathe easier. At least she and Lanny would be long gone before all hell broke loose, before the first wave of rebel troops attacked the capital.

"Something's going on with the war," Catherine said. "In Lima you said something about the calm before the storm. Is that it? Are the rebel troops preparing for attack?"

"Yeah."

"When?"

"Any day now."

"Oh, God!"

He stole a quick glance at Catherine, whose face had paled. "Don't worry. You'll be long gone before it happens."

"I'll be long gone." She nodded her head in agreement as her mind swirled with doubts. More than once Murdock had corrected himself when he had mentioned that *she* would be leaving Zaraza, instead of *they* would be leaving. A frightening suspicion formed in her mind. Murdock wasn't leaving Zaraza! He had lied to Lanny. And he had lied to her. He was planning to stay here in this god-awful country, to help the rebels in some way. Murdock couldn't leave, couldn't walk away and let old debts go unpaid. Even as she wanted to beg him to go with her, a part of her, begrudgingly, admired his sense of loyalty—to Lanny and Juan Sabino, the men who had saved his life twenty years ago.

"You aren't flying with me to Lima this afternoon, are you?" She knew the answer before she asked the question, but she needed to hear him confirm her dark suspicion.

Without moving a muscle, his expression unchanged, Murdock replied, "Once I see you safely off on the flight to Lima, I'll be heading down the Rio Negro to find Vicente before he reaches San Carlos."

"Why?" Her heartbeat accelerated as she waited for his answer.

"Because Vincente's life is in danger."

"How do you know that?"

"Lanny was given some information before he left the prison that Vincente's most trusted bodyguard, Domingo Sanchez, plans to assassinate Vincente the day he takes control of San Carlos."

"Why would—"

"Some people don't want peace," Murdock explained. "Without a Sabino to lead the rebels, they'd splinter back into factions and the war would never end."

"You can't leave the job of saving Vincente to someone else, can you? You can't let the Zarazaians fight this war without you. Oh, no, not Aloysius Murdock. Not the mighty warrior who's willing to die for 101 causes the world over, but isn't willing to live a normal, decent, unexciting life with a wife and children.''

Where had all that anger come from? she wondered. From the resentment she still felt for her father? Yes. Maybe. Probably. But she had to admit that some of her wrath stemmed from her unwanted feelings for Murdock. She despised the weakness in herself that made her care about this man—this carbon copy of Lanny McCroskey!

''Who are we talking about here, Catherine, me or Lanny?''

''Both of you. You're two peas in a pod. Same kind of men. Same kind of reasoning.''

''Care about Lanny,'' Murdock told her. ''He's your father and I think you've got a good chance of rehabilitating him. But don't care about me. I'm a lost cause.''

''Don't flatter yourself thinking I care about you one way or the other, Mr. Murdock.''

''Yeah, sure. You and I don't mean anything to each other, do we? We're together only because of Lanny.'' Murdock pulled the car into the alley behind the hotel and killed the motor. With one arm draped over the steering wheel, he glared at Catherine. ''But care about each other or not, if we stayed together much longer, we'd wind up doing the horizontal tango, just to get it out of our systems.''

She wanted to deny his statement, to tell him that hell would freeze over before she'd ever have sex with him. But denying it didn't change the truth. She did not like Murdock. Did not want to become involved with a man so much like her father. But try as she might, she couldn't tell him he was wrong.

''Then it's a good thing we won't be together much

longer," she said. "Because I'd hate myself if I let you...if we... I don't even like you!"

"Yeah, I know, honey." He reached out, grabbed her by the back of the neck and hauled her forward until her mouth was almost touching his. "You don't like me, but you want me."

She held her breath, knowing he was going to kiss her and that she was helpless to stop him. *You don't want to stop him,* an inner voice taunted. Murdock's gold-flecked hazel eyes burned with barely contained passion. His hand momentarily tightened around her neck. His parted lips hovered over hers. Her heartbeat accelerated with anticipation.

With a sudden thrust, Murdock shoved Catherine away from him. Shivering from head to toe, she stared at him, her gaze questioning his actions.

"Consider yourself lucky," he said. "I could have had you. Right here. Right now. In the car. And you wouldn't have done a thing to stop me."

Catherine gasped as she willed her heart to slow its breakneck speed. Lifting her hand to slap him, she screamed, "You arrogant son of a bitch!"

He deflected her blow, taking the brunt of her attack on the shoulder. She flung open the car door, jumped out and raced to the hotel's back entrance. Murdock groaned. Damn! He pocketed the car keys and then got out and followed her. She was his responsibility and it was his duty to protect her, no matter what. But once he put her on that plane this afternoon, she'd be Lanny's problem. He figured his old buddy had his work cut out for him to regain Catherine's respect and love.

Two things he would never have, he reminded himself.

* * *

When Catherine and Murdock arrived at the San Carlos airport shortly before one, they found the place buzzing with activity. Manuel whispered to Murdock, as he handed their suitcases to him, that he'd been told every flight out of Zaraza was booked solid. Had the rumors of Sabino's first wave attack on San Carlos reached the public? Murdock wondered. Or had the populace simply sensed something in the air? His own sixth sense was certainly acting up, sending off warning signals, but he couldn't pinpoint the danger. Just a general uneasy feeling. The sooner he got Catherine out of the country, the better.

"I will say goodbye." Manuel shook hands with Murdock, then nodded to and smiled at Catherine. "Safe journey, *señora*."

"Thank you, Manuel. Safe journey to you, too."

When Manuel left them, Murdock guided Catherine through the customs check. All the while, he stayed on guard. Waiting. Watching. Halfway expecting the worst. But they passed inspection quickly, without a moment's pause.

Murdock checked his watch. "They should start boarding soon. Your flight leaves at one-fifty."

"I'll be so glad to get out of this country." Clutching her purse containing her passport, boarding pass and billfold, Catherine sat down to wait for her flight's departure.

"When I get back to the States, I'll come by to see Lanny." Murdock squeezed his big body into one of the narrow airport seats.

"Don't you mean *if* you get back to the States?"

"I plan on making it back. Sooner or later."

Catherine folded her arms across her chest, tilted her

nose slightly, as if she'd smelled something unpleasant, and deliberately turned her head away from Murdock.

"I'm glad Jose got a call through to us before we left the hotel," Murdock said. "It's good to know that Lanny arrived safely and that Jose whisked him off to a private sanitarium."

"I want to take Lanny back to the United States as soon as I can. That's where he'll get the best medical treatment possible."

"Lanny may need to spend a few days in Lima. Enough to build up his strength some more, before the long flight home."

Catherine cleared her throat. "If...when you get back to the States, please, let us know. Lanny will worry about you."

"Yeah, honey. Sure thing. I wouldn't want Lanny worrying about me, would I?"

"And you're welcome to visit us in Huntington any time you'd like."

Murdock grinned. Catherine was trying so damn hard to act like a lady, to remember her manners and to pretend that he didn't mean anything more to her than any old friend of Lanny's would. All right, he told himself. Two can play that game. After all, they were both better off ignoring their attraction to each other.

"Don't expect too much too soon from Lanny," Murdock advised.

"I don't expect anything from my father," she said, gracing Murdock with one of her snooty little looks. "I intend to see that he receives the best medical care possible and afterward offer him a home with me. Lanny may be my father, but he's a stranger to me, as I am to him. I assume it will take some time for us to become acquainted and to find out if we can build any type of relationship together.''

''Ever the dutiful daughter.''

''You have your loyalties and I have mine,'' Catherine said. ''Nothing is more important to me than family. Where you've chosen a jaded life-style that leaves no room for love or family, I want love and a family and a lifetime commitment. No matter what Lanny has done, no matter how much he disappointed me and hurt my mother, he is still my father.''

''And he's a fortunate man. I'm glad you're willing to give him a second chance. He deserves it.''

''You take care of yourself.'' Temporarily lowering her defenses, Catherine looked at Murdock, concern in her eyes. ''If anything happens to you, I'm afraid Lanny might blame himself. After all, he's the one who told you about the assassination threat.''

''If Lanny was physically capable of doing this job himself, he'd do it,'' Murdock told her. ''He paid with twenty years of his life to aid Sabino's rebels. I can't let Juan Sabino's death, twenty years of your father's life, and a just cause go down the tubes.''

''No, I don't suppose you can.'' She lifted her hand, but refrained from actually touching him. ''Good luck. I hope—'' her voice cracked ''—you accomplish your mission.''

Before he could reply, the announcer called Catherine's flight and said that they would begin boarding passengers immediately. Catherine and Murdock stood, exchanged a long, tense glance and then Catherine stuck out her hand. Murdock stared at her hand for several seconds, then grasped it in his.

''Goodbye.'' Catherine clutched his hand tenaciously,

as if she never meant to let go. "And thank you for helping me get my father out of Zaraza."

Murdock tightened his grip on her hand, then pulled her forward. She almost tripped in her effort to avoid their bodies touching. He grabbed her shoulders to steady her. She gazed at him, her feelings so plainly visible in her expression.

Catherine Price was damn lucky to be leaving today, he thought. Otherwise, he'd never let her go. "Go. Now."

She nodded, pulled her hand from his and practically ran toward the departure gate. Don't look back, she told herself. And don't cry. Don't you dare cry!

The pain in Murdock's chest radiated out and spread through his body. God help him, he didn't want her to leave him. He'd never needed a woman. Not ever. Not even when he'd been madly in love with Barbara. But on some basic level and for reasons he couldn't even begin to fathom, he needed Catherine.

But she already had everything she needed—a great career, a hefty bank account and her father back from the dead. She sure as hell didn't need him. No way. She was better off without him. If he really cared about her, he'd let her go—now and forever.

She'd been right when she'd said he had his loyalties and she had hers. Her life was back in Tennessee, presiding over that fancy private school and hobnobbing with the social elite. She'd take care of Lanny, shower him with love and attention and ease him into her world. A world guys like Aloysius Murdock could never enter. He had his own life, back in Atlanta, working for Dundee. But before he could return, he had a mission to accomplish. An assassination to prevent. A nation to save.

Suddenly and without warning, an explosion rocked the airport. Billowing smoke. Screaming people. Confusion and fear. Murdock froze as he assimilated what had happened. Something had blown sky-high outside on the runway—where the plane to Lima was boarding.

Catherine! He had to get to Catherine.

Before he could form a plan of action in his mind, another explosion ripped through the terminal, sending debris and body parts flying through the air.

The airport was under attack! A strategically planned attack to hit the airport when the most planes were on the ground. Damn! Why had the rebels moved up the day of the attack? Manuel had been so sure that the assault on San Carlos was days away.

Where the hell was Catherine? Had she boarded the plane before it had been destroyed? Or was she trapped between the airstrip and the terminal? He didn't care where she was as long as she was still alive. He had to find her!

Murdock hadn't prayed much over the years, but he prayed now. If there was any justice in this world, any at all, then he'd find Catherine alive. He had promised Lanny that he'd take care of his daughter and he had arrogantly assumed he could. Hell, why hadn't he stood at the gate and watched her until she boarded the plane?

Shoving his way through the horde of frightened and wounded people, Murdock sought the woman whose life he'd be willing to exchange for his own. While he searched, another explosion ripped through the parking area, setting cars aflame and shooting fire into the sky. Screams of the injured and dying echoed in Murdock's ears as he frantically hunted for any sign of Catherine.

Fear more powerful and deadly than any he'd ever known took firm control of him. Like a madman on a suicide mission, Murdock ripped through the airport, calling out Catherine's name. He had to find her. He had to find her alive!

"Murdock!"

As utter chaos ruled, he barely heard his name being screamed through the racket of human suffering and panic. He scanned right and left, forward and behind, uncertain from which direction the voice had come.

"Murdock!"

Then he saw her. Clawing her way through the mass of frightened people trying to escape the burning building. At six feet tall in her heels, she stood out in the crowd. Her beautiful face was covered in soot. Her filthy blouse had a rip in the sleeve. But she was alive and standing. And calling out to him from thirty feet away.

Stomping his way toward Catherine, his presence alone parted the crowd that separated him from his objective. Catherine accelerated her approach and started running. Murdock hurled himself toward her, his arms open, reaching out for her. Their bodies collided in an emotional reunion. He swept her off her feet. She wrapped her arms around his neck and hung on for dear life.

"Oh, God, Cat, I thought I'd lost you!"

Their gazes met and held as they visually devoured each other. And then he took her mouth in a ravaging kiss, plundering her in a show of possession and thankfulness. She clung to him, returning his kiss, responding with the same fervent gratitude and passion that commanded his actions.

Murdock ended the kiss, then ran his hands over her face and down her arms. "Are you all right?"

She nodded. "Yes. Just shook up a little and scared senseless. What happened?"

"My guess is that Sabino's front guard has arrived in San Carlos and that putting the airport out of commission was their first order of business."

"What—what are we going to do?" she asked.

"We're going to get the hell out of here."

"But where are we going?"

"I have to get you out of the city as soon as possible. You aren't safe here. No one is." Murdock wrapped his arm around her waist and led her over and around the rubble and through the confused crowd of people, who were still trying to figure out what had happened.

When they entered the street, Murdock realized that the rebel troops had bombed more than the airport. Rows of nearby buildings lay in crumbled ruins. Bodies littered the streets. And in the distance, they heard the distinct sound of artillery fire drawing closer and closer.

"We've got to find a safe place to hide, until I can make plans to get us out of the city. It'll be safer leaving late tonight." Taking her hand, he guided her away from the airport and in the opposite direction of the burning buildings.

"Why can't we go back to *Hotel Dulce de Rosa?*" she asked breathlessly, as she tried to keep step with his longer gait.

"It's too far away. Besides, unless I miss my guess, General Ramos's army will have all the main streets blocked. Our best bet is to head in the other direction."

Catherine tugged on Murdock's hand, temporarily halting him. "I'm scared," she admitted.

He pulled her into his arms and hugged her ferociously. "I'm going to take care of you. Do you hear me? No matter what it takes, I'll get you out of Zaraza!"

"I know you will."

"Come on."

He grabbed her hand and together they ran into a nearby alley. The escape route ended abruptly at a six-foot wooden fence that separated one alley from the next.

"I'll give you a boost over," he told her.

She nodded agreement, then lifted her leg and placed her foot in Murdock's open palm. He gave her a forceful shove. She caught the top of the fence with both hands and hoisted first one leg and then the other over the wooden rails. Jumping without looking, she landed on something large and soft that partially cushioned her fall. Using her hands as leverage, she placed them, palms down, on each side of her and pushed herself onto her feet. That's when she saw what had eased her downward plunge. A body! A dead soldier! And to his left, lay another unmoving form. Another soldier!

Catherine screamed. Murdock scaled the fence and dropped to the other side in a split second. Then he saw what had frightened Catherine. Damn! He grabbed her shoulders and shook her soundly, until she stopped screaming.

"Take a couple of deep breaths," he told her. "I know this isn't a pleasant sight, honey, but you'd better get used to it. I'm sure there's worse ahead of us."

"I'm all right. I've just never... Who are they?"

"By the their uniforms, I'd say they're Zarazaian soldiers who got caught in a bomb blast."

When he noticed Catherine shaking, Murdock shoved her up against the fence, spread his hands out on either side of her head and looked her square in the eye. "Our best bet of getting out of the city in one piece is if we hide until night and head out sometime after midnight. And we'll have a better chance, in case we're seen at a distance, if we're posing as soldiers. Since my guess is that Ramos's army has control of this part of San Carlos, then we're lucky we ran across these two.''

"What—what do you mean we're lucky we ran across these two?"

"The smaller man—" Murdock pointed to the young man whose body had broken Catherine's fall "—is about your size. His entire uniform should fit you. And it's in pretty good shape. Looks like he got it in the head. The blood that's on the uniform is dried, so—" He left his sentence unfinished the minute he noticed the horrified look on her face. "This other one—" he nodded to the heavyset man who lay facedown several feet away "—is big enough that I think his shirt might fit me. Even if his pants weren't in shreds, I figure they'd be way too short."

"Are you saying that we…that you expect me to—"

"I expect you to follow orders. Remember what I told you on the way to Lima—that if I have to stop to explain my orders, that delay could cost us both our lives."

Shivering uncontrollably, Catherine shook her head and keened softly. Murdock grasped her face between his big hands.

"You can do this, Cat. I know you can."

He released her and then hurriedly stripped the young soldier down to his underwear. After tossing Catherine the tan uniform, Murdock removed the other man's shirt. He hurriedly tugged his own shirt over his head and replaced it with the tan shirt bearing the Zarazaian government emblem on the sleeves.

Catherine stared at the uniform she held in her hands. These garments belonged to a dead man and had only moments before been on his body. She swallowed hard, then slid the pants up under her skirt, jerked up the zipper and snapped them closed. She removed her skirt, tossed it onto the dirty street and then removed her blouse.

Murdock inspected the soldier's weapons—a pair of M-16s. He slipped the rifles away from the stiff bodies and then retrieved the ammunition belts. When he glanced up at Catherine, he saw how badly she was still shaking, so much so that she couldn't button the shirt she'd just slipped into.

After slinging one M-16 and both ammunition belts over his shoulder, he reached out for Catherine. She fell hard against his side. He forked his fingers through her disarrayed hair and held her head against his shoulder.

"I'm sorry you're a part of this," he said, his voice deep and soothing. "All I can do now is take you with me. And that means you're going to have to not only cooperate, but you're going to have to be strong and brave."

She wrapped her arms around his waist, but when she felt the weapon and the ammunition belt, she withdrew from him and stared at the offensive objects.

Murdock grabbed her chin. "I need for you to show me that you're Lanny McCroskey's daughter. Can you do that?"

She closed her eyes for a moment, then when she reopened them she nodded and said, "Yes. I can do that."

"Good!"

Murdock lifted the other M-16 and handed it to Catherine. Her mouth rounded in a silent gasp, but she gripped the gun tightly and then slung it over her shoulder. Murdock picked up the soldiers' berets. He stuck one cap on his head and then lifted Catherine's hair and shoved it under the other beret before he pulled it down over her ears. He looked into her familiar blue eyes and saw her father's grit and determination. Hell, he thought, they just might have a chance to come out of this alive, after all.

Chapter 8

Murdock led Catherine along the nearly deserted back streets and alleys of San Carlos. When a squad of Zarazaian soldiers swept through Tripoli Avenue, Murdock jerked Catherine into a doorway and motioned for her to go up the stairs leading to the second floor of a deserted building that had once housed a restaurant. She held her breath as General Ramos's men marched by, their weapons drawn and ready for combat. As their boot steps echoed in her ears, Catherine reached the top of the stairs. Halting at the closed door, she grabbed the handle and found the door locked.

"This might be a good place to stay until dark," Murdock whispered.

After setting her aside, he rammed his shoulder against the door. The force of his powerful body broke the lock. The door swung open, giving them a view of a long, narrow hallway. Catherine followed him down the corridor. He flung open three doors, checking the upstairs rooms for any occupants. Empty. Behind the fourth and final door at the end of the hallway, they found a small, partially furnished apartment.

Murdock flipped the wall switch. Nothing. Just as he suspected, the electrical power had been cut off—either when the building had been vacated or due to a citywide blackout caused by the rebel attack.

"This is better than I'd hoped," he said. "A bathroom and a bed. We can clean up and get some rest before we head out."

Bone weary and mentally fatigued, Catherine removed the M-16 from her shoulder, laid it on the floor and slumped down into the nearest chair. "Why do we have to leave the city? Why can't you just hook up with the rebel soldiers and tell them you have a vital message for Vincente Sabino?"

Murdock pulled the curtains over the windows, protecting them from being viewed by anyone on the street below. He jerked the beret from his head and forked his fingers through his damp hair. "Because the rebel soldiers are going to shoot first and ask questions later. Any soldier worth his salt would. They're in the middle of their first major attack on San Carlos and anyone crossing their path will be eliminated. And as far as my telling them I have a message for Vincente—they don't know me from Adam. And unless we could find Manuel or Andres, both of whom I suspect have gone underground, we'd have no one to vouch for us. Besides, I'm not sure we can trust Manuel or Andres one hundred percent."

"So our only alternative is what? Try to find Vincente ourselves?" Catherine glanced down at her scuffed heels as she stretched her legs.

Murdock's gaze followed her. "Too bad that soldier's feet were so big. You could have used his boots."

She shrugged. "What are the odds we can get out of San Carlos tonight?"

"Pretty good, actually, if we can find some sort of transportation."

"Like what?"

"Like a car."

"How do you propose we get a car?"

"Later, when it's dusk, I'll go out and see what I can find." A quirky grin arched his lips.

"I'd like to wash up and get some of this soot and grime off of me and out of my hair. Do you suppose there's any water in the bathroom?"

"Only one way to find out." Murdock kicked open the bathroom door, stepped into the tiny room and turned on the sink faucet. Water flowed freely into the cracked porcelain bowl. "You've got cold water. No hot."

"Cold water is just fine with me." She sighed, thinking about how wonderful it would be to splash that cold water over her face and body.

"Here's some old soap, too." Murdock picked up the yellow, cracked remains of a partially used bar of soap. "No towels. But as warm as it is, you'll dry in no time."

With soap in hand, he emerged from the bathroom. Catherine kicked off her shoes. She sighed when she noticed the huge run in her stocking. When she'd slipped into the soldier's pants, she hadn't bothered removing her panty hose. That's something she'd rectify as soon as she got a chance. She looked up as Murdock approached. He tossed her the soap, which she caught in her right hand.

"Clean up," he said. "I'm going to make a trip downstairs and see if I can find any canned food. When the restaurant closed down, they might have left behind a few things.''

Grasping the soap in her hand, Catherine forced her tired legs to stand. ''I'm not really hungry.''

''You will be later.''

''Maybe.''

Murdock picked up the M-16 she'd laid on the floor and handed it to her. ''I'd better give you a quick lesson in handling this baby before I leave you alone.''

She listened while he explained the basics of using the weapon. She nodded as if she understood what he was talking about when he mentioned the rifle had been upgraded and had a two-stage trigger.

''Pull back a little for semiautomatic fire and pull back fully for full auto fire,'' Murdock told her. When he started out the door, he paused and cautioned, ''Take that gun into the bathroom with you. And if anyone besides me enters this room, shoot him!'' With that said, he left her alone.

Catherine stared at the rifle she held. She didn't own a gun. Knew practically nothing about them. And had always associated weapons of any kind with her father. *I need for you to show me that you're Lanny Mc-Croskey's daughter. Can you do that?* Murdock's words reverberated inside her head. All her life she'd been Mae Beth McCroskey's daughter in every way. A well-educated, mannerly, Southern lady. But the traits she had inherited from her mother wouldn't cut it in this situation. She needed to reach down inside herself and draw on the traits Lanny had surely passed on to her. She'd known what Murdock meant by asking her if she could show him she was Lanny's daughter. And yes, dammit, she could and would do whatever necessary to survive, to get out of this horrendous country and reunite with her father.

By the time Murdock returned carrying a burlap sack filled with canned goods and a manual can opener, Catherine had not only stripped down to her panties and bra, but she'd washed her hair. He walked in to find her sitting on the bed, with her head held down and her damp, shoulder-length hair tossed over her face. The fact that she hadn't bothered putting on any clothes before his return surprised him. What had happened to Catherine's ladylike modesty?

When she heard his approach, she flipped her hair out of her eyes, grabbed the M-16 lying beside her on the bed and aimed the weapon directly at him.

"Hold your fire, Cat. It's only me."

"I need to put a damn bell around your neck, Aloysius. You didn't make a sound."

"Found us a supply of canned goods." He dropped the burlap bag onto the round table in the kitchenette area. "And look what else I found." He pulled a couple of flashlights from his back pockets. "One for you and one for me." He tossed one onto the bed.

Catherine laid the M-16 on the floor, then eased her long legs over the edge of the bed and stood. Murdock looked his fill, surveying her from the strands of light-brown hair dripping moisture onto her shoulders, over her high, firm breasts pushing over the cups of her bra and down to the square of cream silk that barely covered her hips. Her arms and legs were long, slender and shapely. And she possessed a well-proportioned body, with curves in all the right places.

Murdock's sex sprang instantly to life. What kind of game was she playing? he wondered. She couldn't be so naive that she didn't realize the effect her half-naked body would have on him. Practically panting, he watched her as she picked up her discarded Zarazaian uniform shirt and slipped her arms into the sleeves. When she reached down for the pants, Murdock crossed the room in three giant strides and grabbed her around the waist. Catherine gasped. He hauled her up against him, pressing her mound against his arousal.

"What do you think you're doing?" she asked.

"Giving you what you were asking for," he said.

"What I was— I wasn't asking for this! It's hot up here and we can't open any windows. I just wanted to cool off for a while. That's all."

Murdock glared skeptically at her, then released her and shoved her toward the bed. She fell backward and was barely able to break her fall by catching the bed's footboard.

"Cooling off sounds like a good idea," he said.

When Murdock smiled that way—cocky, mischievous—Catherine knew she'd better be prepared for anything. She retrieved the pants from the floor, then stuffed her legs into them and whipped up the zipper.

Murdock laid his M-16 and the two ammunition belts in a ragged armchair in the corner, then unbuttoned the uniform shirt, stripped it off and tossed it onto the back of the chair. He scratched his chest, then spread his arms out and stretched.

Catherine couldn't take her eyes off him. Off his broad chest, his extremely wide shoulders, his huge arms and his thick, heavy muscles. Her femininity tingled and throbbed. The man was a sight to behold.

Ignoring her completely, he marched into the bathroom. He plugged the sink, then turned on the faucets. Using his hands as a scoop, he dipped up the water and poured it over his head, then repeated the process several times, until his head was drenched and watery rivulets cascaded over his face, down his neck and created clean streaks on his dirty chest. Droplets glistened in his dark chest hair.

Catherine closed her eyes to shut out the sight of him. But his image wouldn't disappear; it was burned into her consciousness. Everything female within her reacted to the primal urges that the sight of his big, hard body awakened within her.

Miles away the artillery fire grew weaker and less frequent. Outside the late-afternoon tropical sun beat down unmercifully, raising the temperature inside the boarded-up building.

"Sounds like the battle is dying down." Murdock emerged from the bathroom. "Let's get some rest. If I can find us a car, you'll be driving most of the night."

"What do mean I'll be driving?" Catherine glowered at him.

"It only makes sense. You drive. I ride shotgun."

His wicked smile tempted her to smack him. But she knew better than to touch him, in any way.

"Why does it make sense?" she asked.

"Because it's obvious you don't know a damn thing about guns. Besides, I'm trained to be aware of my surroundings and be alert to danger. And I'm a soldier, capable of killing. You're not."

"All right. Since you explained it that way, it does make sense for me to drive."

Murdock picked up the *borrowed* shirt, wiped his damp face with it and then ran it over his chest. "If I remember right, the nearest village that's situated on the Rio Negro is a little place called Chota. We should be able to book passage on a boat headed downstream and be at Vincente's Santa Teresa camp within twenty-four hours—if we don't run into trouble. I just hope we can make it there before Vincente begins his march toward San Carlos. Otherwise, we'll be following him back to the city.''

''If we're going to be following him, why not wait here for him?''

''Because I have a better chance of getting through to him if I show up at his stronghold. His men might take us captive, but if I can persuade them that I know Manuel and Andres, they just might let me see Vincente. Here in San Carlos, every soldier will be trigger-happy and we could both wind up dead.''

''I know you feel obligated to save Vincente, but wouldn't it be smarter if we just stayed on the boat and kept on going down the Amazon until we reach the Brazilian border?''

''I can't leave Zaraza until I've warned Vincente about the traitor in his midst. And I can't send you alone down the Amazon.''

''So I'm trapped here in Zaraza with you.'' Catherine flopped down on the side of the bed. ''When we don't show up in Lima, Lanny's going to be terribly worried.''

''Yeah, I know. And don't think I haven't figured my promise to him into this equation.'' Hell! If he had a choice he'd never involve Catherine in this wild search for Vincente and endanger her life. For Lanny's sake, he told himself. But he couldn't let this twenty-year war end in defeat for Sabino's rebels. Not after all the sacrifices that had been made to rid Zaraza of General Ramos. ''I can't let Ramos win this war.''

''I don't want General Ramos to win. After seeing firsthand what he and his goons are capable of doing— to people like my father—makes me realize that I'd like to help you make sure Vincente Sabino takes control of this country. I'd like to see the general hung from the highest tree in San Carlos!''

Murdock's lips twitched. ''Getting a little bloodthirsty aren't you, honey?'' He crossed the room, then sat down beside her, his weight sagging the bed. ''What would the blue bloods back in Huntington say about your newly acquired thirst for revenge?''

She turned up her snooty little nose. ''Hmph! What's that old adage about 'when in Rome?' Well, the way I see it, I'm in Zaraza, caught in the middle of an ugly war and it's either fight or die.''

''You learn fast.'' Murdock shoved her over in the bed. ''Get some rest. It'll be sunset before long.''

After she scooted to the far side of the double bed, Murdock stretched out beside her. They lay there, only inches separating their bodies. Catherine closed her eyes and tried to pretend that the nearness of his big body, naked from the waist up, didn't disturb her in the least. The instant he touched her arm, her eyes flew open and she shot straight up.

''Take off that shirt. You'll be cooler,'' he said.

Hesitantly, she did as he had suggested. Of course, he'd been right. Without the shirt, she felt much cooler. But she also felt a lot more vulnerable. You're not naked, she reminded herself. You're still wearing your bra.

Within fifteen minutes Murdock was snoring. Catherine glanced over at him, surprised and amazed that he could fall into such a deep sleep so quickly. But at least, if he was asleep, she, too, could rest without worrying about him pouncing on her.

Murdock opened his eyelids and quickly checked his surroundings. Quiet and shadowy. A peaceful lull had settled over the city. No artillery fire, not even in the

distance. The last rays of golden sunlight crept from beneath the curtains and fingered out over the bare wooden
floor. He felt a warm, soft weight on top of him. Catherine lay cuddled against him, her head nestled on his
chest. Lifting his hand, he cupped her head and caressed
the silky strands of her hair. If he had all the time in the
world, there was nothing he'd like better than to spend
the night making love to this woman. But he didn't have
that luxury. Not now.

Murdock eased her off his chest and into his arms.
She whimpered, then wriggled until she'd wrapped herself around him. He kissed her forehead and then her
cheek.

"Catherine," he whispered her name into her open
mouth.

"Hmm..." Still half asleep, she kissed him. Softly.
Tenderly.

With one swift, adept move, he flipped her over on
her back and straddled her. Her eyelids flew open. She
glared up at him with a startled, uncertain expression.

"What are you doing?"

"Waking you," he said, a deadpan expression on his
face.

"Well, you succeeded. I'm awake." She shoved
against his chest.

He remained unmoved. "How about a quickie before
I go out into the cold, cruel world to look for some
transportation for us?"

"What!"

Murdock rolled over and off the bed, then burst into
laughter. "Wish you cold see the look on your face, Ms.
Price. You'd think I just asked you to drown newborn
kittens."

Catherine sat up, ran her fingers through her disheveled hair and glowered at Murdock. "Very funny. But I don't care for your sense of humor."

"I think I like you better when you're half-asleep," he said. "You're more...much more...so much more—"

"Dammit, I didn't realize I was kissing you! I thought I was dreaming," she admitted.

"About me?" He grinned, not having a doubt in his mind that awake or asleep, he'd been the man she had kissed.

Her face flushed. She didn't respond. Instead she got out of bed, put the uniform shirt on and searched for her heels.

"We've got to find you some other shoes," he said. "But for now, those will have to do."

"I'm not staying here alone while you go in search of a car to steal," she said. "Where you go, I go."

"I wouldn't have it any other way, honey."

"Good. Then we finally agree on something."

"Yeah, finally," he teased.

"Are we staying in these uniforms?"

"Yeah. Why do you ask?"

"What if we run into rebel troops?"

"Our chances of being seen by Zarazaian troops is much more likely since my guess is they still control this part of the city," he explained. "I think, for the time being, we're safer with these—" he pinched the material of her shirt where it buttoned between her breasts "—than we would be without them."

Ten minutes later, each with an M-16 in hand, Catherine and Murdock emerged from their temporary hideaway. He had strapped on the two ammunition belts and turned the burlap bag into a makeshift knapsack that he'd hung on his back. In the dark shadows of twilight, they might pass for a couple of Zarazaian soldiers, but if they came face-to-face with the enemy their disguises wouldn't hold up under close scrutiny.

Keeping watch behind them and their backs close to the storefronts they passed, Catherine and Murdock prowled the empty streets searching for a car. Minutes ticked by, like a bomb inside her head. Pressure building. Fear mounting. Nerves rioting. Where were they going to find a vehicle? she wondered. So far, they hadn't seen a living soul or spotted even a bicycle. Undoubtedly, once the attack had started, people had fled, using every available means of transportation to escape.

After scouring a two-block area, Murdock led her into another alley. Just as she started to protest by asking him how he thought they'd find a car in this alleyway, Murdock cupped his hand over her mouth and pulled her into a dark corner. That's when she heard the sweet sound of a car's motor.

"Stay here," he whispered as he removed his hand from her mouth.

"Where are you going?"

"To check things out."

She nodded, crouched farther into the darkness and watched as Murdock sneaked silently down the alley and toward the street. She waited, her heart beating fast and her mind reeling with a dozen frightening scenarios.

Gunshots! Repeated firing. Human cries. A loud crash. Splintering glass. And then silence. Catherine's heart skipped a beat. Tremors racked her body. Please, dear God, she prayed, let Murdock be all right.

Within seconds, she saw a large figure moving toward her in the semidarkness of the alley. Her senses recognized the big man before her vision acknowledged that Murdock was running in her direction. He motioned for her to come to him. She slipped from her hiding place and rushed toward him. He reached out and grabbed her shoulders.

"The car's a jeep, belonging to a Zarazaian officer and it's out there waiting for us," Murdock said. "I think I scared off the rebel soldiers who shot the major and his driver."

"Did the rebels see you up close?"

"No, I'm sure they think I was a Zarazaian soldier and that there are probably a lot more government troops around somewhere close. They didn't hang around to find out." He pulled her back against the side of the brick building. "We'll stay right here for a few minutes. If we don't see any rebel troops in the next five minutes, then we're going to make a mad dash for the jeep and head out of town."

They waited. And waited. Each moment like an hour. No more gunfire. No troops marching. Not even artillery fire in the distance. All Catherine could hear was the sound of her own breathing.

"Stay behind me, until we reach the jeep. Keep your eyes open and be ready to use your rifle," he told her. "Then as soon as I get the jeep started, hop in quickly."

She nodded, then followed him down the alley and out onto the sidewalk. The hood of the jeep kissed the smashed storefront window. Shards of broken glass littered the surrounding area. One soldier lay across the steering wheel. Another—the major—hung halfway out of the vehicle, his head almost touching the pavement.

"I'll clear things away," Murdock told her. "Keep your back to the wall and warn me if you see anything moving. And remember, shoot first and ask questions later."

Catherine thought her heart was going to leap from

her chest, but there was nothing she could do to slow its frantic beating. She scanned the area. Left. Right. Up. Down. Nothing. Only fragments of trash swirling about in the twilight breeze.

Murdock dumped the lifeless bodies onto the street, hopped into the jeep and tried to start the motor. A groaning hum repeated over and over. Catherine's gaze kept a constant vigil, waiting and watching for any sign of trouble. Murdock tried again. The groaning hum and then a hesitant cough shouted failure. *Hurry up and start, dammit,* Catherine's frightened inner self pleaded silently. A third try. A growl. A cough. And then ignition.

Murdock hailed her with a wave of his arm. She scurried toward him as fast as she could run, weighted down by the M-16 and the fear of being shot in the back. The moment she jumped into the jeep, Murdock shifted into Reverse and backed the vehicle onto the street.

"You're driving, remember," he told her as he indicated for them to exchange places.

Without saying a word, she removed the rifle from her shoulder, handed it to Murdock and took her place behind the wheel. Before Murdock was seated, she shifted gears and revved the motor. As she took off, Murdock fell into the seat.

"Floor it," he told her.

And she did.

Following Murdock's instructions, she turned right, then left and headed west. She didn't think. Didn't feel. She simply drove. Like a bat out of hell. Just as they neared the outskirts of the city, shots rang out, whizzing over their heads. Crying out, Catherine gripped the steering wheel with white-knuckled ferocity. Murdock swerved around, aimed his M-16 and fired at the small band of soldiers behind them.

Rebel soldiers! Damn! The rebels saw a government jeep with two uniformed soldiers inside. If he tried to identify himself, he and Catherine would be shot and killed before he got out the first word.

"Those aren't Zarazaian troops following us," Catherine said.

"Yeah, I know."

"What are we—"

"No matter what happens, keep driving. Due west," Murdock told her. "Chota is a straight shot from here."

Murdock didn't want to kill rebel troops, but he had to defend himself and Catherine. He was a good enough shot to wound without killing. At least he hoped he was. And if he could aim one of the grenades in the back seat so that it would tear up the road and disable their truck, then maybe he could halt the small group of rebels chasing them.

He crawled over into the back seat, placing his body directly behind Catherine. She could feel his movements, but had no idea what he was doing. He squeezed off another round of rapid fire. Enemy shots pierced the jeep's tailgate and fractured the rearview mirror. In her head, Catherine screamed and screamed and screamed. But while her silent cries reverberated in her mind, she kept her gaze directed on the road ahead.

Suddenly she heard a rocking explosion. Stealing a quick glimpse in the one remaining mirror shard, she saw fire and smoke in the street behind them. Before she had time to assimilate the facts, Murdock hauled his big body over and into the seat beside her.

"There are hand grenades in the back of the jeep,"

he said, grinning. ''And a small arsenal of weapons. We hit the jackpot when we confiscated this jeep.''

Tears streamed down Catherine's cheeks, but she didn't even attempt to wipe them away. With the humid wind bombarding her face and the echoes of warfare resonating in her ears, she gripped the steering wheel as if it were a lifeline.

She sensed an execrable truth—Murdock was in his element right here in the middle of this war. He was a trained soldier. An expert. The horrors of what she was experiencing were nothing new to him.

She glanced at him out of the corner of her eye and noted the self-satisfied expression on his face. His triumph showed plainly in his expression. How could she expect a man like him to ever understand the importance of the gentler human feelings that ruled her life?

Murdock hated to see her cry. He wanted to wipe away her tears. Longed to take her into his arms and comfort her. But he didn't touch her. Didn't speak to her. Since coming to Zaraza she had witnessed carnage unlike any she'd ever seen before in her life. Not on a TV or movie screen. But up close and personal. Death. Human suffering. The ravages of war.

A woman like Catherine needed the cleansing relief of tears. God, how long had it been since he'd cried? Since he'd felt that kind of tenderness? Suddenly he saw this war through Catherine's eyes. Fresh. New. Never before experienced. The very thought shattered his reserve. She must think him a monster, a heartless killer.

Why do you care what she thinks of you? an inner voice asked. *You don't owe her an explanation or a justification for the life you've lived. The only thing you owe her is the vow you made to her father—to keep her safe.* And he intended to keep that sacred promise, even if it meant sacrificing his own life.

Chapter 9

Despite the sheer terror Cathcrine experienced during their escape from San Carlos, the trip to Chota came off without a hitch. Not one incident. No sign of either rebel or Zarazaian soldiers, which Murdock had said probably meant the battles were being fought farther inland, and not along the banks of the Amazon. She had never driven at night when the only light came from the quarter moon above and the headlights of her vehicle. The un-illuminated road stretched before them, taking them closer and closer to the jungle and ever nearer to the Rio Negro.

"Chota shouldn't be far now," Murdock told her.

"Just how big is this town?" she asked. "Will we be able to find a hotel room?"

Murdock chuckled. "Chota won't have a decent hotel and the place isn't really much of a town. It's more like a large village. And I need to warn you that the natives probably won't be all that friendly to a couple of Americans without money.''

''Great. What should I expect? Flogging in the town square or being tarred and feathered and run out of town?'' Humor was the only thing that could save her sanity at this point and she knew it. She was in way over her head in this situation. And truth be told, she was scared senseless.

''Nothing that drastic. More like some vicious stares and maybe a rotten tomato thrown in our general direction.''

Her arms ached, as did her back and neck. And she suspected that once she removed her hands from the steering wheel, her fingers would be permanently curled.

''There!'' Murdock nudged her arm. ''Look straight ahead.''

In the distance she saw the village lights and could hear the faint sound of music. ''This village has electricity?''

''Yep. It's the last civilized village before you enter the jungle,'' he explained. ''And unless things have changed a lot in twenty years, which I suspect they haven't, there's at least one or two boats a day stopping here on their way down the Amazon.''

''Explain to me again why we're taking a boat instead of continuing our trip by jeep?''

She vaguely remembered that at some point in their two-hour journey, Murdock had given her the particulars of finding Sabino's headquarters. But for the life of her, she couldn't recall the details. Maybe she'd been too busy concentrating on keeping the jeep out of the ditches and her eyes focused on the dark road ahead. Or perhaps her mind had simply wandered into thoughts of safety far away from Zaraza. Home in Tennessee. Back at

Huntington Academy. Or dreams of a hot bath, a soft bed and a decent meal.

"There are no roads into the jungle," Murdock told her. "The Sabino rebels are headquartered at a place called Santa Teresa, a mountain hideaway they've been able to defend for twenty years. If we go downriver, we can reach Santa Teresa, by foot, in about three hours."

"Three hours on foot, climbing a mountain? I can hardly wait."

Ignoring her sarcastic remark, Murdock said, "Once I've talked to Vincente and exposed Domingo Sanchez, we can hike back to the river, hitch a ride on the next boat going downstream, be in Brazil like that—" he snapped his fingers "— and then we'll take a flight out of the first airport we find in Brazil."

"Sounds way too simple to me. Expose the bad guy. Save the good guy. Be heroes. Sail off down the river and then fly away to safety. Yeah, sure. What are the odds of that actually happening?" She cut her gaze toward him quickly, then focused back on the road.

"I gave you the best case scenario," he admitted. "If we don't run into any kind of problems, it could happen that way."

Chota sprang to life in front of them as Catherine drove the jeep down the main street of the village. Two-story buildings danced with light and activity. Natives swarmed about on the streets and walkways as music drifted from several of the *cabañas*. She slowed the jeep to a leisurely crawl in order to avoid running over anyone.

"What is this place?" Catherine asked. "It's lit up like a banana republic version of Las Vegas. Don't these people know there's a war on?

"Chota is Sin City." Murdock's laughter rumbled

from his chest. "Gambling. Prostitution. Drugs. Smuggling. The merchants are rebel sympathizers, but they'll take anybody's money. Even Zarazaian soldiers are welcome if they have gold to spend."

"You're kidding." Suddenly realizing that she was gazing slack-jawed as she scrutinized the strange town, Catherine shut her gaping mouth. This little town Murdock had called Sin City was flanked by the jungle on one side and the Amazon on the other. How had it developed into a cesspool of illegal vices?

Gazing out from arched doorways, their faces painted like Kewpie dolls, prostitutes waved and smiled. Some even called out to passersby. One amply endowed woman opened her blouse to give potential customers a preview.

"Just where are we going?" Catherine asked. "Do I keep driving until we've passed through the village or are we actually going to stop somewhere?"

"I'm looking for a place called *El Paraiso del Diablo.*"

"You're looking for what?" Catherine tried to translate for herself. *Diablo* meant devil, didn't it? And *paraiso* meant paradise. Good grief! Was he looking for a place called The Devil's Paradise? "Just what is this place?"

"It used to be a brothel," he replied. "I once knew some of the…er…girls who worked there. And the proprietor was Juan Sabino's sister-in-law's cousin. Hernandez. If the place is still in business and Hernandez is still alive, then he'll help us."

"You're taking me to a whorehouse?"

"You'll be perfectly safe there, Cat. If anybody comes on to you, just give him one of those snooty little looks of yours and you'll stop him dead in his tracks."

"Ha, ha. Very funny."

"Down there. On the right." Murdock pointed to a building painted a hideous shade of hot pink. "Just pull the jeep into the alley and be sure to pocket the keys."

El Paraiso del Diablo sparkled like a vulgar pink Christmas tree draped with scantily clad fallen angels in colorful, gossamer silk robes. Women lined the porch of the fuchsia two-story structure. And from every upstairs window, ladies of the evening lured potential customers with their come-hither gestures.

Catherine eased the jeep into the alley between the brothel and a gambling hall. *This is something out of an old western movie,* she thought, as she killed the motor and pocketed the key. *I must be asleep and having a nightmare. This town can't be real.*

"Give me my rifle," she said. "I think I'll stay here and wait for you. I really don't want to go in there."

"I know you're joking, honey." He handed her the M-16. "Where I go, you go. Remember?"

"Yes, but I'd like to forget."

Murdock hopped from the jeep, checked his weapon and ammunition belt, then rounded the hood and held out his hand to Catherine. She accepted his offer of assistance and stepped onto the ground. "Don't forget that you're my woman." He hauled her up against him.

"I beg your pardon?" Glaring at him, she snatched her hand from his and stepped backward.

"Act the part," he said. "Nobody's going to touch you if they think I might blow them to smithereens."

"I have a gun, too, you know." She readjusted the strap on her M-16. "Maybe they'll think I'd blow them to smithereens!"

"Yeah, I'm sure they will." He grabbed her arm, jerked her to his side and growled menacingly. "But just in case they don't, then let's get our parts straight right now. Me Tarzan. You Jane.''

Catherine snarled at him. But when he gave her a gentle shove, she fell into step alongside him as they headed toward the brothel. All heads turned in their direction when they walked onto the porch and although the ladies whispered and the ogling gentlemen stared, no one attempted to stop them. The double doors of the establishment stood wide-open, making access to the huge foyer quite easy. The interior boasted the same gaudy colorfulness as the exterior, the hot pink being replaced by varying shades of red and purple.

When Murdock entered the room containing an enormous bar, a gigantic man with a heavy beard and patch over his right eye laid his meaty hand on Murdock's shoulder. He spoke in Spanish, saying what Catherine assumed translated into something like ''What do you want here?'' Murdock brushed the man's hand off his shoulder and turned to face him. The two stood eye-to-eye, both the same height. A couple of Mack trucks preparing to collide. But where Murdock was pure muscle, the other man was fat.

Speaking rapidly in Spanish, Murdock asked for Hernandez. The bouncer shook his head and replied, then grabbed Murdock's shoulder again. Catherine held her breath. Without saying another word, Murdock knocked the man's hand off his shoulder a second time.

Oh, God, he's going to have to kill this big bear! She cringed just thinking about what would happen to them if Murdock shot the brothel's bouncer. The grizzly man growled like an animal, then spread out his ham hock arms and took a wrestler's stance. Oh, great, Catherine thought, the idiot wants to fight. Didn't he realize that Murdock would wipe the floor with him?

"Paco!" a strong feminine voiced called out from behind them.

The bouncer glanced over his hefty shoulder at the woman standing on the stairs. All gazes turned toward her, including Catherine's. Dressed in a tight-fitting yellow silk dress that accentuated every well-rounded curve of her body, the petite brunette descended the staircase and glided over to the bouncer. She placed her hand on his arm and smiled, then spoke to him in a quiet, soft voice. Apparently dismissed, the big man nodded and then disappeared into another room.

The gorgeous woman, whom Catherine guessed to be only a few years older than she, turned to Murdock and opened her arms. "Murdock! Do you not remember me?"

"Landra?" Murdock's gaze traveled appreciatively over her full breasts, tiny waist and wide hips. Then he grabbed the woman off her feet and swung her up into his arms.

Catherine moved away from him as a very ugly emotion took root in her heart and spread quickly through her body. *Get your damn hands off him,* she wanted to scream. *He's mine!*

"Where have you been all these years, *viejo amigo?*" The lovely Landra planted a welcoming kiss on Murdock's lips.

Catherine balled her hands into tight fists. *Wonder how she'd like to have her cute little button nose rearranged?* a demonic inner voice asked. *Or maybe she'd like that jet-black hair pulled out by the roots!*

When Murdock set Landra back on her tiny feet, Catherine took a step forward, placing herself directly at his side. He draped his arm around Catherine's shoulder.

"Landra, this is Catherine. Catherine, meet Landra."

The two women sized each other up, like prizefighters preparing to shake hands and come out fighting. Catherine towered over the small, voluptuous Landra.

"Who is she?" Landra asked, running her gaze up and down Catherine's body.

Catherine realized that she must look a fright in the ragged, bloodstained, military uniform. She jerked the cap off and raked her fingers through her hair.

"Catherine?" Murdock rubbed his hand up and down Catherine's arm. "She's my...traveling companion."

Catherine jabbed him in the ribs with her elbow, then smiled at Landra when Murdock groaned. "How do you do," she said, with all the good grace she could muster at the moment. She felt like a huge, gawky frump compared to the silk-clad, perfume-drenched Landra.

"I do very well, *señorita*. Or is it *señora?* How do you do?"

Landra's English was quite good, Catherine thought. Much better than my Spanish, that's for sure. The smile on Landra's face seemed genuine, which puzzled Catherine, considering that she had despised this woman on sight.

"It's *señora*," Catherine said, but when Landra's smile widened, she hastily added, "I'm a widow."

Landra reached out and clasped Catherine's hand. "I am so sorry, señora. I, too, am a widow." Landra winked at Murdock. "You are fortunate to have this one as your man, now. Murdock, he is *muy hombre,* is he not?"

Translating quickly in her mind, Catherine figured out that the woman had asked her if she didn't agree that Murdock was very much a man. "Oh, yes. *Sí.* Murdock is indeed *muy hombre.*"

Murdock cleared his throat. "Not that I don't enjoy

having two lovely ladies discussing my merits as a man, but I'm looking for Hernandez. Is that old buzzard still running the show around here?''

Landra's smile weakened and a sad, rather faraway look entered her eyes. ''Hernandez died five years ago. A knife fight with one of Orlando's men.''

''Damn! I was hoping Hernandez could help us. We need to book passage on a boat headed downriver and I'm afraid we're short of funds. About all we have to barter with is a government jeep.''

''Come with me.'' With a wave of her hand, Landra invited them to follow as she strolled out of the bar, across the wide foyer and to a set of French doors.

Murdock leaned over and whispered in Catherine's ear, ''Pull in your claws, Cat. Landra's not your enemy.''

They met up with Landra just as she opened the French doors. A room of pale-lavender walls, deep-purple drapes and ornate mahogany furniture greeted them. Landra sat in a lush plum-and-gold stripped chair and indicated for them to take seats on either the purple velvet settee or the magenta wingback chair across from her. Murdock chose the chair. Catherine sat on the edge of the settee.

''Hernandez left *El Paraiso del Diablo* to me,'' Landra said. ''I was always his favorite, you know. And about a year before he died, we got married and I started overseeing the other girls.''

''Well, congratulations,'' Murdock said. ''So all this is yours, now, huh?''

''Yes. All mine,'' Landra said. ''So, tell me what I can do to help you.''

''We need to book passage on a boat going downriver.'' Murdock crossed one leg over the other, bracing his right foot over his left knee. "We need to get to Santa Teresa as soon as possible."

"To Santa Teresa. But why?" Landra's black eyes rounded questioningly.

"It's urgent that I get to Vincente Sabino before he reaches San Carlos. I have information that is vital to the cause."

"Vincente is no longer at Santa Teresa." Landra stood, walked across the room and closed the French doors. "Vincente is already on the move with several regiments of his troops. He should arrive in Yanahuara by day after tomorrow."

"How can we get to Yanahuara?" Murdock asked.

"I'll arrange for you and your traveling companion to go downriver and disembark near Celendin," Landra said. "And I will send you with money and a message to someone there who can arrange to take you to Yanahuara."

"How soon will a boat going downriver come along?" Catherine asked.

Landra smiled. "There is a supply boat leaving tonight, making a round-trip to Senona. I will arrange things with the captain for him to stop along the way and let you and your traveling companion—" Landra narrowed her gaze as she smiled at Catherine "—off near Celendin."

Murdock stood. Catherine followed suit. Landra sauntered toward Murdock, then reached out and grasped his big hands when she drew close.

"Thank you for not asking questions." Murdock kissed Landra, first on one cheek and then the other.

Landra caressed Murdock's chest, then let one hand rest over his heart. "I do not forget that you are a true friend to the Sabino family. And I do not forget that you are a good man.''

Without further ado, Landra walked across the room and pulled a tapestry cord that summoned a servant, who appeared almost instantly. She spoke to him in rapid-fire Spanish, making it impossible for Catherine to understand a word. When she finished instructing the servant, Landra turned to her guests.

''You may use my room, upstairs, to bathe and change clothes,'' she informed them. ''Fresh clothes will be available and I'm having a light supper sent up to you.''

''*Señora,* you're very kind.'' Catherine wanted to dislike this woman—this whorehouse madam—but how could she harbor any ill feelings toward someone who was treating them so graciously? ''Thank you. *Gracias.*''

''For Murdock, anything.'' She nodded to the waiting servant. ''Go with Erasmo. I will send word to the captain of the *Dama de la Libertad* that he will have passengers on this trip. You have less than three hours before he departs.''

As Murdock and Catherine walked past Landra, she gently grabbed Catherine's arm and urged her to come closer. Whispering softly she said, ''Have no worry in giving yourself to him, *señora.* He is *muy buen amante.*''

Catherine offered the other woman a weak smile, then followed Murdock and the servant out into the foyer. As they climbed the stairs, Murdock asked what Landra had said to her.

''I'm not sure. But when I figure it out, I don't think I'm going to like it.''

''Want me to translate for you?''

Catherine hesitated. ''She said you were a—'' she whispered the words to him ''—*muy buen amante.*''

As they reached the landing at the top of the stairs, Murdock laughed. "Why that little devil. I think she was trying to make you jealous, Cat. She told you that I was a very good lover."

Catherine rolled her eyes, but the flush that stained her cheeks destroyed the cavalier attitude she had hoped to project. "Don't go feeling so macho. She remembers what you were like twenty years ago, when you were a lot younger. I'll bet you aren't the man you were then."

He grinned. "You're right, honey. I'm more experienced now."

Catherine blew out an exasperated breath, then followed the servant into Landra's private room. The moment they entered, Catherine gasped. Gold and white silk and satin covered every inch of the bedroom. Ornate gold mirrors hung on every wall and the entire ceiling was mirrored.

"Good grief!" Catherine planted her hands on her hips. "Talk about being obvious. If this isn't the epitome of a whorehouse madam's bedroom, I don't know what is."

"And just what would you know about a whorehouse madam's bedroom?"

"Not nearly as much as you do, I'm sure." She circled the room, gazing at the ostentatious decor. "Was the room where Landra discovered you were a *muy buen amante* anything like this?"

"When I knew Landra, she was one of Hernandez's girls," Murdock reminded Catherine. "I don't remember what her room looked like back then. It was twenty years ago."

"And I'll just bet there have been a lot of rooms and a lot of women since then!" Catherine scanned the doors, wondering which were closets and which led to the bathroom. She'd had just about all she could stand of *muy hombre* Aloysius Murdock.

"What can I say?" Murdock held up his big hands in a show of defeat. "I like the ladies and they like me."

"Well, here's one lady—" she thumped her chest "—who'll be glad when she's seen the last of you, *muy hombre!*" Catherine flung open one door after another until one revealed the bathroom. "I'm getting out of these filthy clothes. When your old buddy Landra sends up something for me to wear, just crack the door and toss them in to me."

"Want me to come in and wash your back?" Murdock asked teasingly.

"In your dreams, Aloysius!"

They boarded the *Dama de la Libertad* before eleven-thirty. The captain himself, a rebel sympathizer, welcomed them aboard and told them that when they wanted to rest, they could use his cabin. He then explained to Murdock that he would wake them when they reached the roadway that led into Celendin. If the trip went as usual, they'd reach that destination around dawn.

The *Dama de la Libertad* was an old gunboat, which was now used to deliver equipment, supplies and medical aid to the natives in remote areas along the river. As well as arms to Sabino's rebels.

Standing on deck as the boat began its twelve-hour round-trip journey, Catherine and Murdock looked out over the dark waterway in front of them.

"I wish you could see this river in the daylight," he said. "There are places on the Rio Negro where schools of small fish jump out of the water and where dolphins play. There are palm swamps and giant butterflies.

And…you'll see it for yourself, when we go upriver and into Brazil.''

''I'm beginning to think we'll never get out of Zaraza,'' Catherine told him. ''I've been in this damn country for less than a week and I feel as if I've been here a year!''

Murdock draped his arm around her shoulder. She tensed, but didn't pull away from him. ''I'm sorry you got stuck here with me.''

''It wasn't your fault.''

''No, but I could take you straight into Brazil and say to hell with warning Vincente.''

Inclining her head to the right, she gazed at him in the shadowy darkness. The gas lanterns inside the pilot house cast a dim glow out across the covered deck and spotlighted Murdock's big silhouette.

''You can't do that and we both know it,'' she said. ''I wouldn't let you, even if you wanted to. Not now.'' She laid her hand atop his where it rested on the starboard rail. ''If Lanny were physically able, he'd be making this journey with you. My father can't do this one last thing to bring victory to the rebels and peace to this country. But I can.''

The humid breeze rippled along the river, tripped through the towering tree branches and caressed Catherine's face and bare arms. Murdock latched his fingers around the side of her neck and stroked her chin and bottom lip with his thumb.

''You're quite a woman, Catherine Price.'' And far too good a woman for the likes of me, he thought.

''And you're *muy hombre,*'' she teased.

''I'm glad you're not still angry with me over Landra.''

''Have there really been a lot of women?''

"Hellfire, Cat! You don't ask a man a question like that."

"All right, I'll rephrase the question. Are you really a womanizer?"

"Damn!" he cursed under his breath. "Let's just say the older I got the more discriminating my tastes became. I go more for quality than quantity these days."

"So, you're not quite the hell-raiser you were when you were younger, huh? Then why did you want me to believe that—"

He tightened his hold around her neck, drawing her toward him. She lifted her face to his and waited, with bated breath, for his lips to descend. As the boat passed a clearing along the riverbank, the moonlight broke through and washed the edge of the deck with shimmery light.

"Mi hermosa gata," Murdock whispered against her lips.

"What—what does that mean?" Her lips quivered as they sought his and her hands crept up the front of his shirt.

"My beautiful cat," he told her, then covered her mouth with his.

The kiss robbed her of breath and weakened her knees, but Murdock ended it abruptly. "That's why I told you about my bad-boy ways, Miss Catherine. I want you to know exactly the type of man I was and am and the kind of life I've lived."

"Don't you think I have a pretty good idea? I knew before we ever met that you were a man like Lanny and...no matter how strong the...er...the sexual attraction is between us, I could never...I would never allow myself to...to—"

"To care about a guy like me." He finished her stuttering sentence for her. "Maybe I don't want you to care. Maybe all I want is to work off a little frustration in the sack."

Her back stiffened. She withdrew from him. Physically. Emotionally. "Then I suggest you stick with women like Landra."

Gazing out over the dark water and listening to the faraway echoes from the jungle, Catherine and Murdock separated themselves, each wary of the intense emotions the other aroused. They stood side by side, not touching, not speaking, for endless moments. After what seemed like an eternity to Catherine, Murdock broke the silence.

"Let's take advantage of the captain's offer for us to use his cabin."

"What?"

"I'm tired. You're tired. And come morning, we have a long trek on foot to reach Celendin. Let's try to get some sleep."

Murdock turned to go, took several steps, then glanced back over his shoulder. "You coming?"

The last thing she wanted was to spend the night in close quarters with Murdock. To share another bed with him. To lie at his side and not touch him. To ache with a need almost beyond bearing.

"Yes, I'm coming." She followed him toward the captain's cabin.

Chapter 10

The captain's bed hadn't been built for a man of Murdock's size, let alone to be shared with a woman as tall as she. Murdock's feet hung off the end and his massive shoulders took up more than half the mattress space. He had offered to sleep on the minimum floor space and Catherine had said she could sleep in the chair. They had quarreled to the point of ridiculousness, then simultaneously agreed that in order to spend the next few hours resting instead of wasting time in a no-win argument, to just share the bed. That had been at least an hour ago and Catherine lay there wide-awake, clinging precariously to the edge of the bed butted against the wall. If she moved two inches, she'd be touching Murdock.

The hum of the gunboat's motor rumbled in her ears. Indistinct cries echoed from within the jungle that flanked the Rio Negro tributary that wound its way along the Zarazaian border and into Brazil. The constant lap-

ping of the river and the light rainfall blended softly with
the other noises until they became a monotonous rhythm.
Sleep. Sleep. Sleep.

She closed her eyes again and tried to concentrate on
pleasant things. A faculty luncheon. An evening at the
symphony. An afternoon spent in the backyard swing
reading a good book.

But Murdock disturbed those pleasant thoughts. He
showed up at the faculty luncheon, wearing the camouflage fatigues Landra had provided. And he sat beside
her at the symphony, his big hand resting on her bare
knee. And she lay with her head in Murdock's lap, in
the backyard swing.

Damn! The man wouldn't stay out of her thoughts! If
she didn't stop thinking about him, she'd never get any
sleep.

Count sheep, she told herself. Or count the women in
Murdock's past. *Stop that!* her inner voice called. *You're
doing it again. Relating everything to Murdock.*

Her shoulder and hip ached from lying in one position
for so long, but if she tried to turn over, she would end
up halfway on top of her *traveling companion.* That's
how Murdock had referred to her when he'd introduced
her to Luscious Landra. The woman had immediately
assumed a certain relationship existed between Catherine
and Murdock and hadn't been able to hide her jealousy.
Landra had immediately jumped to the conclusion that
although they were not yet intimately involved, it was
only a matter of time before Catherine and Murdock
became lovers.

Why didn't she just tell her that she and Murdock
were already lovers? Catherine asked herself. That she
knew exactly what a *muy buen amante* Murdock was.
She could have told Landra that she was reaping all the

benefits from his years of experience! That would have dulled the other woman's brilliant smile a bit.

"Hmpph!"

"Did you say something?" Murdock asked, his voice low and rough.

Catherine jumped as if she'd been shot. "Dammit, Murdock, I thought you were asleep. You scared me to death."

"I thought *you* were asleep. You haven't moved a muscle since we lay down." He rolled over onto his side so that their bodies spooned together. Her back to his chest. His groin to her buttocks. "What's wrong? Can't you sleep?"

Her first instinct was to melt against him, to absorb all that manly aura and drown in an overdose of testosterone. But her second instinct was to claw her way through the wall she faced in order to escape. No good can come from this, she warned herself. All he wants is *to work off a little frustration in the sack.* Making love won't mean anything to him. *But it will to you,* her conscience reminded her. *Remember that simple little fact.*

But why does it have to mean something to me? she quarreled with herself. She had a great deal of frustration that needed to be worked off, too, didn't she? It's not as if she was back in Huntington, Tennessee, living a normal life. She was far removed from everything and everyone important to her. She was stuck in a nightmare, not of her own making. She had a right to act out of character. To give in to her baser instincts.

"Catherine?"

He draped his big, hairy arm across her waist and over her belly. Every muscle in her body tightened painfully. She opened her mouth into a wide oval as she pulled air into her lungs in a shuddering gasp. The quivering began in her head and slowly radiated down her shoulders and into her arms.

"Cat, honey, what's wrong?" He grabbed her waist and flipped her over to face him. "Are you sick? Hurting?"

Moonlight bathed the tiny cabin with a pale, creamy radiance and cast soft shadows across the bed. Catherine looked directly at Murdock's face. That hard jaw, darkened by beard stubble. Those chiseled cheekbones. The lines at the corners of his eyes and around his mouth. The gray that streaked his short sideburns and peppered lightly through his dark hair.

"I've never had sex except when I was in a committed relationship," she told him, her voice an uncertain whisper. "But I don't care. I want you. I want you so much."

Murdock felt as if he'd been slammed in the belly with a sledgehammer. The last thing he had expected was an invitation to fulfill a fantasy that had plagued him since the moment he set eyes on Catherine Price. He had thought about taking her. Had considered a dozen and one things he wanted to do to her and have her do to him. Hard and fast and white-hot. Slow and sweet and earth-shattering. He on top. She on top. From the rear. From the side. Standing up, bracing her against the wall. Her sitting in his lap. His hands all over her. Her hands stroking him. His mouth on her, tasting, plunging, loving. Her mouth on him, pleasuring him.

His sex grew hard and heavy. Turning on his side, he lifted himself into a semisitting position. Without saying a word, he unbuttoned the camouflage shirt she wore and spread it apart to reveal the naked flesh beneath. He'd been well aware that she had discarded her bra back at *El Paraiso del Diablo* when she'd shed the dirty Zarazaian uniform.

Catherine didn't move. Barely breathed. Murdock cupped one full, firm breast in his hand and strummed the tip with his thumb. She shivered. As he continued the assault, she closed her eyes and arched her back. With practiced ease he slipped the shirt off her shoulders and down her arms, then quickly discarded it before unbuttoning his own shirt.

When his mouth covered the begging nipple of her unattended breast, Catherine keened, the sound reverberating from deep in her throat. As he tormented each breast, she arched her back, then reached for him and threaded her fingers through his hair. Opening his mouth, he flicked out his tongue in repeated forays on one tight point and gently pinched the other between his thumb and forefinger, until Catherine writhed and cried out, pleading. Grasping the strands of his hair curled about her fingers, she held his head to her body, wild with need.

"Please…please…" she mumbled.

With his mouth still on one breast, he reached down to unsnap and then unzip her pants. Not bothering to do more than drag the camouflage trousers a couple of inches lower on her hips, he slid his hand inside the red silk panties Landra had provided for her and cupped her mound. She bucked against his hand and for just a minute, he thought he was going to lose control.

"Easy, Cat. Easy, honey."

He slid his hand farther beneath the red silk, gliding over the soft triangle of hair, delving between her satin folds, dipping into the hot, damp depths of her receptive sheath. Instinctively she tightened around his probing fingers, holding him in place. As he plunged his fingers in and out, he sought her lips and quickly began a foray into that wet depth, both acts seductive and arousing.

He ached to be inside her, to fill her completely and bury himself to the hilt in her sweet body. But dammit, he couldn't risk it, could he? Why the hell hadn't he asked Landra for some condoms? How was he going to pleasure Catherine, give himself some relief and at the same time protect her?

Just how experienced was she? he wondered. How would she react if he suggested a different kind of coupling?

All Murdock knew was that he had to do something and soon—before he exploded. If Catherine were anyone other than Lanny's daughter, he might consider just taking her and to hell with the consequences. After all, what were the odds that he'd get her pregnant? He knew he was safe, medically speaking. And with a woman like Catherine, who didn't sleep around, there would be no other risks.

Deciding not to chance scaring her off, Murdock opted to give her pleasure first and hoped she'd reciprocate.

Deepening the kiss, he ran the tip of his finger over her protruding little kernel. She shivered uncontrollably and rubbed rhythmically against his massaging finger. He released her lips and proceeded to plant a row of kisses down her throat and then back to her breasts. With his huge body draping her like a massive, muscular canopy, he ravaged her with a practiced skill that soon had her trembling. When he explored her sweet, hidden depths with his tongue, the tension inside her tightened unbearably. Deep, wide, heavy strokes. Torturous, tingling kisses. With the mastery of his lovemaking, Murdock brought her to the brink, then held back, until she clawed at him and begged for more. Finally, one delicate, precisely placed touch pushed her into an explosive, climactic release. With the urging of his mouth and fingers, he forced her to the limit, demanding she feel more and more and more, until she screamed with a pleasure that drained her completely and left her sated beyond her wildest dreams.

Lifting his head, the taste of her still fresh on his lips, he rose up and over her once again to capture her cry of fulfillment. He dragged her over and on top of him. Kissing her cheeks, her chin, her throat, he urged her to straddle him, then laid her hands flat on his perspiring chest.

She reveled in the feel of him, his chest hard with muscles, damp with sweat and matted with thick, dark hair. His tight male nipples begged for her mouth. She flicked one and then the other with the tip of her tongue and elicited an animal moan from him.

His sex throbbed intimately against her. When he bucked up, thrusting against her, she understood what he needed. What he expected.

She hadn't been with a man in years. And sex with Rodney had never been like this. Never untamed. Never a primitive urge that overruled common sense. But she knew how to do this, she reminded herself. She had used her hand to pleasure a man before. But Murdock had used more than his hand, more than his talented fingers. Did he expect her to…to…

"Please, Cat," he growled. "I need you."

With trembling fingers, she undid and unzipped his pants. Without the incumbrance of underwear his sex sprang free immediately. Catherine's mouth rounded in a silent gasp, surprised by his lack of briefs and by the sheer size of him. Singing an ancient mating song, her blood pounded in her head, drummed in her ears and heated in her veins.

"Don't torture me, honey," Murdock groaned.

She slid the tip of her index finger over the plum-shaped globe and was rewarded with a deep, dangerous growl. Continuing down the shaft, she added more fingers to the exploration, curling them about his sex. She stroked and caressed, fondled and gently pumped. Arching off the bed, Murdock urged her to further action.

With her other hand, Catherine tugged his pants down to his knees. Lowering her head, she spread tiny, nipping kisses over his muscular thighs. Then her tongue replaced her lips as she created a damp path upward and over one hip, across his washboard-lean belly and down the other hip.

He cupped the back of her head with one huge hand and persuasively invited her to take him as he had taken her. Overwhelmed with a primitive desire unlike any she'd ever known, Catherine claimed him. Encompassed him. Gave him a pleasure equal to what he'd given her. Spurred on by her own passion, she loved him with her mouth and tongue, all the while her own body danced with excitement.

His words barely coherent, Murdock told her graphically how he felt and what he wanted. Then he slid his hand between her thighs. Finding her wet and hot, he stroked her nub and when his release hit him full force, he held on long enough to give her that final nudge over the edge to a second climax.

He pulled her up his body and into his arms, then wiped the perspiration from her face with his shirt. He kissed her soundly, then curved her over onto her back and rested her head on the pillow. He slipped off the corner of the bed, pulled up his pants and zipped them, then searched the semidark room until he found a bottle of whiskey on the captain's desk, which was attached to the aft wall. Lifting the liquor, he uncapped the lid and took a giant swig. He coughed several times as the liquid singed a path down to his belly. Taking the bottle with him, he returned to the bed, sat down and then lifted Catherine to his side.

"Here, honey. Drink a little of this."

Without question, she took several sips, then burst into a coughing fit. Tears stung her eyes. He slapped her on the back. She dropped her head to his shoulder and wrapped her arms around his waist. After recapping the bottle, he dropped it to the floor, then took her into his arms as he eased them down on the bed. He held her, wanting to say something worthy of the moment. But what the hell did you say to a woman like Catherine after a hot session of unparalleled lovemaking? Thanks? Or maybe, this was great, let's do it again every chance we get?

Instead he held her close, kissed her forehead and said, "You're quite a woman, Catherine Price."

Sighing contentedly, she kissed his shoulder. "And you, Aloysius Murdock, are *muy hombre!*"

Murdock heard the captain's footsteps before the man reached the door. He'd been holding Catherine in his arms, watching her while she slept for the past half hour. He'd gotten a couple hours of sleep after their lovemaking, but he had awakened suddenly, as if his internal clock had sensed dawn approaching. The knock on the door came hard and loud. Catherine stirred in his arms.

"Be ready in ten minutes!" The captain's voice carried plainly through the closed door.

The moment Catherine opened her eyes and looked at him, Murdock knew she was fixing to go all remorseful on him. He could just imagine what she would say. *Our*

*indiscretion was a mistake. We can't let it happen again.
I don't know what came over me. I want to forget all
about it, pretend it never happened.*

But she surprised him completely when she said,
"You're right, Murdock. Working off a little frustration
in the sack was just what we both needed."

She eased out of his loose embrace, crawled over him
and hurriedly put her clothes in order, then stuffed her
hair up under her camouflage cap. "You'd better get
moving, if we're going to disembark in ten minutes."

"Yeah. Sure."

Well, she was taking things awfully well, he thought.
Acting as if she played the I'll-show-you-mine-if-you'll-
show-me-yours game all the time. But he knew better.
His gut instincts told him that what they'd shared in the
wee hours of the morning had been a first for her. She
was no inexperienced girl, no shy virgin, but giving and
receiving the type of pleasure they'd exchanged was new
to her. And maybe that's why her cavalier attitude bothered him. It wasn't in character for Catherine to treat
something so intimate, so extremely personal, as if they
had done nothing more than give each other a good back
rub.

Hell, man, be glad she didn't cry and carry on and
blame you for taking advantage of her, he told himself.
And be damned grateful that she didn't misinterpret your
passion for something more. Like love. If she thought
love was involved in your relationship, she'd start talking about marriage and kids and a dull, safe life back in
Tennessee.

*And what would be so dull about spending the rest of
your life with Catherine?* a nagging inner voice asked
him.

Dismissing the question, Murdock hurried Catherine

out the door and up onto the deck. They gathered their rifles, ammunition belts and knapsack of supplies, some taken from the restaurant back in San Carlos and some provided by Landra. The captain offered them steaming cups of rich, black coffee and slices of crusty hard bread.

"Good luck on your mission to find Sabino. You should be able to meet up with him in Yanahuara tomorrow. But perhaps he has sent a scouting team on ahead and you can make contact with them," the captain said in Spanish, which Murdock relayed to Catherine in English.

The gunboat docked near a small, decaying pier just as dawn spread her scarlet arms and pink fingers out over the Amazonian sky. Murdock and Catherine departed, leaving civilization behind. While the *Dama de la Libertad* chugged on down the river, they stood on the bank and watched their best means of escaping Zaraza disappear around the bend.

"No sense waiting here wishing we were going with them," Murdock said. "The sooner we head out, the sooner we'll reach Celendin and be able to find someone who can take us on to Yanahuara."

"Don't tell me that this is the road to Celendin." Catherine gave the wide, dirt pathway leading into the jungle a snooty little glance. "That's not a road."

"It's what passes for a road out here in the jungle," he told her, then swatted her on the behind.

She glared at him, but said nothing. They fell into step alongside each other, neither speaking as they began the journey inland. A morning fog, formed from the night's tropical rain, surrounded them, then slowly cleared as they continued walking.

A steep hill, covered with stands of thick trees, rose to their right and a tiny stream wove its way over a rocky bed several feet to their left. The buzz of insects made Catherine glad she'd taken Murdock's advice and used the repellent the captain had provided.

Here and there, the jungle darted out spiny fingers of new growth, edging close to the cleared pathway. The first rays of morning sunlight bored through the verdant canopy that all but encompassed the narrow road. Shooting, bright beams of warmth highlighted spots of verdant foliage as vibrant as sparkling emeralds.

How was it possible, Catherine wondered, that this vast, green wasteland seemed deceptively inviting? The walls of greenery grew high and wide, each individual plant, each tree indistinguishable as it vied for sunlight and nourishment in the crowded garden. So full of trees and vegetation, the nearby forest seemed oddly devoid of wildlife. The cicada's grating song only underscored the eerie silence. Occasionally a shrill birdcall intruded on the monotonous insect chorus.

"Why aren't there any animals?" Catherine asked.

"Oh, they're out there," Murdock told her. "You just can't see them. There are monkeys high in the treetops. And in those same trees, there are flying squirrels the size of house cats. And arboreal snakes are wrapped around limbs, just waiting for breakfast to walk by."

"Oh." Catherine inched her way closer to Murdock's side, then stroked the barrel of her rifle. "They stay in the jungle, right?"

"We're relatively safe from the animals," he told her. "What we have to worry about are the humans."

"Aren't the natives friendly?" She kept in step with Murdock, making sure to stay at his side.

"These people know it doesn't pay to be friendly when you're caught up in the middle of a war. Unless you know the person, he...or she...could be an enemy."

"I suppose war does breed distrust, doesn't it?"

Murdock chuckled, the sound a sarcastic rumble. "Yeah, and distrust is the least of the evils war breeds."

"I have to confess something to you." She reached over to grab his arm, halting his rapid march.

When he gazed at her, irritation and wariness in his eyes, she squeezed his arm. "Not about us. Or about what happened between us. My confession is about me." She paused, took a deep breath and said in one big rush, "I'm terrified. I mean really terrified. I don't belong out here in the jungle. I don't belong anywhere in Zaraza. I should be back home, wearing a neat suit and silk stockings and drinking tea in the teacher's lounge. I don't think I'm equipped to handle playing soldier. Honest to God, Murdock, I'm about ready to scream."

He grasped her shoulders gently and looked her square in the eye. "It's all right to be afraid. I'm a trained soldier and I'm scared."

Her bottom lip quivered. She trembled uncontrollably. He captured her face between his hands and caressed her chin with his thumbs.

"I shouldn't have brought you with me. I should have gotten you out of this damn country and then come back alone."

"No. You couldn't do that. By the time you returned and found Vincente Sabino, Domingo Sanchez might have carried out the assassination plot. You had no choice but to bring me with you, so don't go blaming yourself for this situation."

Easing his hands down each side of her throat, he curled his fingers around and locked them behind the back of her neck. "As long as I'm alive, I'll protect you. Nothing and no one is going to harm you without going through me first."

"I know. It's just that I don't want anything to happen to you while you're trying to protect me or trying to save Vincente Sabino." She laid her hands on his shirt, above where the ammunition belts crisscrossed his chest. "If anything happened to you, I—I—"

Gunfire ripped through the jungle stillness, like a chain saw chewing through metal. Booted feet running. Muffled cries and angry shouts. Rapid bursts of repetitive shots.

Murdock grabbed Catherine's arm and dragged her with him into the jungle. After tossing her down on her knees behind the sinuous buttresses of a massive tree trunk, he lifted the M-16 and scanned the dense forest for signs of a battle.

Her heart thudded with deafening force. Moisture coated her palms as she removed the rifle from her shoulder. *Oh, God, don't let me have to shoot someone. I don't think I can do it. And I know Murdock is depending on Lanny's warrior genes to surface and take hold of me in a crisis. And this is a major crisis!*

Suddenly the bushes rustled. Murdock took aim, preparing to defend himself and Catherine. Out of nowhere a child appeared. A tiny, black-haired little girl, wagging a tattered cloth doll. Tears streamed down her dirty face.

Bullets zinged over the child's head, coming from left and right. Catherine's heart leaped to her throat when she realized the little girl was caught in the crossfire.

"She's going to get killed," Catherine cried. "Do something, Murdock. Please, do something!"

"Can you cover me?" he asked.

"Cover you? You mean—"

"I mean send out a blaze of gunfire in both directions, while I go out there and get her."

"Oh!" Could she? she wondered. Was she capable of

using the weapon she held, possibly wounding or even killing someone?

Without waiting for her reply, Murdock made his move. Instantly Catherine positioned the M-16 against her shoulder, and remembering Murdock's instructions, pulled the trigger back fully and opened fire to her left and then to her right. The impact of the rapid action rattled her teeth and jarred her bones. She stopped thinking, stopped feeling and simply allowed the adrenaline rush of fear to pump through her and give her the strength and the will to do what had to be done.

Murdock swung the child up onto his hip, and aiming his M-16 the best he could, added his firepower to Catherine's as he made a mad dash back to the safety behind the horizontally spreading tree roots.

"Here, take her." Murdock handed the little girl over to Catherine, who laid aside her rifle and wrapped the whimpering child in her arms. "You did good, honey. Real good."

Murdock kept the M-16 aimed and ready, while the combat between the rebels and Zarazaians continued. With the child on her lap, Catherine scooted closer to Murdock.

"What's going to happen?" she asked.

"That depends," he replied.

"On what?"

"On who wins and who loses this skirmish."

She understood, without him explaining further, that if the government soldiers triumphed, there was a good chance they would die. With one arm draped comfortingly around the child, Catherine laid her hand on Murdock's arm.

"No matter what happens, I want you to know that I—I care about you, Aloysius Murdock. As a matter of fact, I'm probably in love with you."

Chapter 11

The miniskirmish lasted less than thirty minutes, leaving seven government soldiers dead and one badly wounded. The rebels hadn't faired much better, with five dead, one wounded and a nervous young lieutenant uncertain how to proceed. Catherine carried the child in her arms as she followed Murdock and marveled at the way he took charge of the situation. Not knowing whether more Zarazaian troops were in the area, they didn't dare risk taking time to bury the dead. Making quick, life-and-death decisions, Murdock had no choice but to leave behind the badly wounded enemy. He handed the man a bottle of whiskey that he'd retrieved from their supplies and placed his rifle within his reach, if he crawled a couple of feet for it. Even an enemy deserved the right to end his own misery.

Turning to Catherine, Murdock said, ''I can help the lieutenant take care of his man on the way to Celendin.

Have you got everything under control with the kid? Do you think you can carry her and a rifle for four miles?''

"Yes. She's a tiny thing and not heavy at all.''

The child stared at Catherine. Her huge brown eyes filled with tears. Catherine tried talking to her, but the little girl kept jabbering in Spanish and she couldn't make out a word.

"She's telling you that her mama and papa were killed when the soldiers raided their village,'' Murdock translated. "From what she says, I think this must have happened months ago.''

"Then what is she doing here, now? How did she get here, all alone and in the middle of the fighting?'' Catherine wiped the child's face with her fingertips.

Murdock questioned the child, who replied almost hysterically. He turned to Catherine and said, "She was shuffled from one family to another in her village and finally sent to another village to live with distant relatives of her mother. When the soldiers came to that village, she escaped by running into the jungle.''

"Oh, this poor baby!'' Catherine hugged the little girl close to her. "Tell her that we'll take care of her and find her a place to stay.''

Murdock translated quickly and the child nodded, but instantly grabbed Catherine around the neck and babbled the same words over and over.

"She wants to stay with you,'' Murdock said. "Look, Cat, we've got to get to Celendin as soon as possible. Two men, a wounded soldier, a woman and a child won't have much of a chance against a squad of Zarazaian soldiers. And we have no guarantees that the jungle isn't swarming with government troops.''

"I understand. I'm—'' she cupped the child's head

with the back of her hand "—we're ready whenever you are."

Murdock caressed the little girl's cheek and asked her name. *"¿Cuál es su nombre?"*

"Benita," she replied.

"You take care of Benita," Murdock said. "And I'll take care of you. Understand?"

"Yes." Didn't he know by now she understood only too well that, whereas he was totally in his element in a situation like this, she was not. And she was smart enough to follow his orders without question.

"Young Lieutenant Vargas over there—" he nodded toward the fresh-faced kid who was attending to his wounded comrade "—says that he and his men were to meet up with Sabino's troops in Yanahuara tomorrow. So we're going to take the wounded soldier and the kid to the priest in Celendin. Vargas says that they've got a makeshift hospital set up there and are already taking care of a dozen orphans whose parents have been recently killed. Then first thing tomorrow, we three will head out to meet up with Sabino."

"Can Lieutenant Vargas get us straight to Vincente?" she asked.

"I doubt it, but once we're in Sabino's camp, he's promised to try to get a message through to him."

She nodded, then fell into step behind Murdock, who lifted the wounded rebel soldier up into his arms and issued the lieutenant an order the youth instantly obeyed.

The four-mile trek from the battlesite to Celendin was fraught with weariness, wariness and tropical warmth. Taking a break every mile proved a necessary delay. Ever mindful of the danger, both from animals and humans alike, Catherine looked to Murdock for inspiration and strength. He now revealed the side of himself that she had wrongfully assumed was the entire sum of his worth—the trained warrior, the cunning animal capable of killing in order to survive and to protect others. But she realized that this Murdock was simply a part of the whole man. And it was the complete Aloysius Murdock with whom she was falling in love. The trained soldier. The mercenary. The sophisticated Dundee agent. The reformed womanizer. The hellion who had mellowed with age. The loyal, caring friend. The passionate lover.

The village of Celendin, carved out of the jungle, lay in a two-mile square clearing and consisted of thatch-roofed huts and wooden buildings. The largest structure turned out to be the church and residence of the Catholic priest and village nurse, a Catholic nun.

After leaving the wounded soldier in the makeshift clinic, Murdock told the priest that Benita's parents were dead and they had found her wandering in the jungle. He immediately agreed to keep the child and to do what he could for her.

When Catherine set the little girl on her feet, Benita hesitated briefly, then looked up at Murdock when he explained that she'd be staying with Father Galtero.

"No, por favor, no. Yo quiero quedarme con ustedes." As she begged to stay with Murdock, she grabbed his leg and locked her little arms just above his knee. *"¡Usted sera mi padre!"* She glanced over at Catherine and cried, *"Ella sera mi madre. No me dejen."*

Catherine fought her own emotions, so touched by the pain she sensed in the little girl's heartfelt pleas. She didn't understand everything Benita said, but she realized the child was asking Murdock to be her father and

Catherine to be her mother and pleading with them not to leave her.

The expression on Murdock's face surprised Catherine. The stern, cold exterior of the big, bad soldier melted away to be replaced with a compassionate expression. He looked as if he were about to crack into a thousand pieces. He lifted the child up into his arms and spoke to her in a calm, gentle voice. Benita wrapped her little arms around Murdock's neck and kissed his cheek. His big arms stiffened. His jaw clenched.

He set Benita on her feet, then placed her hand in Catherine's. ''I've told her that she can't go with us when we leave in the morning, that we have an important mission and it wouldn't be safe for her to go with us. But that you'll stay with her here at the church, until she goes to sleep tonight.''

''Please tell her that I will come back for her,'' Catherine said.

''I won't lie to that child!''

''You won't be lying to her,'' Catherine told him. ''I have every intention of—''

''Have you lost your mind? You can't come back for her.''

Benita tugged on Catherine's hand, apparently confused by the adult argument, which she couldn't understand.

''It's all right, sweetheart,'' Catherine said and smiled, then frowned at Murdock. ''You're upsetting her.''

''This child came into your life less than three hours ago. You aren't thinking straight. You're allowing your emotions to—''

''Fine! You don't have to tell her anything. I'll get Father Galtero to translate. I noticed that his English isn't too bad.''

"Do whatever the hell you want to do!"

"I will!"

With Benita in tow, Catherine searched for the priest. She realized that her decision to take on responsibility for Benita was sudden, not well thought out and based entirely on emotions. Maybe Murdock was right. She shouldn't make any promises she couldn't keep. But in her heart of hearts, she truly felt that this precious little girl was meant to be hers. It was as if God had personally placed the child in her arms for safe keeping.

Murdock stalked off toward the makeshift clinic, presided over by a friendly, middle-aged nun, called Sister Naiara. After checking on the wounded rebel soldier he'd carried in from the jungle and finding him resting peacefully, Murdock met up with Lieutenant Vargas. Young Vargas knew the location of the local gin joint, a place where the village bootlegger provided a native concoction in wooden cups, served by his accommodating, nubile daughters.

He needed time away from Catherine. The woman had his head spinning with thoughts of love and commitment and children. He felt she'd be safe at the church, at least long enough to give him some breathing room. He'd be close by so that if trouble broke out, he could get to Catherine quickly. He wished he could leave her here in Celendin while he sought out Vincente Sabino, but he didn't dare risk leaving her. What if the village was attacked while he was gone? What if something happened and he couldn't come back for her? No, regardless of the risks in taking her with him, the risks in leaving her were far greater.

A few drinks with Vargas while they enjoyed the scenery was just what he needed. Catherine was one fine looking woman, but she wasn't the only woman in the world. He'd be better off sticking with the type he knew and didn't fear. Getting involved with Catherine was like playing with fire—and he'd already been burned by her passion.

Murdock and Vargas entered the saloon, which was little more than a one-room shack, situated on the opposite end of the village from the church. Appropriate, Murdock thought, as they entered the poorly lit interior of the establishment. Half a dozen tables dotted the creaky, unfinished wooden floor. A toothless old man with weathered brown skin grinned at them from where he stood behind a bar made out of logs. Vargas called out an order as he and Murdock sat down at an empty table near the door. Within minutes a black-eyed young woman, wearing a thin cotton dress and no underwear, set two wooden cups in front of them. Vargas patted the woman on the behind. She giggled and sashayed away, leaving the young lieutenant drooling.

"If you want her, she won't cost much," Vargas said.

There had been a time when Murdock wouldn't have hesitated taking advantage of the opportunity, but those days were long gone. The woman was young and pretty and more than willing. But he didn't want her. God help him, he didn't want any woman except Catherine!

"Thanks," Murdock said. "But I think I'll pass."

"The tall *señorita,* she is your woman, yes?" Vargas grinned as if he understood that Murdock didn't need the services of a whore when his own woman was only a couple of blocks away.

"Yeah," Murdock said, then downed the strong native liquor. The homemade brew packed quite a wallop, hitting his stomach like a two-ton brick.

"Another?" Vargas asked.

"One's enough for an old man like me."

Laughing, Vargas slapped Murdock on the back.

With little Benita glued to her side, Catherine helped Sister Naiara in the clinic. She had no experience in nursing, but with the nun's coaching, she quickly learned to take over some of the menial tasks that freed the sister for more important work. Benita eagerly assisted with feeding those too weak to feed themselves and replacing filthy, soiled linens with fresh ones, as well as sweeping and mopping the floors.

Catherine had hesitated about letting Benita, whom Father Galtero told her was six years old, expose herself to the sick and dying patients. But the kindly old priest had reminded Catherine that this precious child had already been exposed to far worse. And being near Catherine seemed to comfort Benita.

Father Galtero had agreed to translate for Catherine, but explained that he had told Benita that the *señora* wanted to return to Celendin someday and if God so willed it, that Benita could then go live with the *señora*. But only if God willed it to be. The loose translation had been acceptable to Catherine and welcomed with gratitude from Benita.

As the day wore on, Catherine began picking up more and more Spanish words and phrases—from Sister Naiara, from the patients and especially from Benita. Catherine turned much of the work they shared into a game, one in which Benita taught her Spanish and she in turn taught Benita English.

Late in the day, Sister Naiara placed her hand on Catherine's shoulder and said, "We go to eat, now. Then you and the little one will rest."

Nodding and smiling, Catherine said, *"Sí. Gracias."*
When she sat down to the meager evening meal she

shared with Father Galtero, Sister Naiara, Benita and the
other children, Catherine kept thinking about Murdock,
wondering how he had spent his afternoon.

Benita asked Father Galtero if she could say the bless-
ing. With a benevolent, understanding spirit, he agreed,
then afterward, translated for Catherine in a whispered
voice.

"She thanked God for leading her to you and Señor
Murdock. And she asked that our Heavenly Father take
care of her mother and father."

"Has she told you when her parents were killed?"
Catherine asked.

The priest shook his head, but Sister Naiara spoke up.

"Yes, she told me. She is most fortunate that you and
Señor Murdock found her," Sister Naiara said, enunci-
ating each word carefully.

"Señor Murdock, he is your husband?" Father Galtero asked as he broke his bread into pieces and crumbled them into his soup.

"No, Señor Murdock is not my husband. He is
my...my traveling companion."

The priest's deep-set brown eyes narrowed as he
frowned. "A woman should have a husband. Señor Murdock is a fine man. Yes? You marry him and come back
to Celendin for little Benita."

"I—I—" How could she reply to such a statement?
she wondered. "I'll certainly consider your suggestion,
Padre."

"You know what your man has been doing today?"
the priest asked. "He and the young soldier, Lieutenant
Vargas, have been instructing the men of our village on
how to protect us if we are attacked by the government
soldiers."

Time away from Murdock had helped her put her feelings for him into the proper perspective. She was physically attracted to him. They had shared a passionate intimacy that she'd never forget. And she admired his abilities as a warrior and protector. But loving him would be a waste for them both. Plain and simple—he didn't want her love.

Aloysius Murdock would probably rather eat glass than even consider a permanent commitment to one woman. But she was the kind of woman who wanted and needed marriage. And she truly wanted a child. This had been confirmed for her by the maternal feelings Benita conjured in her. She couldn't picture Murdock as a father. Then suddenly, the image of Benita in his arms flashed through Catherine's mind. The tender way he'd caressed the little girl's cheek and the kindness in his voice when he'd spoken to her had given Catherine a glimpse of the good man inside the hard-hearted warrior. But she also remembered the stricken look on his face when Benita had hugged him and kissed his cheek.

She and Benita were both better off without a man like Murdock. What she and the child needed was someone they could count on not just for now, but for all the years to come.

Murdock stood in the doorway, his gaze riveted to the tired, disheveled woman sitting on the floor beside the pallet on which the child lay. As Catherine lifted a hand to fork through her hair that curved around her neck in disarray, he noticed that her shirt hung loosely around her hips and the sleeves were rolled up to her elbows.

She leaned over the cot and brushed Benita's bangs out of her eyes, then caressed her cheek. The look of maternal longing in Catherine's eyes created a hard knot in Murdock's stomach. He'd seen the way she'd been with Lanny—caring, nurturing, loving. And now, here with this orphaned child, she had found an outlet for all that love inside her.

A woman like Catherine has more than enough love for everyone in her life, he realized. Father. Child. Lover.

She looked as weary as he felt and he suspected she longed for a bath and a soft bed. He couldn't offer her love or a long-term relationship, but he could—and would—take care of her needs for as long as possible, while she was under his protection.

She glanced up when she heard his footsteps crossing the creaky wooden floor. No smile. No warm word of greeting. Just a look that said *Take care of me.*

He reached down, grasped both of her hands and hauled her up on her feet. "Come with me, Cat."

She hesitated, her gaze plainly revealing her reluctance to leave Benita and go with him. "I can sleep here."

"I know you can, but you're not going to." He tugged on her hands. "You need a bath, some supper and a good night's sleep."

"And you're going to provide all three I suppose." She issued the comment as if it were a challenge.

"As a matter of fact, I am."

Her eyes widened and she stared at him with renewed attention. "You aren't kidding me, are you?"

"Come with me and find out."

She allowed him to lead her from the room at the back of the church, used to house the orphans, and take her out into the night. Using the flashlight he had confiscated at the deserted restaurant in San Carlos to guide them, Murdock led her through the village and toward an outcropping of trees, mostly palms, with a couple of jabuticaberia trees, ripe with fruit, off to one side. The mountain terrain formed a semicircle of protection, cutting off the area from the rest of the world. A glow of warm light hovered from within the secluded thicket.

Nestled in the center of the grove, a small tent awaited them. Large lanterns hung on high poles around the tent, illuminating the area and casting shadowy light far and wide. Catherine halted abruptly and looked from the tent to Murdock. When she heard the ripple of water, her questioning gaze intensified.

"Lieutenant Vargas and some of the men helped me put up the tent," Murdock explained. "We can stay the night here in relative safety. The mountains surround this spot. The only way in or out is through the village. Over there is a small pond, fed by an underground spring. And some of the women prepared supper for us."

"I don't believe this." Catherine circled the tent. "You're a magician. You wave around your machismo and men and women alike gladly do your bidding."

"Are you complaining?"

"No, just making an observation." Exasperated and irritated, she threw up her hands in frustration. "Does anyone ever say no to you? Do you always get what you want?"

"What's wrong, Cat? And don't give me some glib answer. I want to know what's really wrong with you." He came up behind her, planted his huge hands on her shoulders and leaned his head over to brush the side of her face with his stubble-rough cheek.

She jerked away from him, then halted her retreat and faced him. "*You* are what's wrong with me," she admitted. "You. Aloysius Murdock. The most complicated man I've ever known. I have spent this entire day vacillating between wishing I'd never met you and wanting you to be a part of my life forever."

"Cat…honey…"

He reached for her. She sidestepped him.

"I had no idea where you were this afternoon or what you were doing. I didn't know where you'd gone. Or who you were with."

"I was at the village showing the natives how to protect themselves."

"I know that!" When he took a step toward her, she backed away from him. "Father Galtero told me at supper what you'd been doing this afternoon."

"I didn't know you'd already eaten," he said. "We've got a nice meal inside the tent."

"You eat it!"

"So, if you know you had nothing to worry about as far as where I was today, why are you so angry with me?"

"Because…because…dammit, just because!" Flustered by his direct question, she grumbled and fumed.

"Because why, honey?"

"Stop calling me honey! And don't try seducing me with a tent and food and a pond where I can take a bath. It's not going to work. None of it. I have no intention of giving you an encore of this morning's performance."

"What if I told you that I'm not interested in an encore?"

"I wouldn't believe you."

He moved forward; she retreated.

"All I want to do is take care of you," he said.

"All you want is to *work off a little frustration in the sack.*"

"As I recall, you rather enjoyed our last little frustration-relieving session."

His broad grin irritated her unbearably. He was deliberately goading her, but she couldn't seem to stop herself from rising to the bait. She hated the fact that he was right. She had more than enjoyed their sexual encounter in the early hours this morning on the gunboat. But damn him for being ungentlemanly enough to remind her. That's the problem, she told herself, Aloysius Murdock isn't a gentleman. Not even back in Atlanta, ensconced in the trappings of a civilized man. And most definitely not here in the middle of the jungle, when he was the consummate warrior-protector.

She glowered at him, her expression daring him to say or do anything more to provoke her. He accepted the challenge by moving in on her, slowly but surely reaching out for the kill. Inch by steady inch, she continued backing away from him. And inch by determined inch he stalked her, forcing her to retreat.

Suddenly, without warning, she lost her footing and plunged into the pond behind her. Flailing arms and sprawling legs. Wide, startled eyes. A cry for help. And then a resounding flop, followed by a loud splash. Catherine fell flat on her behind, straight into the shallow pond. Landing on the gritty bottom, she gasped as water rose to her neck and slapped her in the face.

Murdock stood on the bank, laughing.

Using her hands as leverage, she hoisted herself up onto her knees and then onto her feet. With menace in her eyes, she stomped back onto dry ground. Without acknowledging his presence, she sat down at the edge of the pond and removed her boots and socks. Then she stood. Allowing her toes to mire up in the mud surrounding the water's edge, she unbuttoned her shirt and tossed it aside. With her naked back to Murdock, she ignored him completely as she unzipped her pants and then tossed them aside. Her only remaining garment was the red silk panties Landra had given her.

She could hear Murdock's ragged breath and knew exactly what she was doing to him. Swinging her hips provocatively, she dabbled her muddy toes into the water. Tossing back her head, she flung her hair over her shoulder and then glanced at Murdock.

"I'm going to take my bath now," she told him. "If you still want to take care of me, then why don't you go rustle me up some towels and come back with them in about half an hour."

She plunged into the cool spring water and swam the length of the pond. Just as she neared the opposite bank, she heard the thunderous splatter of Murdock's big body entering the water. She smiled secretly, all the while plotting his demise. It was high time someone taught the overconfident Mr. Murdock that he couldn't always have what he wanted.

Chapter 12

Catherine was toying with him. Tempting him. She was giving him a glimpse of what he so badly wanted, but his guess was that she had no intention of following through with her seduction. The witch just wanted to make him suffer. However, he didn't think she'd figured her own needs into the equation. She might be able to resist him, but could she deny her own desires?

By stripping in front of him and luring him to come after her, Catherine was acting out of character. He'd bet his life that if they were back in the States, she couldn't shed her clothes or her inhibitions so easily. But here, in Zaraza, with danger and possible death facing them in the days ahead, it was easier for her to throw caution to the wind. And it was easier for him to take what he wanted without torturing himself about the consequences.

Murdock swam across the small pond, reaching Catherine in minutes. Waiting for him in the shallow end, she stood there, waist-deep in water, with moist droplets beading on her bare breasts and a come-hither smile on her softly parted lips.

Emerging from beneath the water, he towered over her. Catherine suddenly realized that he was naked. Completely naked. Where the dark water concealed her from the waist down, it hit him midhip. The upper thrust of his erection bobbed just above the surface. She closed her eyes, but couldn't blot out the sight of his powerful arousal. *Get hold of yourself! You're the one in charge,* the confident seductress within her said. *Don't let him reverse the roles and become your seducer.*

"Enjoying your *bath?*" he asked, but deliberately didn't touch her. "If you need someone to scrub your back, I'm available."

"I forgot to bring any soap." She smiled sweetly, deceptively. "You don't happen to have any in your pocket, do you?"

"Nope. I'm afraid I don't have any pockets."

"Oh, really? I hadn't noticed."

Murdock's chuckle shook his muscular chest. He eased closer to the bank, then stepped forward, leaving only his feet still submerged in the pond. "See. No pockets."

He's daring you, Catherine told herself. Do not let him intimidate you. Garnering all her courage, she looked at him. Big mistake! Like a well-formed giant sculpted from flesh-colored marble, he stood there in all his masculine glory, the moonlight spotlighting him and the glow from the lanterns dancing across the water to lap about his feet. Her hands itched to touch him. Running her tongue across her lips, she recalled the taste of him. Her nipples tightened, beading to sensitive points. A deep, purely feminine ache throbbed between her legs.

Big as a mountain, massive and powerful, the very epitome of manhood at its finest, Murdock smiled at her. A hundred crazed butterflies exploded into flight inside her belly. Her femininity clenched and unclenched, moistening and swelling in preparation.

You're still in charge, she tried to convince herself. Just because your body is betraying you, doesn't mean you can't resist temptation. Show this man he can't snap his fingers and make you come running. Make him beg for what he wants. Make him get down on those big, rock-hard knees and say please. Don't be like every other woman in his life. Make him remember you!

Catherine walked out of the pond, rivulets of water cascading over her breasts and plastering the red silk panties to her belly and cupping them seductively to her mound. Murdock swallowed hard. Like an Amazon princess, tall, lithe, well-proportioned and possessing a strength of will and purpose, Catherine approached him. Then when she was within two feet of him, she stopped. Clasping her left hand around her hair, she squeezed the moisture from the tips, then ran her hand over her shoulder and slowly spread out her palm as she slid her hand from the top of one breast to the other.

Murdock stared, watching her every movement as a hawk would zero in on its prey. She lifted her right hand to join her left, then glided them over and then under her breasts. Murdock's mouth opened. His eyes narrowed to slits. His sex swelled, growing harder by the minute. Taking her own sweet time, she spread her open palms out over her belly and then carried them across to her hips. Hooking her thumbs under the waistband of her panties, she smiled at Murdock.

She's enjoying herself tremendously, he thought. She knows just what she's doing to me and she loves the feeling of power it gives her. If she wanted to be the one in charge, the one to control the situation, then he'd gladly allow her the upper hand. For now.

She teased him by lowering the panties just a bit, then stopping. For a novice at this sort of thing, she was doing a damn good job of torturing the hell out of him. As if swaying to some sort of music in her head, she bumped her hips back and forth, then with leisurely finesse dragged the panties over her hips and down her thighs. The puff of red silk dropped to her ankles. Murdock sucked in a deep breath. When she kicked the panties into the water, he closed his eyes and gritted his teeth.

Her tinkling laughter rippled along every nerve ending in his body. He opened his eyes to find her staring at him, a triumphant twinkle in her eyes.

"I think I'll take my bath now," she said. "Even without any soap, I should be able to rinse away the dirt and grime."

While he stood on the bank and watched, she eased back into the pond, but only up to her hips. Dipping the water with her hands, she splashed it over her body, from face to navel. Using her hands like a washcloth, she scrubbed herself with a soft, circular motion.

Time to stop observing and take action, Murdock thought. Give her a little of her own medicine and see if she likes the taste of it.

He went after her, his attack swift, but gentle. Before she knew what hit her, he plunged into the pond and grabbed her around the waist. Crying out, she pummelled his chest with her fists.

"Let go of me!"

He manacled her fists in one hand, holding them between their wet bodies. Then with his free hand he gripped the back of her neck and held her in place, pressing her firmly against him.

"This is what you wanted, isn't it, honey?" He mouthed the question, his lips almost touching hers. "This is what you were asking for and we both know it."

She squirmed, trying to escape from his tenacious hold. "I wasn't asking for—"

"No, Cat, you weren't asking, you were begging for it." Tightening his grip on her neck, he nudged her closer, until her trapped hands pressed between her breasts and her belly flattened against his erection. "You don't wave a red flag in front of a raging bull unless you want him to attack."

"Is that what you're doing, attacking me?" Her voice quavered every so slightly as she tilted her chin and gave him that haughty little look he so despised. "I thought you were a man, not an animal."

"You should know that I'm both. Most men are. And when it comes to sex, I'm more animal than man."

She glared at him and he suspected that it took a great deal of courage on her part to confront him so boldly. He loosened his grip on her hands, allowing her to tug them free. But in doing so, she inadvertently brushed one hand across the top of his bulging sex. He jerked. She gasped. Their gazes locked and held. She eased her hands up his body, stopping when she reached his shoulders.

Forking his fingers, he slid them up her neck and into her hair to cup the back of her head. "If you're going to dish it out, you've got to learn to take it."

"I—I can take it," she assured him in an uncertain tone.

"Sure you can, Cat." He grinned wickedly. "Why

don't you show me just how much you can take?'' Lifting one of her buttocks with his free hand, he ground her into his arousal.

She trembled from head to toe. ''I can take you…or leave you, Mr. Murdock. Unlike you, I'm capable of controlling my animal urges. If I want to.''

''Is that so? Mmm-hmm.'' He nuzzled her neck as he patted her behind. ''Do you want to?''

''Do I want to do what?'' she asked, breathlessly.

''Do you want to control your animal urges.''

''I—I— You don't mean any more to me than I do to you.''

''Is that right?''

''I know that this morning, when we were caught in middle of the battle, I told you that I was probably falling in love with you, but—''

''This morning you thought you might die,'' he finished the explanation for her.

''Right!''

''And in retrospect, you realize you were mistaken about your feelings for me.''

''Yes, that's it exactly,'' she said.

''Well, then, we don't have a problem, do we?'' He nibbled on her ear, while he caressed her spine, from neck to hips.

''No, we—we don't have a problem.'' She grasped his shoulders, loving the feel of his hard muscles beneath her fingers.

''I don't mean anything more to you than you do to me,'' he repeated her declaration.

''That's right.'' Her breasts rose and fell with each labored breath, as Murdock's masculine presence surrounded her, seeped into her body and took possession.

As he clasped her chin, he circled her lips with the

inside of his thumb. "You know that I want you. You can feel just how much. The question is, are you willing to admit that you want me, too?"

If she admitted that she wanted him as desperately as he wanted her, she realized that she would be admitting defeat. All her efforts to show him that he couldn't always have what he wanted would have failed miserably. In seducing Murdock, she had unwittingly been seduced.

"I can have sex just for the sake of having sex, the way you do," she said, trying to convince herself as well as him. "But neither of us have any contraceptives, so…we'd have to—to be very careful."

His mouth took hers in a kiss that robbed her of breath and rational thought. With his lips still on hers, he swept her up out of the water and into his arms. She flung her arms around his neck and buried her face against his throat. He carried her onto the bank, then stormed toward the tent.

Once inside the small tent, he lowered her to the pallet of blankets on the ground, then straddled her hips. Hovering over her, big, hard and powerfully aroused, Murdock studied every inch of the woman beneath him.

More than anything he wanted to find release within the depths of her body, but he would have to settle for less. If he could control the urge to mate with her, he'd be able to give her pleasure and accept pleasure in return, without any risks. But the primitive need to plant his seed inside her rode him hard.

Easing down beside her, he wrapped her in his embrace and held her close, drowning in the sweet scent of her feminine body. Catherine. Beautiful Catherine. A woman like no other. Strong, smart, courageous. His equal in every way. His superior in many.

Why had she retracted her confession of love? he

wondered. Had he wounded her pride by not reciprocating and declaring his undying love for her? What difference does it make? He didn't want Cat to love him, did he? No! Definitely not! An uncomplicated affair was what they both needed and what they both wanted. No messy emotions to cloud the issue. Sex for the sake of sex. Nothing more.

"I do care about you," he told her, his voice a growling whisper. "As long as we're in Zaraza, you'll be my woman, but once we cross the border—"

She covered his lips with her index finger. "Shh... I'm not asking for more than tonight and however many nights we have together. This isn't real...this passion between us. It's part of the nightmare I entered the day I found out that Lanny was still alive. You and me, my father's rescue and my being trapped in Zaraza with you are all moments out of time, separate and apart from my real life back in Huntington. Once we leave here, it's over for us. I know that better than you do."

"And you're willing to accept what I can offer you...here, now? With no plans for the future. No love. No commitment."

"Very few women are given the chance to live a fantasy, to know this kind of passion." She slid her hand down his body and circled his erection. "I ache with wanting you."

No woman had ever called him her fantasy. Catherine's admission that he was hers blew his control to smithereens. He wanted to tell her that she was his fantasy, too. That she was all he could ever want in a woman—and more. But instead of saying the words, he would show her how he felt. He would turn their fantasies into reality.

"I'm going to love you all night." His kiss possessed, ravaged and aroused.

Her response equaled his attack. Their lips clung, thrust and devoured. Their bodies entwined. Arms and legs wrapping and locking. Rolling and tumbling, they slid off the pallet and then back on. He whispered hot, savage vulgarities as his big hands explored her body. She urged him, encouraged him, seduced him with her actions and her own crude language. They touched and kissed, licked and bit, sucked and nibbled, until there wasn't an inch of unchartered flesh on their bodies.

Using his fingers, as well as his tongue and teeth, he caressed her to the point of madness, giving her repeated pleasure. She writhed and squirmed and cried out as yet another shattering climax claimed her.

Every time she tried to ease his frustration, he stalled her, putting her off, suffering the torment of the damned. But he finally reached the breaking point. Nothing mattered except claiming this woman in the most basic, elemental way a man can claim a woman. Nothing less would satisfy the raging hunger clawing inside him like a caged animal demanding freedom.

Straddling her, he lifted her hips, seeking the entrance to her body. Clinging to him, she arched her back and thrust her hips upward, opening herself to him. He lunged into her, diving deeper and deeper until her sheath fully encompassed him. This was heaven, he thought. Pure, sweet, worth-dying-for heaven!

She tightened around him, fitting him snugly within her. She had never known such ecstasy. He was big and hard and filled her completely. She had been created for this man, this moment, this indescribable pleasure. What they shared was more than passion, even more than love.

Their bodies began the mating dance, slowly, rhythmically, each savoring the delicious sensations spiraling around inside them. With each thrust and parry, the tension built, the passion swelled.

He wanted to make it last—just a little longer. If only he could hold on. Wait. Wait for the earth-shattering climax. But his libido paid no heed.

She wished this moment could last forever. She longed to postpone the completion as surely as she craved release. But the tightness, the pounding ache grew stronger and stronger. She couldn't hold on, couldn't stop the inevitable.

She broke first, her release washing over her like a tidal wave. The force of her climax shuddered through her, its strength diminishing slowly, lingering, sensitizing her whole body so that when he lunged one final time to achieve his own fulfillment, a second shock wave hit her full force. As he jetted into her, she held him, loving him, glorying in the harsh, guttural cries rising from his throat.

He collapsed on top of her, completely drained, totally satisfied and astonished by the power of the connection between Catherine and him. Sliding to her side, he enveloped her in his embrace. She snuggled against him, kissing his shoulder, his neck and then lifting herself just enough to reach his lips.

"I loved making love with you," she told him. "I've never known anything...never experienced anything remotely like... It was wonderful. You were wonderful. I was wonderful." Tears glazed her eyes as she looked down into his face.

He cupped her face between his hands. "It was the best damn sex I've ever had."

"It was for me, too." A stray tear escaped her eyes and hung precariously on the end of her eyelashes.

Murdock licked the tear off her eyelashes, then covered her face with kisses. "It was more than sex," he admitted. "With you, Cat, it was all my fantasies fulfilled."

I love you! I love you so much it hurts! she wanted to scream, wanted to shout it from the rooftops.

"Murdock, I..." she paused. Then deciding not to ruin the moment with words she crawled over on top of him and straddled his hips, letting her breasts dangle over his chest. He kissed her. Thoroughly. Passionately. Wrapping her fantasy up with a perfect pink bow.

"Thanks, Murdock." She lay down on top of his huge, damp body, her own body small in comparison.

He stroked her back with tenderness. "Go to sleep now," he said. "I'm going to make love to you again after a while and I want us both rested."

She sighed contentedly and closed her eyes, breathing in the musky scent of the man she adored.

All but one of the lanterns had burned out, leaving the singular light alone to aid the moon in illuminating the tent site. Murdock roused first, waking with a hard-on thumbing against Catherine's hip. She lay at his side, one arm thrown over his hip, her lips almost touching his shoulder.

He wanted her again. As much as he had hours ago. Maybe more. Yes, definitely more. Now that he knew how good it could be between them. Their time together in Zaraza would end soon—either by their returning to the real world or by a less pleasant fate. Either way, only a few days stood between them and a final separation. He didn't intend to waste one minute of his precious time with her.

Running his index finger between her breasts and nuzzling her ear, Murdock urged her to awaken. She mumbled and stirred, but didn't open her eyes. Lowering his head, he covered one breast with his open mouth and sucked greedily on her nipple. Her eyelids flew open. She gasped and then smiled.

"Fantasy time again," he told her.

Her smiled widened as she skimmed her hand over his chest and down his belly, halting before she reached his jutting erection. Before she realized what he was doing, he hauled her up and over on top of him, crushing her breasts into his chest hair.

"Ride me, Cat." He bucked his hips, then rubbed his sex against her mound.

"Ah!"

She sucked in a long, deep breath and exhaled slowly. Then she reared up, bracing herself with her knees. Reaching between their bodies, she circled him, drew him up and into her. She eased her body down over his, impaling herself on his shaft. When he was fully embedded within her, he grasped her hips and lifted her up and down, setting the pace of her ride.

The feel of him inside her set off rockets of aching need, compelling her into action. Fitting herself around him, exposing her femininity to the strongest amount of friction possible, she rode him frantically. The harder she pounded, the farther her body lowered onto his, until she draped him like a shawl.

Her breasts dangled over his mouth, tempting him to taste them, and Murdock complied by laving first one and then the other nipple. His ardent attention further stirred her desire. And when he sucked at one nipple and stroked the other with his fingers, she accelerated the pace.

"That's it, Cat. Harder and faster!"

When completion claimed her, she cried out from the force of her release. Aftershocks pelted through her nerve endings as Murdock jackhammered into her, renewing her climax and accomplishing his own.

This *was* a fantasy, Murdock thought. Nothing could really be this good.

Catherine sprawled out on top of him, replete, sated beyond her wildest dreams. I'm not living a fantasy, she thought. This is more than a fantasy. Undoubtedly, I've died and gone to heaven.

Chapter 13

Morning arrived too soon. Reality set in immediately. The harsh fact of being in a war-ravaged country woke them with the echoes of gunfire. Murdock shot straight up. Early-morning light seeped through the partially open tent flap. He grabbed Catherine.

"Stay here. I'll go to the pond and get our clothes."

She nodded that she understood. He rushed out of the tent and went straight to the pond. After gathering up their scattered garments and boots, he scanned the horizon. From what he could tell, a battle had just begun in Celendin. After returning quickly, he flung her shirt and pants at her, then tossed her boots on the ground. They dressed hurriedly, taking no time to tuck in their shirts or close every button.

Murdock snatched up a blanket lying in the corner of the tent, where he had stashed the two rifles and ammunition belts. He slung the belts over one shoulder and the rifle over the other, then handed Catherine's M-16 to her.

"Is the village being attacked?" she asked.

"From what I could see at this distance, I'd say yes, that's exactly what's going on."

"Benita!" Catherine cried. "And the other children."

Murdock grabbed her arm and dragged her out of the tent. "Stay with me. We'll go straight to the church to make sure Benita is all right."

"Thank you," she said, then followed him toward the village.

They made their way into Celendin, Murdock ever mindful that the unknown faced them around each corner. The doors and windows of every house and building they passed were sealed tight. Shutters closed, doors locked. Only a few chickens and one lone dog roamed the empty streets. As they drew nearer to the church, they saw a group of native men, weapons of various sorts in their hands, congregating in front of the town elder's home.

When one of the men saw Murdock approaching, he lifted his rifle and shouted a greeting.

"Stay behind me," Murdock told her.

They joined the group of about twenty men, Catherine remaining discreetly one step behind Murdock. She listened while Murdock conversed with the leader, making out a word here and there, but not enough to comprehend what was being discussed. Within minutes she realized that Murdock had taken charge and was issuing orders. The men formed four separate groups and quickly dispersed.

"A small band of rebels, several of them wounded, showed up here about thirty minutes ago," Murdock explained to Catherine. "It seems a squad of Zarazaian soldiers followed them here and now the rebels are trying to hold them off and protect Celendin.''

"What are their chances of holding off the government soldiers?'' she asked.

"Pretty good. It's a small squad. And I've just set a plan into motion.'' He grasped her shoulders. ''I need you to go to the church and wait for me there.''

"No! I want to go with you.'' She shook her rifle. ''I know how to use this thing now. I can fight alongside you.''

He squeezed her shoulders. ''I know you can, honey. But I need you at the church. We can't spare a man to guard and protect the children and Father Galtero and Sister Naiara. I'm counting on you doing that for me.''

"Oh. I see.''

"Can you handle this, Cat? If any of the enemy soldiers make it to the church, can you shoot them? Can you kill them?'' Clutching her chin between his thumb and forefinger, he forced her to look him directly in the eye.

"Yes. I can do it. To protect the children. To keep Father Galtero and Sister Naiara and those innocent children safe. Yes, I can shoot anyone who tries to harm them. I—I—'' her voice cracked ''—I can kill, if I have to.''

"Good.'' He kissed her—hard and quick. ''I'll walk you to the church. When you get inside, barricade the doors and don't let anyone inside, unless Father Galtero or Sister Naiara knows who they are and gives you the okay.''

"I understand.''

He saw her safely to the church, where Father Galtero opened the locked door for them. Standing in the open doorway, Murdock draped one of the ammunition belts over her head and across her chest.

"Remember, if in doubt, shoot first and ask questions later," he told her. "Better to be sorry than dead."

And then he disappeared. Out the door, down the steps and around the corner. Quickly, Catherine and Father Galtero locked the doors, then she turned to him and suggested that they shove several of the wooden benches against the door for reinforcement. Once that task was accomplished, she motioned from him to follow her.

In the back room the orphans huddled together, their dark eyes filled with fear. Sister Naiara came running up to Catherine.

"Thank our blessed Lord that you are safe," the nun said.

"Are all the doors locked and the shutters closed?" Catherine asked. "Is there any way someone can get inside the church without bursting through a door or window?"

"There are no other entrances. Father Galtero and I have secured the doors and windows," Sister Naiara assured her, nodding toward the back door in that room. She gazed at the rifle in Catherine's hand and then at the heavy ammunition belt draped across her body. "You look like a soldier. Has Señor Murdock sent you here for your safety or as our protector?"

"Both," Catherine said. "I won't let anyone harm you and Father Galtero or the children."

"We must pray." Sister Naiara folded her hands together and dropped to her knees.

The children gathered around the nun, but Benita went straight to Catherine, wrapping her arms around Catherine's leg. She knelt in front of Benita, wrapped one arm around the child and caressed her cheek.

"I know you don't understand what I'm saying, but I want you to know that I'm going to take care of you."

Benita laid her hand in the center of her chest and said, "Me—" then she laid her hand on Catherine's chest and said, "—you." She repeated the English words *me* and *you* as she moved her hand back and forth from her chest to Catherine's.

Catherine grabbed the child's hand, stilling it over her heart. She nodded and smiled. "Yes, Benita. You and me. Together. *Juntas.*"

Minutes ticked by. Hours began to blur together. Time became meaningless. Father Galtero led the children in several songs that temporarily took their minds off the sound of warfare surrounding the church. Sister Naiara insisted on attending to the wounded in the clinic, which was reached by a long hallway that dissected the church building. When Catherine went with her to check the doors and windows, they marched the troop of orphans with them.

With the doors and windows secured, the noonday heat soon turned the interior into a sweatbox. The children grew restless. Father Galtero gave them all water to drink and distributed a piece of fruit to each child.

How long could the battle continue? Catherine wondered. Who was winning? And was Murdock all right? She tried not to even consider the possibility that he could be killed. No matter what happened, they would survive! And they'd get out of Zaraza alive and together!

Only an occasional blast of gunfire sounded in the distance. And the quiet within the church allowed her to hear her own heartbeat. The weary, frightened children sat around on the floor, silent and still. Several had even fallen asleep. Benita sat beside Catherine, huddled against her.

Suddenly loud shouts outside the back door alerted Catherine to trouble. Although she couldn't understand what the men were bellowing, she could tell by the terrified look on Father Galtero's face that whoever was pounding on the door was an enemy.

"What are they saying?" she asked.

"They are demanding that we let them in," the priest told her. "They say if we do not, they will punish us."

"Take the children and get in that corner—" she pointed the direction "—and stay out of the line of fire."

He did as she instructed. When Benita refused to leave her, Catherine walked with the child and placed her hand in Father Galtero's. And then they waited. The shouting continued, as did the horrific pounding on the door. The rusted metal hinges began to loosen. The old wooden door cracked under the force of the attack. Catherine took cover behind a heavy wooden table, then knelt, braced the M-16 against her shoulder and prepared herself for battle.

Two Zarazaian soldiers burst through the door. Catherine sucked in a deep breath. The men began shooting, splintering the wooden furniture and ripping apart the floor. Sister Naiara came running from the clinic. Catherine screamed for her to go back. But not in time. In a knee-jerk reaction, one of the soldiers aimed and fired. Sister Naiara took a bullet in the shoulder, then fainted dead away.

Huddled in the corner, the children screamed and screamed and screamed. The sound of their fear echoed inside Catherine's head. The moment the two soldiers turned their weapons on the children, Catherine acted purely on instinct. She gunned down the men before they knew what had hit them.

Trembling from head to toe, tears blurring her vision,

she eased the rifle from her bruised shoulder. Father Galtero rushed past her. He dropped to his knees and lifted Sister Naiara into his arms.

When the children started to move away from the corner, Catherine cried out for them to stay where they were, then realizing they didn't understand her, she held up her hand in a gesture for them to stop. With the door open, they were exposed to the outside world and to all and any dangers. She lifted the rifle and moved hurriedly to block the doorway. Only she and this weapon stood between the children and anyone who might harm them.

When Murdock returned to the church, he found Catherine crouched in the doorway, her hands gripping the M-16 with white-knuckled fierceness. The rebel soldiers who accompanied him stopped dead in their tracks when they saw her.

"Catherine!"

"Murdock?"

"Battle's over," he shouted. "We held the village and put the government boys on the run."

She wanted to get up and rush to him, to throw her arms around his neck, to kiss his face and tell him she was glad they'd both survived. But she couldn't move.

Murdock dropped to his knees beside her and prised the M-16 from her hands. "You can let go now, honey. It's all right."

When he laid the rifle down beside her, she toppled over into his arms. He wrapped her securely in his embrace and kissed her forehead. "Was it bad, Cat?"

"I—I killed two men." She gripped his shirtfront. "They shot Sister Naiara. They would have shot the children!"

"You did what you had to do," he told her, rubbing

her back.

Scanning the room, Catherine searched for the nun. She heaved a sigh of relief when she saw that Sister Naiara was sitting up and smiling weakly at Father Galtero. "How is she?"

"She will be all right," the priest said. "The bullet went through her shoulder."

"Come on." Murdock grabbed Catherine's arm. "Let me get you up on your feet. We have to leave in a few minutes."

She stared at him questioningly. "What do you mean we have to leave?"

Lifting her to her feet, he supported her by draping one arm around her waist. "Vargas is hooking up with this band of rebels. We've already missed our chance to connect with Vincente in Yanahuara, so our best bet of catching up with him is to go with these men. They're joining up with the rest of the rebel army before they march on San Carlos."

"What about Benita?" Catherine asked.

"We can't take her with us. She's safer here."

"Is she?"

"The war is moving downriver," he explained. "General Ramos's army is preparing to defend the capital. I doubt there will be any more troop movements through Celendin."

"How long...how much time do we have before we leave?"

"Ten or fifteen minutes. The troops are preparing to move out."

"I'm going to find a way to get Benita out of this country," Catherine said. "Somehow, someway, I'm going to bring her to the United States."

"Sure you will, honey." He soothed her with his agreement, but in the back of his mind a niggling doubt remained. What were the odds that little Benita would ever leave Zaraza?

An hour later, Catherine and Murdock marched with the rebel troops, who hacked their way through the jungle when necessary, followed the winding paths by the river and took whatever existing roads they could find. By midafternoon they stopped in Yanahuara, a village half the size of Celendin. They were offered bread and water by the natives and rested there for half an hour before their leader resumed the journey. Before nightfall the band of rebels with whom Catherine and Murdock traveled joined with two other troops, all following the trail Vincente Sabino was blazing toward the capital city.

Conspicuously American, Catherine and Murdock's presence had to be repeatedly explained, usually by Lieutenant Vargas. Every time Murdock tried to tell them that he needed to get an urgent message to Sabino, he was asked to relay that message through the officers. But Murdock insisted that what he had to say to Sabino had to be delivered personally. He soon realized that, unfortunately, the more he tried to convince them that his seeing Sabino was a life-or-death matter, the more they distrusted him.

"I've tried giving them as much information as I dare," Murdock told Catherine as they sat beneath a palm tree, just out of hearing range of the nearest soldiers, and ate the meager rations they'd been given for supper. "Vargas got me in to see Captain Delgado—" Murdock pointed to the row of three tents, in which the leaders of each rebel faction resided for the night "—and I think I finally convinced the man that I'd once fought with Juan Sabino."

"Then he'll help us, won't he?" Catherine leaned her head back against the tree trunk.

"Only if I share my information with him first," Murdock said. "And there's no way I can risk trusting anyone, not even the captain. Domingo Sanchez may intend to act alone, but he's bound to have sympathizers in the rebel army. I have no way of knowing who those people might be. Besides, there's a good chance that if I trusted Delgado and told him about the assassination plot, he wouldn't believe that Vincente's most trusted bodyguard plans to kill him."

"Is there any way we can go off on our own, leave the camp tonight, and try to reach Vincente Sabino without anyone's help?"

"We have to follow the rebel army," he told her. "They know the exact route Sabino is taking and we're not more than half a day behind. If we go out on our own and try to catch up with Sabino, the guards around his camp will shoot us on sight. The only way we can get to Sabino is with an introduction."

"Without the captain's help, how will we accomplish that?"

"Vargas is going to see what he can do to get me an audience with Major Montero."

Catherine finished off the strong, bitter coffee in the tin cup she'd been issued. "Do you trust Vargas? He seems awfully eager to help us."

"I trust Vargas as much as I trust anyone I don't know well." Murdock stretched out on the ground, then placed his crossed arms beneath his head. "He and I fought side by side back in Celendin. We've become comrades, of a sort. I've told him about how your father and I fought with Juan Sabino and that you and I came to

Zaraza to pay a hefty ransom to gain your father's freedom from *Prision de las Puertas al Infierno*."

"Did you tell him about the assassination plot?" she asked.

"That information goes straight from my mouth to Vincente Sabino's ear."

"What if we don't get to him in time?"

"I'll find a way. No matter what."

Catherine shivered. The determination she heard in Murdock's voice frightened her. *No matter what* could mean anything, including sacrificing his own life.

She scooted closer to him, then leaned over and stared down into his face. "Promise me that you won't take any unnecessary risks."

"Ah, Cat, don't make me spell it out for you." This was the very reason a soldier didn't become involved with a woman while he was on a mission. No matter how strong, how fierce a warrior the woman might be, if she cared about a man, she was going to get sentimental. And when it mattered to your woman whether you lived or died, you were in trouble.

She grabbed his chin. Looking him square in the eye, she said, "*No matter what* means that if you have to, you'll die in order to save Vincente Sabino."

"Ah, Cat. Don't!" Hell, she was going to cry. He could hear it in her voice.

"I don't want you to die. I don't think I could bear it if anything happened to you."

He pulled her down into his arms. She wrapped herself around him as he held her close.

"This is the nightmare," she told him. "I want the fantasy back."

"I'm afraid they go together. Can't have one without

the other. The nightmare and the fantasy are all a part of our mission in Zaraza.''

''At least I know my father is safe and getting medical treatment in Lima,'' she said. ''If only we could have gotten Benita out safely, too. Every time I remember the look in her eyes when we said goodbye, I— Oh, God!'' *Don't cry!* she warned herself. *Not again. You've cried way too much lately.*

''Don't do this to yourself.'' Murdock wouldn't admit to Catherine that he was worried about Benita, too. Something about the kid, about the way she and Catherine had bonded, had touched some tender spot inside him. And no matter how hard he tried to forget it, he kept remembering the way the child had wrapped her arms around his leg and asked him to be her father.

So, the kid obviously had lousy taste in men, if she'd picked him out to be her new father.

What kind of father would he be anyway? He didn't know the first thing about being a parent. *But what if you had Catherine around to teach you?* a hopeful inner voice asked. *If you married Catherine and the two of you adopted—* Wait just a damn minute here! What the hell was he thinking? Marry Catherine? What was the matter with him? Had he lost his freaking mind? Had he allowed himself to blur the lines between fantasy and reality?

There is no hearth and home, no wife and kiddies, no woman like Catherine for a man like him. He was an old soldier, with all the regrets and fading battle scars to prove it. Even Catherine knew that what they had together wasn't real, that it was an illusion.

He held her—protectively, possessively. This was all they had. All they would ever have. He'd find a way to get her out of Zaraza, even if he had to sell his soul to the devil. He might not make it out of this hellhole alive, but Catherine would. He'd make sure of it.

Before dawn a messenger arrived. Murdock woke when he heard the faint commotion of men stirring about in the darkness. By the time he was fully awake, lanterns around the tents had been lit and waking soldiers mumbled among themselves. His gut instincts warned him that whatever the hell was going on, it wasn't good. Not for Zaraza. And not for Catherine and him.

He roused Catherine. She stared up at him, yawned and then smiled. "Morning."

"Get up, Cat. Something's going on and I don't like it."

She snapped up into a sitting position, glanced around and frowned. "What happened?"

"A jeep came whirling into camp a few minutes ago," he told her. "I'd say it's bad news from Sabino."

Standing, Catherine stuffed her shirt into her pants and raked her fingers through her hair. "Look! There's Captain Delgado."

"Yeah, and look who's with him."

"Is that Captain Montero?" she asked.

"Whatever's happened, it's bad."

"They're coming this way." She grabbed Murdock's arm. "Why are they heading toward us?"

"Stay calm, honey. Let me handle things. I'll translate for you later. Okay?"

"Okay." Her stomach did an evil flip-flop as fear shot a rush of adrenaline through her body

Six soldiers accompanied the two rebel captains as they marched through the encampment, obviously headed straight toward Catherine and Murdock. Captain

Delgado issued orders and suddenly the half-dozen men surrounded their American guests.

"What's wrong?" Murdock asked in Spanish. "Why are you arresting us?" He slid his arm around Catherine's waist and pulled her to his side.

"You and the *señora* will be taken to San Carlos, not as our guests, but as our captives," Captain Montero said. "We know that your mission in Zaraza is to kill Vincente Sabino."

"Where the hell did you get that kind of information? It's a lie. Whoever issued orders for our arrest is the person who wants Sabino dead. Not us."

"You will have a chance to defend yourselves, after we have captured San Carlos and Vincente Sabino is recognized as the new leader of Zaraza." Captain Delgado snapped his fingers.

Immediately all six soldiers surrounded Catherine and Murdock. Two sets of handcuffs dangled in one young lieutenant's hand.

"They're going to separate us," Murdock warned Catherine. "Don't fight them. All they're going to do is handcuff us."

"But why?" she asked.

"We're being arrested on suspicion of plotting to murder Vincente Sabino," he told her.

"What!"

"Apparently, somehow word got back to the wrong person that we knew about the plot and were on our way to warn Sabino. *He* has issued orders to arrest and detain us, until after Sabino is declared official leader of Zaraza."

"But...but—"

"Don't say any more," he warned her. "Don't mention any names."

"What are we going to do?"

"Nothing right now. There's not much we can do, except cooperate." Murdock scanned the group of rebel soldiers who watched the proceedings. There, in the back of the crowd, stood Lieutenant Vargas, his keen black eyes focused on Murdock. The two men exchanged a mutual stare, one that communicated their comradery.

They would have to bide their time and wait for the right moment. Then Vargas would make his move. Murdock prayed that the right moment would come in time for them to save Vincente Sabino!

Chapter 14

Catherine and Murdock were being left in a deserted building on the outskirts of the capital city, their hands shackled to an iron rail that ran the length of the low ceiling. Lieutenant Vargas was in charge of the men who deposited their prisoners in the basement room for safekeeping, until the battle for San Carlos was fought and won.

"Charming little place you've found for us," Murdock said to Vargas, in English.

"Yes, isn't it," Vargas replied. "Captain Delgado's choice, actually."

"Be sure to thank the captain."

"I will do that." Vargas's smile broadened. "And I will—personally—return for you, when the time is right."

He came over and checked the handcuffs that bound Murdock to the rusty metal rail. "Old pipes in old buildings." He shook his head, as if saddened by the poor condition of both. ''The door to the basement will, of course, be bolted, so there is no way you can escape. When I return, we shall see what can be done to bring your situation to the attention of Vincente Sabino. Once he has taken control of the city, of course.'' A wicked little smile curved Vargas's lips.

''And before Sabino is officially declared the new leader of Zaraza,'' Murdock said.

The smile vanished from Vargas's face to be replaced by a solemn expression. ''Yes. Of course.''

Catherine caught the visual exchange between Murdock and Vargas, but quickly diverted her attention away from them and toward the four soldiers waiting on the stairs. Apparently none of them spoke English and they seemed totally uninterested in whatever the lieutenant was saying to the American captives.

Vargas winked at her, then turned and issued an order to his subordinates. One of the men handed the lieutenant the lantern he held, then he and the other soldiers scurried up the stairs. Vargas hung the lantern on a dangling metal hook by the staircase. Nonchalantly, he reached in his pocket to retrieve something, then placed the item on top of the wooden beam from which the hook hung. Whistling a marching song, he followed his men upstairs. The door slammed shut with a loud bang. A resounding thud announced that the heavy wooden bolt had been rammed into place.

Catherine veered around and shoved her handcuffs down the metal railing toward Murdock. ''What's—''

''Wait!'' he cautioned, nodding toward the stairs.

Biting down on her bottom lip, she held back all the questions she was dying to ask. Something was going on between Murdock and Vargas, she surmised. Or had she read things wrong? No, she knew a conspiratorial look when she saw one and comprehended double-talk when she heard it. If ever two men were up to something, Murdock and Vargas were.

And just what had that little farewell wink Vargas gave her meant? To anyone watching it might have seemed like a flirting gesture, but she knew better. It was as if Vargas had been reassuring her, even making light of the fact she was chained to a pole and trapped in a dingy basement.

She counted the minutes, waiting for Murdock to give her an all-clear sign. While waiting, she tested her handcuffs. As she pulled on them, metal against metal, they clanged loudly.

"Stop that!" Murdock said. "You'll bruise your wrists."

"I don't care if I bruise my wrists, if I can somehow get loose. We can't just hang here like this all day and maybe all night."

"I'll see what I can do to remedy the situation. Move all the way to end of the pole—" Murdock indicated the direction with a nod of his head "—down there."

"Why?"

"This is one of those times when you're supposed to just do as I tell you to do and not ask questions."

"Oh, all right!"

He waited while she dragged her handcuffs along the metal pole. When she reached the opposite end, she gave Murdock a now-what? glare. He separated his hands as far possible, then grasped the rail tightly and shook it as hard as he could.

"What are you doing?" she asked. "You told me not to do what you're doing."

Ignoring her comment, he continued his efforts. Suddenly, with a shattering crunch of metal, the railing broke in two. Catherine gasped as Murdock slid the broken tip of the rail through his hands, until the jagged end fell through his handcuffs.

"Now, just slid along the pole until you can slip your cuffs over the end," he told her.

She did as he'd instructed. When she reached the broken point of the pole, she noticed that rust had corroded the metal just enough to weaken it. Murdock had known all along that, with his superior strength, he could sever the vulnerable spot.

"Why didn't you just tell me what you were going to do?" she asked.

He lifted his arms and brought them down over her head and around to rest his cuffed hands at the back of her neck. "I wanted to impress you with my manly strength."

She grinned. "Well, you did. I was duly impressed. Even after I noticed the corrosion on the metal."

"Noticed that, did you?"

"Now, if you could just figure out some way to get us out of these pretty little bracelets." Bringing her arms up between their bodies, she stuck her cuffed wrists in his face.

He nuzzled her nose, then kissed the tip. "What will you give me if I can get us out of these?" He rubbed his cuffs against her neck.

"Get me out of these, big boy, and you can name your own reward." She lowered her hands and gave him a quick, preview-of-what's-to-come kiss on the lips.

"I'll want more than a kiss," he said.

"You haven't gotten me out of my bracelets, yet."

He lifted his arms from around her and stalked off across the room toward the stairs.

"Wait a minute!" she called out. "Are you planning on bursting through the door?"

Chuckling, Murdock glanced over his shoulder. "I took a good look at that door and the wooden bolt as we passed it on our way down here. I'm afraid it would take a stick of dynamite to open it from this side."

"So, where are you going?"

"Did you happen to notice that Vargas left us a little present?"

"You mean whatever it was he slid into that notch over the wall brace is a present for us?"

Murdock took the steps two at a time, then ran his hand over the wooden ledge, seeking the gift. When his hand encountered the small metal key, he hooted and whirled around to show her the prize. "Our man Vargas left us the key to the handcuffs."

"Aha! I knew it! You and Vargas. What's going on between you two?" She stomped over the damp dirt floor, avoiding the debris that cluttered the room and held her cuffed hands out to Murdock.

He inserted the key in the lock of her cuffs, switched it over and set her free. As the cuffs dropped to the floor, she grabbed her wrists and rubbed vigorously. By the time she looked up, Murdock had released his wrists and was scouring around in their below-ground prison.

"What are you looking for?" she asked, traipsing behind him.

"Just checking things out."

"I don't suppose there's any chance this place has a bathroom."

"I doubt it," he said. "But we'll figure something out and make do until Vargas comes back for us."

As she followed Murdock around the large, cobweb-infested basement, she began questioning him. "What's going on with you and Vargas? Obviously he tried to help us. But there's more to it than that, isn't there?''

"Look what I found," Murdock said, as he dropped to his knees in front of an old trunk. "A treasure chest. Now, if only there's some dynamite in here and a couple of rifles…''

He lifted the unlocked lid, which creaked as it rose from the base. Murdock rummaged around inside, tossing items out on the floor. "No dynamite. And no weapons. But here's a couple of old blankets." He tossed the threadbare blankets to her.

After catching the cover and then laying it to her side, she demanded, "So explain about Vargas."

"Vargas will be back for us. And he'll come alone. Then he'll do what he can to get us in to see Vincente Sabino, before Sanchez can follow through with his plans.''

"I thought you said you didn't tell Vargas about the assassination plot?"

"I didn't."

"Then why—"

"Vargas trusts me," Murdock said. "He's going on his gut instincts, which tell him that I want to help Sabino, not hurt him."

"Why does Vargas trust you?"

"When men fight alongside each other, the way we did back in Celendin, they get to know each another pretty fast and often have to make instant judgment calls. Vargas trusts me for the same reason I trust him."

"Gut instincts," Catherine said.

"Yeah, gut instincts."

"So, we really are stuck here, in this…basement, until Vargas returns for us?"

"I'm afraid so." Murdock went back to rummaging

through the trunk. "Nothing much else here except some old clothes, a couple of books and—" He withdrew a square wooden box, the top decorated with a faded painting of roses and encrusted with rows of tarnished brass studs.

"What have you got there?" she asked.

He flipped open the lid. "Looks like some sort of music box."

He searched and found the key to wind the internal mechanism. Suddenly the tinkling strands of a familiar waltz filled the dirty, gloomy basement with music.

"How lovely." Catherine reached for the box.

Murdock handed it over to her. "No food. No water. No dynamite and no weapons. But we can have music while we sit around here going stir-crazy!"

Catherine clutched the box to her bosom as the jingling melody played on. "I wish you hadn't mentioned food and water. I'm really thirsty."

"We can survive without water for days and food even longer, but my guess is that it won't take Sabino more than twenty-four hours to put the government troops on the run. And I figure General Ramos found a way to get out of the country right after the first rebel attack."

"So, take another look in that trunk," Catherine said. "Maybe you can find a deck of cards or a checkerboard. Something we can do to pass the time."

"You're being a good sport about this. Some women would be yelling their heads off and demanding I find a way out of here."

Catherine sat down on the stairs, then placed the music box several steps above her. "I thought you'd already figured out that I'm not like most of the women you've known."

Murdock slammed the lid shut on the trunk. "No cards. No checkers. No games of any kind." He stood up, then looked at Catherine. "I realize, only too well, that you're not like any woman I've ever known."

"I hope that's good." She offered him a faint smile.

He crossed the room, kicking aside any clutter that blocked his path, then sat down one step below Catherine. With his gaze focused on a spot between his spread feet, he cleared his throat. "For the record...just so, later on, you won't wonder about... I thought I was in love once. She was the daughter of the richest and most powerful family in Cypress, Mississippi. And my old man was the school custodian and a drunk, to boot. Barbara and I had known each other for years. I'd had a thing for her when I was in high school, but she'd never given me the time of the day. I'd had my teenage heart broken a couple of times, like most guys. But I was a grown man when I got out of the army and became involved with Barbara. I was a fool to think she loved me. All I was to her was a temporary walk on the wild side."

Catherine reached over and grasped Murdock's hand. "Barbara was the fool, not you."

He squeezed her hand, but didn't look at her. "When she dumped me, I went crazy. That's when I joined up with your father and—"

"And became a mercenary," Catherine finished for him. "Did you love her so much that losing her made you not care whether you lived or died?"

Murdock whirled around, grabbed Catherine's shoulders and peered deeply into her eyes. "I haven't loved a woman since then. I purposefully chose a life that wasn't exactly conducive to making any permanent ties. I've avoided commitment most of my adult life."

"And all I've ever wanted was a family," she said

quietly, a soft sad note to her voice. "A husband, children, parents. I thought I had a chance for a real family when I married Rodney. But...we didn't have children and I lost Rodney a few months before our fifth anniversary."

"So, I assume it's safe to say that we've spent our lives pursuing different goals." Murdock released his tight grip on her. "If it hadn't been for our mission to rescue Lanny, you and I never would have met. But we did meet and we've shared some unforgettable moments together."

Catherine sighed. "The most unforgettable moments of my life."

"Yeah. For me, too," he admitted. "And when this is all over—when you go your way and I go mine—I want you to remember that you weren't just another woman to me." He placed his open palm across the left side of her face and caressed her tenderly. "You were my fantasy woman. Everything I could ever want."

Emotion clogged her throat, threatening her breathing. She laid her hand over his and held it to her face. "You turned out to be my fantasy man." She laughed softly. "I told myself that I didn't like you, that you were a carbon copy of Lanny. You were a trained killer, who didn't possess any gentle, tender emotions."

"You were right to feel that way."

"No, I was wrong." She dragged his hand to her lips and kissed his big, hard knuckles. "What I've been through this past week—what we've been through—has shown me how wrong I was about you. It's easy to judge someone when you haven't walked a mile in their shoes. Well, I've walked a lot of miles at your side since we came to Zaraza and I've seen a side of life that no one could imagine unless they've experienced it firsthand."

"I'd give anything if I could have spared you the hell you've been through."

Murdock pulled her off the step, lifted her over onto his lap and draped his arms around her hips. She wrapped one arm around his neck and rested her head on his shoulder.

They sat there on the stairs, not speaking, just holding each other. As one moment passed peacefully into another and then another, Catherine thought about how much her life had changed since she'd met Murdock. She realized that she would never be the woman she'd once been. Now and forever, she would be his woman. No amount of time or distance could ever change that one irrevocable fact. And finally she understood why, after all that had happened between them, her mother had called for Lanny on her deathbed. When you loved a man the way she loved Murdock—the way her mother had loved her father—you loved until the day you died. And probably for all eternity.

"We've got a lot of time on our hands, honey." He nuzzled her throat. "What do you say we make hay while the sun shines?"

She swatted him playfully on the arm. "Aloysius Murdock, I do swear you have a one-track mind!"

"Yes, ma'am, where you're concerned, I believe I do." He traced a fine blue vein in her neck, then crisscrossed his finger back and forth on her chest, opening the top two buttons of her shirt.

She didn't utter one word of protest when he hoisted her into a standing position, undid and lowered her pants to her knees. She lifted one foot and then the other. Murdock tossed her pants over the stair rail, then quickly unzipped his pants and freed his sex. As he lowered her to his lap, positioning her so that she slid onto his shaft, she braced herself by grabbing his shoulders.

"Ah…ah…ah," she sighed when he cupped her hips and forced her to take him completely. Her body swelled and tightened, holding him hard and fast.

Easing one hand between their bodies, he finished unbuttoning her shirt. Then while his lips sought her breasts, his hand delved through her intimate curls and found her core. A torturous tingling zinged between her breasts and her femininity, like tiny lightning strikes preparing to set the world on fire.

Clutching her hips again, he maneuvered her, lifting her up and down, making sure each stroke touched her with tormenting accuracy. Their mating was fast, furious and frenzied. Within minutes she cried out her fulfillment and he followed her quickly, releasing himself within her hot, wet depths.

In the hours that followed, they talked and laughed and made love. And sometimes they simply held each other and listened to the silence. They shared stories from their childhoods, along with their most embarrassing moments and their darkest secrets. He learned that despite all her accomplishments, Catherine couldn't carry a tune. And she found out that his full name was Aloysius Devlin Murdock, but that since his father had been Devlin, Sr., his parents had called him Aloysius, which he had shortened to Al in high school.

And several times, they wound the music box and Murdock waltzed her across the dirt floor. Every moment precious. Every experience only adding to the fantasy.

She had never felt closer and more connected to another human being in her entire life. How was she ever going to let this man go? she wondered. All that mattered to her was holding on to Murdock, now and for the rest of her life.

Vargas returned the next day. Alone. And with bad news! Although the rebels had secured the capital city, the war was far from over.

"General Ramos escaped to Brazil," Vargas said. "But his right-hand man, Colonel Ordaz, has retreated with over three-fourths of the Zarazaian army to Carrizo."

"What about Sabino?" Murdock asked.

"Sabino is alive and well," Vargas said. "Today at noon, he will address the residents of San Carlos in a victory rally in the town square."

"Is there any way I can get to him before the rally?" Murdock laid his hand on Vargas's shoulder. "His life depends on my talking to him."

"I have tried every way I know to gain an audience with Sabino." Vargas shook his head in disgust. "I am only a lowly lieutenant, with very limited influence."

"Don't sell yourself short, *amigo.*" Murdock checked his watch, then slipped his arm around Catherine's waist. "Let's get the hell out of here. We have less than two hours to save Vincente Sabino's life."

Bright morning sunshine nearly blinded Murdock when he stepped out into the light of day. The effects of having spent twenty-four hours in a subterranean dungeon.

"Did you bring me a rifle?" Murdock asked.

"*Sí.*" Vargas pointed to a HK53 carbine propped against the wall. He picked up the compact rifle and handed it to Murdock. "I took this off a Zarazaian soldier. Nice, yes?"

"Very nice." Murdock stroked the retractable buttstock.

"What about me?" Catherine asked. "Shouldn't I have a gun, too?"

"Of course, *señora*." He removed his hip holster, containing a 9mm Glock and handed it to her, then rearranged the rifle slung over his shoulder.

Murdock strapped the leather belt around her waist, notching it in the last opening. It dropped to the top of her hips. "I'll give you some pointers on using a handgun while we're en route."

Vargas jumped in the jeep and motioned for them to hurry. Catherine clutched Murdock's arm, halting him.

"What is it, honey?" he asked.

"You think Sanchez is going to strike at the rally, don't you? And you're going to try to stop him."

He grabbed her arm and hauled her up against him. "It's the only way."

"But what if something goes wrong...what if—"

"Vargas will get you to the American embassy. It'll be the safest place for you. Ambassador Hadley should be able to find some way to get you out of the country." He squeezed her arm. "Worst case scenario, Cat."

She wanted to scream. *No! No! No! Nothing is worth risking your life. If I lose you, I don't care what happens to me.* But she didn't scream. She made no verbal protest of any kind. She simply gazed into his eyes and told him, without words, exactly how she felt.

He gave her a gentle shove. She jumped into the back of the jeep as he got in the front beside Vargas, who immediately revved the motor.

"Okay," Murdock said. "Let's rock and roll."

Chapter 15

Celebrators congested the streets of San Carlos. Soldiers and local citizens alike. Men and women of all ages, from old men aided by walking canes to babes on their mothers' hips. After waiting twenty years for this day, the victory was bittersweet. Although the capital was now in the possession of the rebel army, the war was yet to be won.

Blue skies and tropical sunshine blanketed the city, the day itself as cheerful as the crowds that swarmed through the streets, making their way to the town square. Vargas had abandoned the jeep several blocks back since traffic had slowed to a standstill. The only way to get to the square by noon was on foot.

"Sabino will have guards surrounding him," Vargas said as they wove their way in and around the milling crowd. "Our best bet is for us to separate once we reach the square. Let me try to get a message to Sabino."

"Sure, you see what you can do," Murdock agreed.

"But if I have to, I'll make a scene to attract Sabino's attention. Even if means getting myself arrested."

Murdock kept Catherine's hand tightly clasped in his. The crowd was huge, boisterous and rowdy enough to be dangerous for a woman separated from her man. Even if she were nothing more to him than Lanny's daughter, he wouldn't be able to forget that he had two missions to accomplish—save Sabino's life and make sure Catherine got out of Zaraza alive. But she meant a great deal more to him than simply being his old buddy's daughter. Her safety was always utmost in his mind. And in his heart.

The closer they got to the heart of the city, the thicker the congestion, the wilder the crowds. Many people had stopped in *cantinas* to quench their thirst and rest their feet. Others had opted to take positions in upper rooms, where the windows were draped with rebel flags. But the vast majority trudged ever forward, toward the former home of General Ramos, now the new headquarters of Vincente Sabino and his rebel army.

By Murdock's estimation, it was taking them more than fifteen minutes to cover one block. At this rate, they'd barely make it to the square by noon. His gut instincts told him that Sanchez would assassinate Sabino today, at the square, in front of thousands. If that happened, the war in Zaraza would never end. Not in five years, or ten or even another twenty. If the rebel factions didn't remain a cohesive unit, under one leader, then Colonel Ordaz could easily take over where General Ramos had left off.

As they neared the square a chorus of "¡Viva Sabino!" rang out loud and clear, followed by deafening shouts. A man spoke over a loudspeaker system, sending his voice several blocks in every direction. Damn! Murdock thought. He's congratulating Sabino on his victory. That meant the young leader was already on the podium. And unless he was badly mistaken, Domingo Sanchez was probably standing at Sabino's side, waiting for the perfect moment to betray his friend and his country.

"I will leave you now," Vargas said. "If I get through to Sabino, what do I tell him?"

"Tell him that his father's old friend, Murdock, wants him to know that he has a Judas among his disciples."

"And if he does not believe me?" Vargas asked.

Murdock made a decision based on instinct. He had to take a chance on completely trusting Vargas. "Tell the young man that you know the old code word." Murdock leaned over and whispered into Vargas's ear.

Once Vargas disappeared into the mob, Murdock dragged Catherine along with him as he circled the crowd, slowly but surely inching his way closer and closer to the podium. Finally, thanks to his six-foot-six height, he was able to see Vincente Sabino. He would have known the boy anywhere. He was very much his father's son.

The speaker, an older gentleman in army fatigues, introduced the man of the hour. Murdock's heartbeat accelerated. Sweat moistened his palms. *It was coming down. And soon!* He could feel it in his bones. Years of experience told him that every minute counted now.

"Stay with me," he told Catherine. "But if something goes wrong, try to find Vargas."

She tightened her grip on his hand. In that same instant he noticed the tall, broad-shouldered man, his rifle held in front of his chest, standing guard on the podium, about ten feet to Sabino's right. He wore a rebel uniform and the insignia identified him as a general. Was he Sanchez? Murdock wondered. His every instinct replied in the affirmative.

Catherine tugged on Murdock's hand. "Look, there's Vargas. Two soldiers are dragging him off the podium."

"Damn!" Murdock shoved his way through the crowd, with Catherine running to keep pace.

Vargas struggled with his captors, all the while shouting at the top of his lungs that Sabino was in danger. Sanchez pointed his rifle at Vargas and ordered the guards to get rid of the nuisance.

Murdock and Catherine were less than ten feet away from the edge of the podium, when Vargas called out loudly, "Your father's old comrade, Murdock, has a message for you! Your life is in danger from someone who calls himself your friend!"

One of the guards rammed his rifle butt into Vargas's stomach. He doubled over in agony. Sabino held up his hand in a halt signal.

"Bring this man to me," Sabino said.

The guards obeyed instantly. The crowd quieted, all eyes riveted to the scene before them. Murdock scanned his gaze back and forth from Sabino to Sanchez, all the while plowing forward toward the podium.

Catherine followed him, clinging to his hand, praying harder and harder with each step they took.

The guards dropped Vargas to his knees in front of Sabino, who thoroughly inspected the intruder. "Where is this Señor Murdock?"

Vargas lifted his head. "Murdock is here, in the square. He knows the name of the traitor." Vargas hesitated momentarily, then shouted, "I know the old code word."

"If I am to believe you, then you must tell me the

old code word, the one my father and his American friends used,'' Sabino said.

''Bubba,'' Vargas said, then shouted, ''Bubba!''

The old man who had introduced Sabino to the crowd gasped. The young rebel leader leaned forward and offered his hand to Vargas, then helped him to stand.

Suddenly the world shifted gears. Movement slowed. Sounds blurred. Murdock released Catherine's hand, aimed his HK53 carbine and with one fatal shot, aimed right between the eyes, dropped Domingo Sanchez to the ground. The rifle Sanchez had aimed directly at Sabino fired, but the bullet went wild, just as Sanchez took his last breath. Several soldiers surrounded Sabino, protecting him with their own bodies. One of those men was Lieutenant Vargas. And at the same instant two soldiers tackled Murdock to the ground. He wrestled with them for a couple of minutes before subduing both men, but in the struggle he lost his weapon.

Catherine noticed the man dressed as a rebel soldier, who had been at Sanchez's side on the podium, turn and survey the crowd. His gaze halted on Murdock. That's when she recognized him. Manuel. Their driver when they'd first arrived in San Carlos. So Murdock had been right not to trust the man. He had apparently been the one to tell Sanchez about Murdock and Catherine and Sanchez had ordered their arrest.

Suddenly Manuel lifted his rifle. Her heart stopped for a split second as she realized what was about to happen. No, her mind screamed, no!

With the two soldiers still tugging on his arms, Murdock dragged them into the crowd as he searched for his rifle.

''Murdock!'' Catherine yelled. ''Watch out! Behind you!''

Manuel saw Catherine then and his attention turned from Murdock to her. He smiled as he braced his rifle on his shoulder and aimed. Not at Murdock, but at her. Before she had time to react, to run or drop to her knees, Murdock dove through the air. Two shots rang out simultaneously. Manuel clasped his chest and crumpled to his knees. As blood trickled from his mouth and pumped from his heart, he fell over dead. As he shoved Catherine to the ground and covered her protectively, Murdock's big body blocked the bullet intended for her.

When she wrapped her arms around him, her hand encountered a wet sticky substance on his shoulder. Blood!

"Murdock. Oh, God, Murdock!"

"Stop shouting in my ear, Cat," he grumbled, then rolled off her and struggled to stand.

She hoisted herself onto her feet, then slid her arm around his waist. "You're shot."

"Dammit, woman, don't you think I know that!"

"How bad is it? We'll get you to a hospital right away. You're a hero, you know. You saved Vincente Sabino's life as well as mine. He'll be grateful. He'll see to it that you're taken care of."

She babbled on and on, clinging to Murdock, tears streaming down her face. Even when Lieutenant Vargas brought Vincente Sabino to meet his savior, Catherine couldn't stop rattling or crying.

The man she loved was alive and safe. That was all that mattered right now.

With his arm in a sling, and wearing a clean set of camouflage fatigues, Murdock waited with Catherine at the edge of the airstrip. Now that the rebel forces controlled three-fourths of the country and all flights in and out of Zaraza were at their discretion. Dundee's had flown in a helicopter. The pilot, Matt O'Brien, waited for his passenger.

"Take care of Lanny," Murdock said. "And when he's all well, let him take care of you, too, honey." He caressed her cheek.

She leaned her face into his palm, savoring the feel of his flesh against hers. Then she quickly righted herself and squared her shoulders. "I wish you were coming with me."

"I can't leave," he told her. "Not yet."

"I'd tell you that this isn't your war and they can win it without you, but you wouldn't listen, would you?" She gazed directly into his eyes and knew she had assessed the situation correctly.

"I have to do this. Please, Catherine, try to understand."

"I do understand," she told him. "I understand you."

"You'd better go. O'Brien's waiting for you."

Willing herself not to cry, not go all sentimental on him, she forced a smile. "Take care of yourself. Don't you dare get yourself killed." Her voice cracked. "Do you hear me, Aloysius Murdock!"

He hauled her into his arms and kissed her until she couldn't breathe, then he shoved her gently from him.

"Don't forget our fantasy, Cat. I never will."

While she still had the strength to leave him, she turned and walked away. He stood ramrod stiff and watched her board the helicopter. O'Brien would take good care of her. He'd make all the arrangements to get her and Lanny back to the States. Back to Huntington, Tennessee where she belonged.

Lieutenant Vargas walked up beside Murdock. "You

will miss your woman, but you will see her again. Soon. The war can't last much longer.''

''Catherine's better off without me.'' Once she's back home, she'll realize that he wasn't the type of guy who could fit into her world. For a while, she'll fantasize about what they shared and then she'll meet someone else. Some guy who can be the kind of husband she wants, the kind of man who'll be a good father to her children. And he knew it was highly unlikely that man would be Aloysius Devlin Murdock.

Catherine set the round oak table in the kitchen, where she and her father shared most of their meals, with her everyday earthenware. The oven timer dinged, letting her know the meat loaf was done. As she lifted the pan from the oven, she breathed in the delicious smell. A month ago, just a whiff of any kind of meat sent her straight to the bathroom. Her morning sickness had begun at six weeks and ended promptly at twelve weeks. She and Lanny had been quite a pair during those first few weeks back in Tennessee. He recovering slowly from years of brutality and starvation as well as the tuberculosis the doctors were treating. And she was tormented by vicious bouts of morning sickness.

She smiled as she recalled what Lanny had said when he'd figured out that she was pregnant. ''Damn that Murdock! He'd better not go getting himself killed down there in Zaraza, because I want the satisfaction of blowing his brains out myself.''

Catherine placed the meat loaf on a serving platter, then slid the pan of yeast rolls into the oven and lowered the temperature. As she took the pot of potatoes from the stove eye, she remembered the day she'd realized she was carrying Murdock's child. Exactly three weeks after she'd said goodbye to him at the airstrip. She'd known even before she'd bought the home test kit.

While she creamed the potatoes with a hand mixer, she wondered where Murdock was and what he was doing. The war in Zaraza had officially ended nearly a month ago, but neither she nor Lanny had heard a word from him. Against her wishes, Lanny had contacted the Dundee agency and been told that Murdock hadn't returned to Atlanta. Where was he? And why hadn't he at least called her father?

She knew he wasn't dead. If he were dead, she'd feel it, deep down inside. In her very soul.

Glancing out the window as she dropped the mixer blades into the soapy dishwater, she noticed a snowflake swirling in the wind. One lonely little snowflake.

"Can I help you with anything?" Lanny asked as he entered the kitchen.

"No, thank you, Daddy. Supper's almost ready."

"Looks like we're fixing to get a snow, doesn't it?"

"I believe we are." She spooned the potatoes into a serving bowl. "But it is February in northeast Tennessee. We're due a good snow about now."

Catherine heard a car drive up, then two doors slamming. But from the kitchen windows she couldn't see the front of the driveway where their guests had parked.

"Now who could that be right here at supper time," Lanny said. "You finish on up and I'll go see who it is. You didn't invite anybody to supper, did you?"

"No, I didn't invite anyone for supper. Whoever it is, be polite," she advised. Sometimes her father overplayed his role as father-protector and was unduly rude to people he thought took advantage of his daughter's good nature.

Well, maybe Lanny's rudeness would get rid of their

uninvited guests and they could enjoy their meal. She'd found that lately, her appetite had increased tremendously. And even though her tummy was only slightly swollen, she felt as if she'd gained twenty pounds. In reality, she'd gained eight.

She placed the meat loaf and potatoes on the table, then poured the green peas into a bowl and set them beside the platter. Just as she picked up a pot holder so she could check on the rolls, Lanny swung open the kitchen door.

"There's somebody here who wants to see you," Lanny said.

Catherine dropped the pot holder on the counter, turned and then gasped when she saw who stood in the doorway with Lanny.

"Benita!"

Catherine and Benita started racing toward each other and met in the center of the big kitchen. Catherine dropped to her knees, grabbed the child and hugged her close. Shoving her back a few inches, Catherine grabbed Benita's shoulders and then spread kisses all over her face.

"How did you get here? Who brought you? Oh, Benita, Benita! My sweet, precious little girl."

"I come to live with you, Mama," Benita said in heavily accented English.

Tears welled up in Catherine's eyes. "Oh, yes, darling, yes."

Lanny cleared his throat. "You've got another visitor." He inclined his head toward the living room.

Catherine rose to her feet, but kept Benita's little hand clasped in hers. "Another visitor?"

"Yeah, the guy who brought Benita to you is waiting in there."

"Murdock?" she asked.

"Sí, mi padre," Benita said.

Lanny smiled at Benita and then spoke to her in Spanish. "I'm your grandfather. Your new mama's father."

Benita returned his smile. *"Sí, mi abuelo."*

Lanny took Benita's hand from Catherine's and led the child toward the windows overlooking the backyard. "How about you and I watch it snow?" he asked her in Spanish. "You've never seen snow before have you, sweetheart?"

Catherine hesitated. What would she say to Murdock? Had he come here only to deliver Benita? She laid her hand protectively over her belly. He had a right to know about his child, didn't he?

"Go on out there," Lanny said. "And put the poor guy out of his misery."

"Tell Benita that I'm just going in the living room to talk to Murdock."

"Benita's fine," Lanny said. "The snow fascinates her. Stop stalling and get your behind out there and talk to your baby's father."

Squaring her shoulders and tilting up her chin, Catherine marched out of the kitchen, down the corridor and into the living room. Murdock stood in front of the fireplace, warming his hands, his back to her.

As if he sensed her presence, he turned and faced her. Instantly, she went weak in the knees and butterflies rioted in her tummy. Nothing had changed. Just looking at him aroused every feminine instinct within her. He was so big, so rugged, so powerfully male in every sense of the word. He was *muy hombre*. Much a man. Her man. She wanted to run to him, to throw her arms around him as she'd done Benita, but she couldn't move. All she could do was stand there and stare at him.

"Hello, Catherine."

"Hello." She smoothed her hand over her baggy blue sweater that hung down to midthigh. Damn, she didn't have on any makeup and her hair was pulled back in a ponytail. Would he notice that she'd gained some weight, that her once flat stomach now had a discernible little pooch?

"You look good," he said.

"So do you." Good enough to eat, she thought. *Oh, Murdock if you don't take me in your arms and kiss me soon, I think I'll die.*

"Lanny looks great." Murdock shifted his feet, but made no move forward. "He told me that he's feeling good, too."

Catherine nodded. "How did you get Benita out of Zaraza?"

Murdock shrugged his massive shoulders. "After the war ended, I went back to Celendin to find her, but she'd been shipped out, along with Father Galtero and the other orphans. Vincente Sabino helped me find her and arranged for me to be made her temporary legal guardian. Then I got in touch with Rick Burdett and he pulled a few strings. Took awhile to get things ironed out so I could bring her to the States. But she's here now, with you. And there's nothing to prevent you from adopting her."

"How can I ever thank you?" Tears lodged in her throat.

"Well…I've got something in mind," he said.

"Yes?"

"Lanny tells me that you haven't been dating anybody since… There isn't anyone else, is there, Cat?"

"Actually, there is someone else," she said. "But not another man."

"I don't understand."

"It doesn't matter right now. What is it that I can do to repay you for bringing Benita to me?"

"You can invite me to supper."

"Invite you to—?"

"Yeah, honey. Invite me to supper tonight and every night for the next fifty years."

"The next fifty years?" Catherine's heartbeat thundered in her ears.

"Of course, if I move in here with you, you'd have to marry me. We wouldn't want to set a bad example for Benita, would we?"

"Are you asking me to marry you?" She took several hesitant steps toward him, her heart so full it was about to burst from her chest.

"Yeah, I am, if you'll have me."

He held open his arms and Catherine flew into them. He lifted her off her feet and into his embrace. His head descended as he slid her down his big, hard body. Their lips met in a frenzied kiss. Suddenly, he ended the kiss and set her away from him.

"Stand right there," he said.

"Right here?" she asked teasingly, happiness bubbling up inside her like an overflowing fountain.

He grabbled in his jacket pocket, then pulled out his closed fist and dropped down on one knee. "Catherine Price, I love you. And if you're willing to take a chance on a rough-as-a-cob, old SOB like me, I promise you that I'll spend the rest of my life making every fantasy you ever had come true." He held up an emerald-cut diamond. "It's an antique ring. Jeweler said it's about a hundred years old. The minute I saw it, I knew it was the one for you."

"Get up off your knees." She laughed, recalling the

night she'd sworn she would bring the big man to his knees. She had accomplished that goal in a way she'd never dreamed possible.

Murdock rose to his feet, then reached out for her hand. She offered him her left hand and he promptly slid the diamond onto her ring finger.

"You haven't given me an answer," he said.

"If I give it enough thought, I can probably come up with a dozen good reasons why I shouldn't marry you." She danced her fingers up the front of his shirt. "But I can think of two very good reasons why I should."

"And what are those two reasons?" He draped his arm around her waist and pulled her up against him.

"The most important reason in the world—I love you."

His broad smile deepened the faint lines around his mouth and at the corners of his eyes. "And what's the other reason?"

She laced her fingers through his, then pulled his hand between their bodies and laid it flat over her belly. "I think a woman should be married to the father of her baby."

"What?" His mouth fell open. He stood there, slack-jawed, his eyes glazed over and his breathing erratic.

"I'm four months pregnant," she told him.

"Damn! Damn!" He swept her up in his arms. "We're going to have a baby?"

"I'm very happy about being pregnant. I hope you are, too."

"Happy? Cat, I'm the happiest man in the world."

Lanny and Benita stood in the doorway, both of them smiling as they watched a family in the making. Their family.

Murdock sat down on the sofa, Catherine in his lap

and held out one hand to Benita. Lanny gave the child a gentle shove and she went running. After shifting all of Catherine's weight to one leg, Murdock hoisted Benita onto the other.

"I've resigned from Dundee's," Murdock said. "A family man doesn't need to be in the cloak-and-dagger business."

"So what are you going to do?" Catherine asked.

"Well, I thought Lanny and I might go into the cattle business." Murdock chuckled. "I remember we used to talk about that when we retired we'd buy us a farm and raise cattle."

"Think living a nice, quiet bucolic life would suit two former soldiers?" Catherine grinned.

Murdock winked at Lanny. "What do you think, bubba?"

"I think I like the idea." Grinning from ear to ear, Lanny shook his head. "Who'd have ever thought two old war horses like us could get so damned lucky?"

Catherine tsk-tsked. "The first thing you two old warhorses are going to have to do is clean up your language. We have a little girl who's going to be repeating everything she hears. And I certainly don't want my baby's first word to be something vulgar."

"No cussing, no heavy drinking and what do you want to bet she's not going to let you fool around with other women?" Lanny burst into laughter.

Murdock wrapped his arms around his two best girls. "It's a small price to pay for admission into heaven."

Epilogue

Murdock wheeled the baby stroller across the sidewalk that led to the amphitheater at Huntington Academy, the private school their ten-year-old daughter Benita attended. Four-year-old Devlin was already preenrolled, as was eighteen-month-old Mae Beth. With his hand in his grandfather's, Devlin stopped along the way to pick up a handful of rocks. Catherine paused to retie the bow in Benita's black curls. She caught Murdock staring at her, with a besotted look on his face, as he eased the stroller to a stop.

Ah, life just didn't get any better than this, she thought. A springtime Sunday afternoon in Tennessee, with nature brimming over with new life all around them and an outdoor concert in the campus's amphitheater.

Of course before the concert was half over, Lanny would fall asleep and she'd have to discreetly nudge her father in the ribs a few times. Mae Beth would no doubt need a major diaper change right in the middle of Catherine's favorite concerto. And within thirty minutes Devlin would be squirming and whining. That's when Murdock would suggest they might want to leave early and go on home.

This Sunday outing would end as many others had this spring. With Murdock, Lanny and Devlin eating popcorn and drinking colas while they watched a baseball game on TV, Catherine would gather her two girls up in the backyard swing and read to them until Mae Beth dozed off to sleep. Then she and Benita would discuss clothes and boys, Benita's favorite two topics of late. And just before sunset, Catherine would make homemade ice cream and Lanny would say, as he did each time, that this was the best batch yet.

And later that night, when the children and Lanny were nestled snugly in their own rooms, she and Murdock would lie together in their king-size bed upstairs. And during those precious moments alone, they would learn anew that, for them, fantasy and reality were one and the same.

Catherine finished tying the bow in Benita's hair, then turned to her husband. "Why don't we skip the concert this Sunday? I think I'd like to go home and sit in the swing for a while."

"That's a good idea," Lanny said. "There's a game on TV I'd like to watch and maybe after a while, you could make some ice cream. Make the cherry this time. It's mine and Dev's favorite, isn't it?" He ruffled his grandson's dark hair.

"Yeah, Pops. Cherry's my very best favorite."

Lanny took Benita and Devlin by the hands and walked on ahead of Murdock and Catherine.

"You don't mind missing the concert, do you?" she asked her husband.

He stopped, leaned over and kissed her on the lips. She giggled, then glanced around to see if anyone was watching. "Why, Aloysius Murdock, what will people think, your kissing me like that in broad daylight in the middle of the Huntington campus?"

"They'll think I'm a man who's crazy in love with his wife and is counting the hours until we can put our brood to bed and spend an hour or two setting the sheets on fire."

Catherine's laughter carried on the warm May breeze. Ah, yes, life most certainly didn't get any better than this.

*   *   *   *   *

*Look for EGAN CASSIDY'S KID when
Beverly Barton's exciting series,*

THE PROTECTORS

*continues in
Silhouette Intimate Moments
in July 2000!*

If you enjoyed what you just read,
then we've got an offer you can't resist!

Take 2 bestselling love stories FREE!

Plus get a FREE surprise gift!

Clip this page and mail it to Silhouette Reader Service™

IN U.S.A.	IN CANADA
3010 Walden Ave.	P.O. Box 609
P.O. Box 1867	Fort Erie, Ontario
Buffalo, N.Y. 14240-1867	L2A 5X3

YES! Please send me 2 free Silhouette Intimate Moments® novels and my free surprise gift. Then send me 6 brand-new novels every month, which I will receive months before they're available in stores. In the U.S.A., bill me at the bargain price of $3.57 plus 25¢ delivery per book and applicable sales tax, if any*. In Canada, bill me at the bargain price of $3.96 plus 25¢ delivery per book and applicable taxes**. That's the complete price and a savings of over 10% off the cover prices—what a great deal! I understand that accepting the 2 free books and gift places me under no obligation ever to buy any books. I can always return a shipment and cancel at any time. Even if I never buy another book from Silhouette, the 2 free books and gift are mine to keep forever. So why not take us up on our invitation. You'll be glad you did!

245 SEN CNFF
345 SEN CNFG

Name	(PLEASE PRINT)	
Address	Apt.#	
City	State/Prov.	Zip/Postal Code

* Terms and prices subject to change without notice. Sales tax applicable in N.Y.
** Canadian residents will be charged applicable provincial taxes and GST.
   All orders subject to approval. Offer limited to one per household.
   ® are registered trademarks of Harlequin Enterprises Limited.

INMOM99   ©1998 Harlequin Enterprises Limited

Don't miss Silhouette's newest cross-line promotion,

Four royal sisters find their own Prince Charmings as they embark on separate journeys to find their missing brother, the Crown Prince!

The search begins in October 1999 and continues through February 2000:

On sale October 1999: **A ROYAL BABY ON THE WAY** by award-winning author **Susan Mallery** (Special Edition)

On sale November 1999: **UNDERCOVER PRINCESS** by bestselling author **Suzanne Brockmann** (Intimate Moments)

On sale December 1999: **THE PRINCESS'S WHITE KNIGHT** by popular author **Carla Cassidy** (Romance)

On sale January 2000: **THE PREGNANT PRINCESS** by rising star **Anne Marie Winston** (Desire)

On sale February 2000: **MAN...MERCENARY...MONARCH** by top-notch talent **Joan Elliott Pickart** (Special Edition)

ROYALLY WED
Only in—
SILHOUETTE BOOKS

Available at your favorite retail outlet.

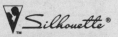

Visit us at www.romance.net

SSERW

MONTANA MAVERICKS
Big Sky Brides

Legendary love comes to Whitehorn, Montana,
once more as beloved authors

Christine Rimmer, Jennifer Greene and Cheryl St.John

present three brand-new stories in this exciting anthology!

Meet the Brennan women:
SUZANNA, DIANA and ISABELLE

Strong-willed beauties who find unexpected
love in these irresistible marriage of
covnenience stories.

Don't miss
MONTANA MAVERICKS: BIG SKY BRIDES
On sale in February 2000,
only from Silhouette Books!

Available at your favorite retail outlet.

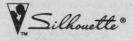

Silhouette ®

Visit us at www.romance.net